TOUCH ME NOT

TOUCH ME NOT

Betty Rowlands

This first world edition published in Great Britain 2001 by
SEVERN HOUSE PUBLISHERS LTD of
9–15 High Street, Sutton, Surrey SM1 1DF.
This first world edition published in the USA 2001 by
SEVERN HOUSE PUBLISHERS INC., of
595 Madison Avenue, New York, NY 10022.

British Library Cataloguing in Publication Data

Rowlands, Betty
  Touch me not
  1. Women detectives – Fiction
  2. Detective and mystery stories
  I. Title
  823.9'14 [F]

  ISBN 0-7278-5602-2

Typeset by Hewer Text Ltd.,
Edinburgh, Scotland.
Printed and bound in Great Britain by
MPG Books Ltd, Bodmin, Cornwall.

Prologue

I t had been a beautiful, liberating experience, as if the gates of paradise had swung open for him to pass through. "Mind-blowing" was how Jennifer would have described it – had in fact done so in a tone of incredulous delight, although of course it would never be possible for him to reveal how the one discordant note in their otherwise perfect relationship had been stilled. The expression was one that would not normally have occurred to Oliver, who was of a different generation, but it certainly seemed to sum up the feeling of exultation and fulfilment that had swept over him during those moments of rapture – moments that were, incredibly, to be repeated again and again during the ensuing blissful weeks. After the long, weary months of frustration and disappointment, it was like being released from what had looked like becoming a life sentence in a prison which held every conceivable comfort and luxury but one.

Jennifer had been so patient, so understanding, despite the repeated failures that hung like a deepening cloud over their day-to-day existence. It had been a downward spiral with no apparent hope of improvement. He had been too shy to discuss it with his doctor, and when Jennifer had shown him the brochure he had been – to put it mildly – sceptical. He was, after all, a man of substance, the owner of a flourishing company, highly respected among his colleagues and competitors alike for his acumen, flair and razor-sharp judgement. The suggestion that he waste good money to sit with a group of sad souls listening to what he suspected would be a load of mumbo-jumbo went against all his business instincts. It was only for Jennifer's sake that he had

1

agreed to give it a try; to his surprise, after the first two or three sessions, he had become aware of a subtle change in his own personality and outlook. A certain lack of self-confidence that he had hitherto managed to conceal but not overcome began to disappear; he spent less time, after making some far-reaching decision, asking himself whether he had done the right thing. Little by little, he felt himself inching towards his true goal, but despite a certain improvement the perfection he and Jennifer sought still eluded him. And so he had screwed up his courage and, during a private consultation, admitted his problem.

The diagnosis was simple; the treatment, when first suggested to him, had seemed shocking, unthinkable. He protested that Jennifer would be horrified, that he would never be able to look her in the face again, but when he was gently reminded that it was for her sake and at her suggestion that he had sought their help in the first place – and that in any case she would never know – he allowed himself to be persuaded. And it had been so amazingly, wonderfully successful that he had never had a moment's regret.

Until now.

One

"Hi, Mum!" Fergus Reynolds came bouncing into the kitchen at half-past six on Sunday evening, swung his bulging holdall from his shoulder and dumped it on the floor before giving his mother a hug. "Had a good weekend?"

"Yes thanks." Sukey returned the hug before nudging the holdall into a corner with her foot. "How many times do I have to tell you not to leave things where we might trip over them?" she said in mock exasperation.

"Sorry! What's for supper?"

"There's some cold chicken left over from lunch. We could have some sauté potatoes to go with it, and there's salad in the frig."

"Sounds fine."

Sukey turned to the sink and began washing earth from her hands. "I've been working in the garden all afternoon, so I haven't had time to cook anything special," she explained. "You could peel the spuds if you like."

"Will do, when you've finished at the sink," said Fergus. A thought struck him. "Where's Jim? I thought he was spending the weekend here."

"He has to attend an inquest in Birmingham first thing tomorrow morning, so he decided to travel up today to avoid the morning rush hour."

"But you had yesterday together?" Fergus gave his mother a quick glance of concern. He had accepted the invitation to spend the weekend with his girlfriend's family in Devon on the understanding that she would not be on her own.

"Oh yes, we went to the theatre in the evening and had supper afterwards." Sukey felt her cheeks glow at the memory of what had happened next and she paid close attention to scrubbing her nails. Not that she had anything to hide: Fergus knew very well that she was having an affair with Detective Inspector Jim Castle and was happy to accept the situation – as she had learned to live with the fact that he had had his first sexual encounter two years ago at the age of sixteen and was still happily involved with the nubile Anita Masters. She wondered if the girl's parents were aware of how far the relationship had gone; whether they were or not, they seemed happy to accept Fergus into their home and had several times invited him to join them for weekends at their country cottage. Sukey had met Anita's father on a few occasions, albeit briefly, when he called to collect Fergus or bring him home from such visits. From the car he drove and his general air of restrained affluence, together with the odd remark her son made from time to time, it was clear that the Masterses, if not exactly landed gentry, were in a different income bracket and moved in very different circles from the Reynoldses. Not that Fergus ever appeared disturbed by the fact and Anita always seemed perfectly at home in the modest semi in Brockworth.

"So, what was your weekend like?" she asked as Fergus began sorting out potatoes. "I suppose you did the usual seaside things?"

"Yes, we swam a bit and went for a couple of bike rides – at least Anita and I did. Cath and Adrian had to spend most of their time looking after Auntie Vera."

"Just a minute, you've lost me. Who are Cath and Adrian?"

"Anita's parents. They said it was all right to call them that."

"I see." Sukey found herself wondering why there should be anything unusual about it; everyone did it nowadays – Anita called her by her first name and she thought nothing of it. Something to do with the age gap, maybe. Anita's parents were in their early fifties whereas Sukey was still – just – on the right side of forty. Aloud, she said, "Who's Auntie Vera?"

"She's Adrian's cousin actually – she's quite old and completely dotty. As a matter of fact, they're a bit worried about her."

"Oh – why's that?"

"Seems she's begun going to some weird place where people sit around having touchy-feely sessions. It's called the RYCE Foundation."

"It sounds like a cookery class."

Fergus giggled. "It's not the stuff you eat with curry," he explained. "It's an acronym, it's spelled R.Y.C.E. and it stands for Release Your Cosmic Energy. Auntie Vera spent most of the weekend banging on about how wonderful it is, and how liberating, but Adrian says the only thing the people who run it are concerned with liberating is the customers' money. They don't call them customers or clients, by the way – they're known as initiates."

"It sounds a bit of an odd set-up – I can understand Adrian feeling concerned."

"It got quite heated once or twice until Cath told him to cool it."

"I read something a while back about one of these cults," Sukey said thoughtfully. "People sit around and meditate while someone chants a load of gobbledegook at them."

"That's what seems to go on at this place. Cath takes the view that if it keeps the old dear happy it can't do much harm. She used to have a friend and they did everything together, but the friend became senile and had to go into a home, so she felt a bit lost. And then another friend was widowed and Auntie Vi thought it might help them both."

"Yes – it's the kind of thing that would appeal to people in that situation. Oh well, at least she's got relatives to keep an eye on her. Now, are those potatoes ready?"

Half an hour later, as they sat down to their supper, Fergus said casually, "By the way, Cath is going to phone you in a day or two."

"What about?"

"She wants to invite you and Jim to dinner one evening."

5

Sukey paused with a forkful of cold chicken halfway to her mouth. "Whatever for?" she asked. "I mean . . . I know you and Anita have been an item for quite a while, but—"

"I suppose they just feel it's time they got to know you better," said Fergus. He was paying close attention to his plate and did not meet her eye.

"It wouldn't have anything to do with this RYCE business, would it?"

"What makes you think that?" he countered. His voice lacked conviction.

"Gus, you aren't very good at dissimulation."

"What's that?"

"Covering up. It's your new word for today. Well?" Sukey persisted as he remained silent.

"I suppose it's bound to come up in conversation."

"You mean, they know Jim's a policeman and they want to pick his brains."

"I'm sure it's not only that – they've been saying for some time that they ought to get to know you better," Fergus repeated. "Truly, Mum. But Adrian really is very worried and, well, I sort of suggested that maybe Jim could advise them . . . or maybe know some way they could check up on the people who run this place."

"You mean, it was your idea?"

"Sort of. You're not angry, are you?"

"No, of course not. In fact, it'll be rather interesting to visit the Masterses after all you've told me about them. They sound really nice."

"Oh, they are," said Fergus warmly, plainly relieved at the way his mother had responded to his somewhat clumsy efforts at diplomacy.

"I'll mention it to Jim when he comes back from Birmingham, but unless the people who run this place have a record or there have been any formal complaints against them, I doubt if the police will be interested. Incidentally, how did Auntie Vera get to know about them?"

"She saw an advertisement – I think it was in one of the national papers. She insists it's all thoroughly respectable and not all the 'initiates' are lonely old ladies – some of them are business people and they seem to get a lot out of it as well."

"That should reassure Adrian. Perhaps he should enrol and see for himself."

"I can't see him sitting in a ring holding hands with a load of strangers and chanting 'ommm'." Fergus giggled again at the picture conjured up by the suggestion; his amusement was infectious and Sukey joined in. "Seriously, Mum, you will listen to what he's got to say, won't you?"

"Of course I will . . . and I promise not to laugh."

Two

"Morning, Sarge. Had a good holiday?"

Sergeant George Barnes, officer in charge of the scenes of crime team at Gloucester City police station, looked up from the sheaf of computer printouts on his desk and said, "Morning, Sukey. Yes, thanks. The weather was great and there was a couple in the hotel with a son the same age as Ben, so we took it in turns to look after both kids to give us the odd day out on our own. Having to come back to work kind of takes the shine off it though," he added with a rueful grimace.

Sukey chuckled. "At least, you had the advantage of going early in the season. Wait till young Ben starts school and you have to go in August – queuing for ice creams and donkey rides, hordes of screaming brats trampling your sand-castle, theme parks full of noisy teenagers . . . it's bad enough when you're young and fit, but for old boys like you . . ." Her impish smile gave her sharp features the elfin look that had long ago won Jim Castle's heart.

"Thanks, you make parenthood sound so rewarding!" said George. As the result of a late marriage, he had become a father at a comparatively mature age and had to suffer a considerable amount of good-natured teasing, all of which he took in equally good part. "How have things been here?"

"Mostly run-of-the-mill stuff. There was a good result on the Drake and Benson break-in: the three villains caught trying to get away via the fire escape turned out to have been responsible for doing at least half a dozen of their stores in other parts of the country and evidence we collected provided a vital link. They've all been remanded in custody while the forces concerned get their act together."

"Brilliant. And how about you – how was your weekend?"

"Busy. Fergus was away so I took the opportunity of the fine weather to tackle some gardening jobs. He's great at helping in the house, but gardening is not his strong point."

"Oh, right." There was a hint of dryness in George's voice. Sukey had a shrewd notion what lay behind the remark; he was probably wondering whether Jim had figured in her weekend arrangements, but was too tactful to mention it. She gave him a keen look and received a bland smile in return. Knowing her troubled marital history, he had shown a paternal concern for her from the time she had joined his section a little under four years ago and she knew – and was appreciative of the fact – that he took an interest in her welfare. Latterly, she had begun to suspect that he guessed how close her relationship with DI Castle had become. He was the soul of discretion when others were around, but now and again he caught her unawares with the odd raised eyebrow or knowing smile. She had never mentioned this to Jim; they had made a pact long ago that they would keep their personal and professional lives strictly separate and she knew he would hate it to be generally known that they were having an affair. Now, as if to reassure her that he had no intention of prying, George went on to say, "Can't say gardening's my favourite thing either. The wife does ours – I tell her it's good for her figure. I cut the grass, though – she can't mow in a straight line to save her life."

"There speaks a typical MCP!" said a new voice as Sukey's colleague Mandy Parfitt entered the room and dumped her bag on her desk. "Morning Sukey and welcome back, Sarge. Have you missed us?"

"You'll never know how much!" said George without a flicker of a smile.

"So what delights have you for us this morning?"

He consulted the printouts, which he had sorted into two piles. "RTA on the A38 involving a tractor, a motorbike and two cars.

Some casualties; uniformed, ambulance and fire crew in attendance. The other two are less exciting: a car previously reported stolen found abandoned and returned to owner in Cam and a break-in at Marsdean. The car owner asked if we could be there before ten to check it over; I said we'd do our best but we couldn't promise.You take these, Sukey. I believe you know Marsdean from a previous case," he added with a touch of irony.

"Don't I just!" Sukey repressed a shudder as she took the papers he handed her. Lorraine Chant's murder had not been the most gruesome she had encountered by a long way, but the sight of a corpse never failed to cause a contraction in her stomach.

"Do the RTA first, of course," George went on. "Uniformed have set up diversions but the traffic's piling up and they're anxious to get the road clear as soon as possible."

"Right-ho, Sarge."

"I'm sending you in the opposite direction, Mandy." George held out a second sheaf of printouts. "There's three here, all in the Tewkesbury area. Attempted break-in at a village store, smash and grab at a filling-station shop – could be the same gang – and a power mower and tools taken from a shed at a private house in Randfield. OK troops, that's your lot for now. On your way!"

"Do I detect a certain reluctance to be back at work?" said Mandy as the two SOCOs made their way to the car park to pick up their vans.

"Could be! I've been rubbing salt in by telling him about how things will be when he has to stick to the school holidays," said Sukey with a chuckle. "See you later, Mandy."

It was not long before Sukey caught up with the tailback of traffic crawling towards the spot where the diversion had been set up. She pulled out and drove past the queue to where the road ahead was blocked by a police car, its engine running and its blue light flashing. The uniformed officer directing drivers on to a side road recognised her and waved her past. A short distance ahead, a breakdown truck had pulled into a lay-by, obviously awaiting the go-ahead to clear away the damaged vehicles. She parked behind it, got out of the van, put on a bright yellow waistcoat with "Police" emblazoned on the back and set off to make a preliminary assesment of the scene.

Up ahead, the emergency services – three ambulances and a fire crew – were at work. One car – a Golf – lay on its roof and a young man in a blood-stained shirt was sitting on the verge being given first aid. Mercifully, he did not appear to have been badly hurt; as Sukey approached he said something to the paramedic, who reached through the smashed window of the car and brought out a briefcase before helping him to his feet and escorting him to one of the waiting ambulances.

On the opposite side of the road a tractor was tilted at a precarious angle, its empty trailer slewed sideways into the ditch. A man in a checked shirt, cord trousers and heavy boots – presumably the driver – was leaning against a tree with his eyes closed, evidently in shock. A woman in a flowered dress – probably the occupant of a nearby house who had heard the crash and rushed to the scene – had one hand on his shoulder and was trying to persuade him to drink from a mug she held in the other. One of the paramedics ran across and spoke briefly to them before hurrying back to the ambulance. As it pulled away it revealed a motorbike lying in a twisted heap by the roadside. There was no sign of the rider.

The second car, a Jaguar, had finished up a short distance behind the tractor. It was still the right way up but it had left the carriageway and hit a tree, evidently at considerable speed. The front end was badly crushed; the fire crew had just finished cutting away a section and the paramedics were lifting the victims, a man and a woman, both bleeding and apparently unconscious, on to stretchers. Sukey closed her eyes for a moment and swallowed hard to counter the familiar surge of nausea. No such sensitivities appeared to trouble the small group who had congregated to watch; it crossed her mind that it was fortunate that there were only a handful of houses along this stretch of the road or the police might have had a problem with crowd control as well. It was a grim reflection on human nature that so many people felt drawn to a disaster; for her part, witnessing the carnage caused by a traffic accident was one of the least attractive aspects of the job. Still, it had to be done. She returned to the van, collected her camera and went to speak to Inspector Greaves, under whose direction other officers were taking measurements and studying tyre marks on the road.

"This looks a nasty one, Guv," she commented. "What happened to the motorcyclist?"

"Already been taken to hospital. Looks like he's had a few bones broken, but fortunately he was wearing a good quality helmet, so no apparent head injuries. Amazingly, the driver of the Golf got out unaided and called us on his mobile. The other two –" he jerked his head towards the last remaining ambulance which was on the point of moving off – "weren't quite so lucky, but at least they're still alive."

"Have you figured out yet how it happened?"

"According to the Golf driver, the motorcyclist started to pull out to overtake, saw him approaching from the opposite direction and pulled back, clipped the back of the trailer and came hurtling across the road towards him. He tried to take avoiding action but the bike caught the rear of his car and rolled it over before catapulting its rider into the ditch. The Jag evidently started to follow through – we think the driver must have slammed on his brakes too hard when he saw the Golf, lost it and wrapped himself round the tree. All going too fast, as usual," he finished glumly.

"I doubt if the tractor was breaking the limit," said Sukey drily.

"We'll be breathalysing the driver just the same," Greaves joked back. At times like these, a touch of black humour could be a great help.

For the next three-quarters of an hour Sukey was hard at work photographing the scene. She walked up and down recording the state of the road, the tell-tale streaks of black rubber and the visibility from every angle before turning her attention to the vehicles. Under Inspector Greaves's direction she took close-ups of the damage and the presumed points of impact. Meanwhile, a reporter from a local radio station, whom Sukey had often encountered on similar occasions, had arrived on the scene and was taping an interview with the tractor driver on a portable recorder. When he had finished he got out his own camera and took a few shots before walking back to his car, which he had left the other side of the police barrier.

It was well after ten o'clock when at last Sukey finished her task and drove on to deal with the case of the stolen car. By the time she reached the village and located the house it was nearly half past. The door was opened in response to her knock by a sleekly coiffured, carefully made-up woman who might have been anywhere between forty and fifty. In her well-cut navy-blue business suit and crisp white shirt, she would not have looked out of place in the glossy brochure of some blue chip company. She glared at Sukey's ID through designer-framed spectacles and snapped, "What time do you call this? I particularly asked for someone to be here before ten. You people are all the same – a man was supposed to come and fix the garage door on Friday and he let me down as well. If he'd come when he said he was going to, the car would have been locked up and it wouldn't have been stolen."

"I'm sorry, but there's been a rather nasty accident a few miles up the road," said Sukey, the minute she could get a word in edgeways. "I had to wait until the ambulances had taken away the casualties before I could finish examining the scene."

"You'll have to come back another time," said the woman, seemingly unmoved by the mention of casualties. "I have to leave here in a few minutes to keep an important appointment."

"I take it you're planning to use the car?" Sukey glanced over her shoulder at the brand new Audi parked outside the front gate.

"Of course I'm planning to use it. How else do you expect me to get to Bristol from here?"

"It's only that you'll quite likely destroy any evidence the thieves may have left," Sukey pointed out patiently.

13

"Well, that's your problem, isn't it?" The woman stepped outside and slammed the front door behind her. "Tell your people to ring for another appointment," she said as she swept past, unlocked the car and threw a briefcase on to the passenger seat.

"It's normal in this type of case for the complainant to call us to arrange an appointment," said Sukey.

"Huh! So much for victim support! You can tell them to forget it." The aggrieved "victim" settled behind the wheel, buckled on her seat belt, started the engine and shot away like a Grand Prix driver leaving the grid, while the scenes of crime officer stood staring after her open-mouthed.

At eleven o'clock Sukey reached Marsdean Manor, a substantial period house of mellow brick on the outskirts of the village. Wrought-iron gates set in a brick wall stood open and a short gravelled drive led to the front door. She parked the van and rang the bell; after a few moments the door was opened by a woman of about her own age. She was casually dressed, but both her jeans and T-shirt sported designer labels and the shining cap of blond hair that crowned her pale, oval face had been expertly cut and styled.

"Mrs Drew? Sukey Reynolds, scenes of crime officer." She held up her ID; the woman barely glanced at it before holding the door open for her to enter. She had a vaguely abstracted manner, as if her mind had been temporarily elsewhere, then appeared to pull herself together. "Well, that's quick work!" she remarked. "My cleaning lady warned me it might be days before you came."

"Oh dear, is our reputation that bad?"

"I don't think so." Mrs Drew gave a wry smile. "She just happens to be one of nature's pessimists. Where do you want to start?"

"If you'd show me where they got in . . ."

"Yes, of course. This way."

Sukey followed her through a door leading out of the spacious hall into a kitchen that appeared to have been recently refur-

bished on an unlimited budget. Nothing in the room itself
seemed to have been disturbed, but the outside door stood ajar,
its wooden frame splintered where it had been prised open.
Glancing round, Sukey spotted a sensor in one corner and said,
"Didn't they set off the alarm?"

"Yes, and a neighbour phoned the police, but by the time they
arrived the thieves had gone."

"Did they get much?"

"Some rather valuable antique pieces. I think they knew
exactly what they were looking for."

"They often do. I'm afraid it's quite common for these break-
ins to happen after you've had workmen in – some of them have
dodgy friends."

"That's terrible. You feel you can't trust anyone nowadays.
My husband's away at the moment – he's going to be very upset
when he comes home."

"You haven't told him?"

"I . . . didn't want to upset him." Mrs Drew bit her lip and
turned to stare out of the window at the back garden, which was
a riot of summer colour.

Sukey set to work on making a cast of the damage to the door
frame; after a minute or two she was aware of Mrs Drew
standing behind her, watching. "Why are you doing that?"
she asked.

"Every tool leaves its own marks – if we're lucky enough to
catch a suspect with a jemmy or other instrument that corre-
sponds to the damage to the door, it'll be useful evidence." Sukey
left her cast to set and began dusting the door handle and the
paintwork for fingerprints.

Mrs Drew was at the sink, filling the kettle. "Would you care
for a cup of coffee?"

"Thank you. When I've finished, I'd love one."

They drank their coffee in a cosy, book-lined room with a
desk facing the window, which looked out on a paved patio.
"This is my husband's study," said Mrs Drew. "I think he
spends as much time looking out at his plants as he does

working," she added, a little wistfully. For a moment, Sukey thought she detected a hint of sadness in her manner; then, as if making a conscious effort to appear cheerful, she said, "Tell me, what made you take on this job and how long have you been doing it?"

"I was a police constable for a couple of years before I got married and had a baby," Sukey explained. "When Fergus was fourteen I decided I'd like to go back to police work, but it was going to be difficult being a full-time officer so I plumped for this job instead."

"It sounds fascinating. What does your husband do?"

"We're divorced."

"I'm sorry, I didn't mean to pry."

"It's all right."

Sukey glanced across at the desk with its neatly arranged accessories. It was on the tip of her tongue to make some polite reference to Mr Drew, but before she could speak, Mrs Drew said, "I'm so worried about Oliver – he went away on Thursday and he hasn't been in touch . . . it really isn't like him. He isn't answering his mobile . . . I've left messages asking him to let me know he's all right, but he hasn't called back."

"Don't you know where he went?"

"No, that's another thing that worries me. He often goes away on business trips, but he always tells me where he's going. This time he just left a note saying he'd been called away urgently. I found it when I got back from a shopping trip to Bath on Thursday afternoon."

"Have you tried calling any of his regular contacts?"

"I intended to, this morning. Then when I came home from a friend's house last night and found this, I . . ." Her voice tailed off and she put a hand over her eyes. "Forgive me, I . . ."

"It's all right," said Sukey gently. "Is there anything you'd like me to do?" She hesitated for a moment; she was about to say, "Had you thought of reporting him missing?" when there was a ring at the front doorbell. Mrs Drew hastily dried her eyes and went out of the room with a murmured, "Excuse me." Through the half-open door, Sukey heard a woman's voice say, "Mrs Drew? I'm WPC Trudy Marshall. May I come in, please?"

"Yes, of course. Do you want to speak to Mrs Reynolds?"

"Sukey – is she here?"

"She's been dealing with our break-in. Is that what you've come about?"

"No, not really, but perhaps we could join her?"

"Certainly – this way." Mrs Drew re-entered the study with Trudy Marshall behind her. A glance at the young policewoman's face told Sukey that she had brought bad news.

Three

" I can't believe it! Why would he want to kill himself?" Jennifer sobbed. "Things have been so much better lately." The words came out in convulsive bursts; her entire body was racked with the violence of her grief. She had listened in silence, with an air almost of detachment and the unspoken question "Why are you telling me this?" in her eyes while WPC Marshall gently informed her that the body of a man had been discovered in a remote Cotswold field in a car registered in the name of Oliver Drew. For several minutes she had sat bolt upright, staring straight ahead and showing no reaction, before collapsing without warning in a storm of hysterical weeping. Trudy disappeared in search of brandy, leaving Sukey trying to calm the stricken woman.

When at last the sobs became less frequent she said gently, "Mrs Drew, I know it looks bad, but it isn't absolutely certain that the man the police found this morning is your husband."

"Please, call me Jennifer." A slim hand reached out and grasped Sukey's arm; swollen eyes swimming in tears gazed pleadingly into hers.

"Of course I will – and my name's Sukey."

"Sukey – is that short for Susan? Well, not short exactly . . . you know what I mean." Sukey smiled and nodded. "I feel you're a friend," Jennifer rushed on. She was taking deep, rasping breaths in an effort to control her weeping. "I don't have many friends . . . not round here. There's only Maureen and she's leaving for Australia this morning. Please, say you'll be my friend."

"Of course I will."

"Thank you." Jennifer's voice sank to a pathetic whisper. "I've been trying to make myself believe it can't be Oliver's body, but there isn't really much doubt, is there? It's his car."

"That's true, but there's always the chance that it was stolen."

"If it isn't him, where is he? Why hasn't he been in touch?" Jennifer put her hands over her eyes; for a moment, emotion threatened to spill over again but she made a valiant effort to control it. "No, I'm almost sure it's him. I suppose I'll have to identify him." The last words were spoken in a tone of hopeless resignation.

"I'm afraid so."

"Will you come with me?"

"Yes, if you want me to, but isn't there a member of your family you'd rather have with you?"

"There's only my mother, and she lives in Cornwall. I know what *she'll* say." Jennifer's voice took on a harsh, bitter note as she appeared to mimic words she had heard many times. "She'll say, 'I warned you against marrying an old man, didn't I? This is what you get for ignoring my advice.' "

Sukey was at a loss to know how to respond, but at that moment Trudy Marshall entered the study carrying a bottle of brandy and a glass tumbler. She poured a stiff measure and offered it, saying gently, "Drink some of this, it'll make you feel better."

Jennifer obediently took a few sips, holding the glass between hands trembling so violently that Trudy had to steady it for her. After a few minutes she grew calmer and said, "What happens now?"

"I'm afraid we have to ask you to see if you can identify—" Trudi began, but Jennifer interrupted.

"Yes, I understand that, but what then?"

"Assuming it is your husband, we shall have to ask you a few questions when you're feeling up to it. Then there'll be an inquest. The coroner will want to try and establish what led him to take his own life."

"I've simply no idea." Fresh tears spilled from Jennifer's blue eyes and rolled down her salt-stained cheeks. "Everything's been so much better since he—" She broke off; for a moment grief was replaced by a fleeting look of embarrassment.

"Don't try and talk about it now. If you've had enough of this –" Trudy took the almost empty brandy glass from the young widow's unresisting hand and put it on the desk beside the bottle – "perhaps you'd like to tidy up a little before we go to the hospital. I'll drive you, of course, and either I or one of my colleagues will bring you home. Is there anyone you'd like us to contact?"

"I've already told Sukey . . . there's no one . . . she's promised to be with me while I . . ." Jennifer got to her feet, swayed for a moment, then steadied herself against the desk, waving away Trudy's offer of help. "I'll be all right, just give me a moment . . ." She took a deep breath and clenched her hands as if bracing herself for the ordeal that lay ahead. "I'll only be a few minutes," she said and went out.

"Is that right? She wants you to go with her?" said Trudy in surprise as the door closed behind her.

"She claims to have no friends in the neighbourhood and a mother who was dead against the marriage and I gather is unlikely to give the poor girl much support. I'll have to check in first and let George Barnes know what's happened, but I'm sure it'll be OK. Hopefully Mandy will be able to deal with any other jobs that come in."

"Fine." After a moment's thought, Trudy said, "Any idea why the mother was so against it?" She glanced round the room, taking in the expensive-looking furnishings. "It doesn't look as if there's a shortage of money. That kitchen must have cost an arm and a leg to install."

"Something to do with the age difference – she implied that he was a lot older than her."

"She told you a lot about herself in a short time."

"She was already worried about his unexplained absence and I was just someone to talk to."

20

"She seems to have taken a liking to you. If you're not careful, you'll end up acting as an unofficial counsellor."

The words were to prove prophetic in more ways than one.

The ordeal of identification was over. One glance, as the mortuary attendant drew back the sheet and exposed the dead face, was enough; Jennifer gagged, put her hand to her mouth and turned away with a barely audible, "Yes, that's Oliver."

Trudy nodded to the attendant, who replaced the sheet. "Thank you, that will be all," she said.

Sukey, who had been standing beside Jennifer, caught a glimpse of dishevelled silvery hair above an unnaturally pink face. At a quick estimate, she judged that there was a good thirty years' difference in age between the dead man and his widow. She noticed that the chin and cheeks were covered in a heavy growth of greyish stubble; Oliver Drew, it seemed, had spent his final days living rough, wrestling in solitude with some as yet unidentified problem for which he had finally concluded there was only one solution.

Back in the anteroom, Jennifer said, "Is it all right if I go home now?" Her face was drained of colour, but she was outwardly composed.

"Yes, of course," said Trudy. "I'll arrange transport and I'll come and see you tomorrow. As I said earlier, I'm afraid I have to ask you a few questions, but I'll make it as easy for you as I can."

"Thank you. Sukey said she'd take me home."

"If you don't mind coming back to the police station and waiting while I write my reports," Sukey reminded her. "It'll take a little time."

"I've got plenty of that now, haven't I?"

Back at the station, having installed Jennifer in a spare interview room with a cup of tea and a young police cadet to keep an eye on her, Sukey made her way upstairs to the SOCOs' room. George Barnes was there on his own, sitting back in his chair with a mug of coffee in his hand.

"You're looking relaxed, Sarge," she said as she dumped her bag on her desk. "Things must be pretty quiet."

"Heaven be praised, they are. A couple of radios snatched from cars in the Brunswick Road area – Mandy's dealing with them so, barring a sudden emergency, it's OK for you to take Mrs Drew home when you've finished here. Tell me more about this drama at Marsdean."

"Tell you in a minute, when I've made myself a cuppa. I haven't had a chance to eat my lunch yet."

On the way back from the vending machine with a plastic cup of tea in one hand and a chocolate bar in the other, Sukey almost collided with DI Jim Castle as he emerged from his office.

"Just the person I wanted to see," he said. "The minute I got back from Birmingham, Andy Radcliffe was on the blower telling me about a break-in at a house in Marsdean and the owner being found dead in his car. He was in George Barnes's office when your call came through, but he was in a rush and didn't have time to get any details."

Sukey followed him back into his office and closed the door. "There's no reason to believe there's any connection," she said. "The body of a man called Oliver Drew, who owns Marsdean Manor, was found early this morning in his fume-filled car." She gave Jim a brief account of the chain of events which led to her accompanying Jennifer Drew to the hospital morgue to identify the body of her husband. "I've promised to take her home," she said when she had finished. "She's waiting downstairs while I write up my reports."

Castle frowned. "Surely uniformed could have arranged transport? Marsdean's miles out of your way."

"It doesn't matter. As it happens, I think I might learn something useful. She claims to have no idea what drove her husband to top himself, but I have a feeling she's holding something back."

"What makes you think that?"

"One or two things she let drop suggested there have been

problems. I might get her to tell me a little more . . . she seems to find me sympathetic."

"Which you are." In a show of affection rare during office hours, he leaned forward and brushed her cheek with his fingers.

"Thank you." She acknowledged the gesture with an affectionate smile. "Shall we see you this evening?"

"I hope so, but I might be held up here. Can we leave it open?"

"Of course."

"Keep me posted on the Marsdean affair, won't you?"

As she left the city behind and drove along an almost deserted A38 towards Marsdean, Sukey said quietly, without taking her eyes off the road, "Jennifer, are you sure you have no idea what made your husband take his own life?"

"No, I haven't – truly."

"You hinted there had been problems."

"Yes, but not bad enough to . . ."

Sukey took a quick sideways glance at her passenger and noticed her colour had risen slightly. "If you don't want to talk about it—" she began.

"But I do," Jennifer said urgently. "I need to . . . I've never discussed it with anyone, not even Maureen . . . we thought we had it sorted . . ."

"We?"

"Oliver and me. It was difficult, when we were first married, I mean. He couldn't seem to . . ." Her voice cracked and died, drowned in a fresh wave of emotion.

Sukey pulled into a convenient lay-by and waited until she was calmer. Then she said, "Look, the last thing I want to do is upset you further. WPC Marshall will be coming to see you tomorrow, if you'd rather wait till then?"

"No, please, I'd rather talk to you." After a moment's hesitation, Jennifer said in a low voice, "It was Oliver's problem really . . . he couldn't . . . not at first. And then I found this place advertised in a magazine, offering some kind of therapy for people with problems."

"You mean, sexual problems?"

"All sorts of problems related to stress. I sent off for the prospectus; I can't remember everything that was in it, but it claimed to help people to escape what they call their internal shackles. I showed it to Oliver and he was sceptical at first, but he was getting pretty desperate and in the end he agreed to give it a try."

"And did it help?"

"Not immediately . . . at least, things got a little better but nothing spectacular. Then one night he came home from a session on such a high – the change in him was unbelievable. He said he'd been liberated, he'd progressed to the Outer Wheel and was on the way to the Unlimited. It all sounded a bit weird, but the main point was that it had worked. Everything was wonderful for several weeks . . . and then last week something happened. I don't know what it was, he wouldn't tell me, but one day I came home to find him sitting in his chair in the office staring out into the garden. He seemed miles away – he never heard me come in and he nearly jumped out of his skin when I spoke to him. I asked him what was wrong; he insisted there was nothing, but I was sure there was. He was very quiet for several days, not himself at all. And now . . ." This time, Jennifer made no effort to hold back her tears. "I don't understand," she sobbed, "If only he'd told me . . . whatever the trouble was, we could have shared it."

"Just have your cry," Sukey said gently. She waited until the young widow became calmer, then restarted the engine. "I'll take you home now."

"Thank you."

"I wonder," Sukey remarked as she turned off the main road and headed for Marsdean, "whether it might be worth asking the people who run these sessions if they can shed any light. Who are they, by the way?"

Jennifer gave a wan smile. "They use the initials of their slogan

'Release Your Cosmic Energy' as an acronym – Oliver used to say it sounded like a scheme for feeding the Third World. They call themselves the RYCE Foundation."

Four

"I'm afraid it's all out of the freezer this evening," Sukey apologised. "I got home too late to cook anything fancy."

"No problem," said Jim, helping himself to crisps. "Where's Fergus?"

"He left a note to say he was going swimming. He'll be back any time." Sukey spread frozen chips in a dish and slid it into the oven. "I didn't really like leaving Jennifer on her own," she went on. "I offered to contact one of the voluntary care organisations and arrange for someone to keep her company tonight, but she refused point blank, said she didn't want a stranger in her home. A bit illogical, really, since that's exactly what I was until a few hours ago, yet there she was, pouring her heart out to me."

"It's your sweet, sympathetic nature that makes people take to you." Jim put down his glass of wine, took her in his arms and nuzzled her cheek. "I do love you, Sook," he murmured in her ear.

She nestled against him. "Love you too."

They clung together for a few seconds before she disengaged herself, took a dish of chicken breasts from the microwave where she had put them to defrost and began brushing them with oil. He perched on the corner of the kitchen table to watch her at work. "You don't reckon she'll do anything foolish, do you?" he said after a moment's thought.

"That's what was worrying me at first, but once she was back she seemed to calm down and became quite practical – went straight to the kitchen and began taking stuff out of the freezer for her supper. That was when I asked her whether she needed

26

company for the night, but she was quite positive she'd be all right on her own."

"Maybe she thought you were fishing for an invitation to stay for a meal," Jim suggested.

"Cheek!" She gave him a playful thump on the chest. "Anyway, I'd already made it clear I had a hungry son to feed."

"You didn't mention a hungry DI, I take it?"

"Hardly." Sukey chuckled, then became serious again. "She said something about needing time by herself to figure things out, yet on the way home she'd been saying how badly she'd been needing someone to confide in."

"Maybe, having got it off her chest, she now feels she needs time to reflect on how to organise her life from now on."

"It's a bit early for that. I'm more inclined to think that what's uppermost in her mind at the moment is the sudden change in her husband's attitude. She spoke as if everything was going swimmingly up to a short time before he took off. It was after she mentioned the RYCE Foundation that she suddenly clammed up.You know –" Sukey finished seasoning the chicken breasts and put them in the oven with the chips – "by an odd coincidence I was hearing about this RYCE Foundation only yesterday. Fergus's girlfriend, Anita, has a slightly dotty elderly relative who's one of their clients – 'initiates' they call them. According to Gus they have what he describes as 'touchy-feely' sessions, chanting mantras and listening to music. It sounds a bit weird but he says Auntie Vera laps it up. Anita's father, Adrian, thinks they're a catch-penny outfit conning her out of her money – I understand she's got plenty."

"And he's worried about losing his inheritance, I suppose."

"So worried that I gather we're shortly to be honoured with an invitation to dinner and, reading between the lines, I suspect he wants us – or rather you – to try and find out if anything is known about them. From what Gus says, it sounds a bit eccentric, but it doesn't seem to be doing the old duck any harm. If that's how she wants to spend her money I don't see how Adrian can stop her – unless he has her declared of unsound mind or the organisers can be shown to be crooks. I rather think he's hoping for the latter."

"You reckon he's taking it that seriously?"

"It sounds like it, but we'll have to wait and see. The invitation hasn't been issued yet. Are you game to accept?"

"I don't see why not."

"You know," Sukey remarked as she tipped frozen peas into a pan of boiling water, "you do hear about these odd cults whose devotees are persuaded to cough up for what are claimed to be charitable or religious purposes, but in fact the money goes straight into the pockets of the leaders. They practise all sorts of mind control techniques to get people to do what they want."

"Oliver Drew was a successful businessman," Jim reminded her. "He doesn't sound the sort to fall for that kind of con-trick."

"It depends on how badly he wanted to believe it. It does seem to have worked in his case, of course – until it all fell apart again."

"There might have been a totally unconnected reason for that. Maybe he had business worries that he couldn't find a way round."

Sukey adjusted the heat under the saucepan of peas, took a mouthful from her glass of wine and began loading cutlery on to a tray. "Given the time scale, I don't think that's very likely," she said. "Jennifer insists that he was in great spirits until shortly before he disappeared."

"He could have been keeping his worries to himself, putting on an act."

"There are some acts a man can't put on," she pointed out meaningly. "No, I'm more inclined to think that it's got something to do with this RYCE Foundation we keep hearing about, and I have a feeling Jennifer Drew thinks so as well. Maybe Adrian Masters has got a point."

There was the sound of a key being turned in the front door. "That'll be Gus," said Sukey. "Perhaps it would be better not to mention today's adventure. It'll go straight back to the Masterses and Adrian will seize on it as adding weight to his case against RYCE."

"Good thinking."

The kitchen door was flung open and Fergus appeared. He exuded youthful health and high spirits; his eyes sparkled, his face had a rosy glow and his fair hair clung damply to his head like a smooth coating of honey.

"Hi, Mum! Hi, Jim! Had a good day?"

"Busy." Sukey answered for both of them. "How about you?"

"Fine. We played tennis and then had a swim. I got your message, Mum. What was the hold-up?"

"The lady of the house where I was working on a break-in was called on to identify a body found in her husband's car."

"Gosh, how awful for her. Did you have to go with her?"

"I didn't have to, but she asked me to."

"Was it her husband?"

"Yes."

"Had he been murdered?" An anticipatory gleam appeared in the lad's eyes.

"No, he'd run a pipe from the exhaust into the car and left the engine running. Look, Gus, it was all a bit stressful and I really don't want to talk about it, OK?"

"OK." Fergus helped himself to crisps and took a can of Coke from the refrigerator. "How was the inquest, Jim? Any gory details?"

"You are the most bloodthirsty young man I've ever met," Jim replied with a chuckle. "And no, it was all very tame by your standards."

"Oh well, I suppose you can't have exciting cases every day."

"Thank goodness. Here." Sukey picked up the tray of cutlery and handed it to him. "Do something useful – go and lay the table."

"OK." As Fergus took the tray the telephone rang. "That'll probably be Anita's mum – she said she'd call this evening."

"I'll take it in the sitting-room. Will you turn the peas off when the pinger goes, Jim?"

The voice that greeted Sukey with the words "Mrs Reynolds? This is Catherine Masters – Anita's mother" was warm and friendly, with a musical intonation and a cultured accent that spoke of elocution lessons at an expensive boarding school. "I daresay Fergus mentioned that I'd be getting in touch?"

"Good evening, Mrs Masters. Yes, he did – and before we go any further, I'd like to thank you for inviting him for the weekend. He did so enjoy it."

"My dear, it was a pleasure to have him with us." It sounded as if she really meant it. "As I've been saying to Adrian for a long time, with our children being such close friends, it really is time we got to know one another properly."

"Yes, that would be nice," said Sukey politely.

"So perhaps you'd like to come for a meal with us one evening? Are you free on Wednesday? Your friend too, of course – Mr Castle, isn't it?"

"Wednesday's fine for me, but I'm not sure about Jim. He's here, as it happens – if you wouldn't mind holding on?"

So far as he could tell, Jim was free on Wednesday, and the call ended with polite expressions of mutual pleasure at the arrangement.

Sukey and Jim left Anita and Fergus arguing good-naturedly over whether to fetch Indian or Chinese from one of the nearby take-away establishments and set off in Jim's Mondeo on the short drive to Churchdown, where the Masterses lived in an old farmhouse on the outskirts of the village. On the way, Jim remarked, "I wonder at what stage in the evening they'll raise the subject of RYCE? What's your guess?"

Sukey thought for a moment before saying, "Probably towards the end – over the coffee and liqueurs, perhaps. Not that you'll be having any of those as you're driving."

"I expect it will be dropped in casually, to try and kid us that they've only just thought to mention it."

"I expect so."

They were both wrong. The four of them – the Masterses and their guests – had barely agreed to waive formality and use first names, and were sitting around a table in an enclosed courtyard, sipping aperitifs and basking in the evening sunshine, when Adrian produced a brochure with a coloured cover from the pocket of his linen jacket and dropped it with a casual gesture in front of Jim. "Ever come across that outfit?" he asked.

"Oh really, Adrian!" his wife exclaimed in an exasperated tone. "Our guests are here for a social evening, not to have their ears bent over your hobby-horse."

"I'm not going to bend anyone's ear, Cath," Adrian promised. "I just wondered if Jim knew anything about them."

Jim picked up the brochure and studied the cover for a few moments without speaking, while Sukey, seated beside him, leaned across to have a look. She saw a photograph of a substantial red-brick house in a garden setting, evidently taken in high summer for the trees were in full leaf and a rose bed in the foreground was a mass of variegated colour. Above the house, the legend "The RYCE Foundation" was printed in dark green capitals against a cloudless blue sky and beneath it, in smaller letters, the words "At One with the Cosmos".

"I can't say I do," said Jim cautiously. "Is it some kind of health farm?"

Adrian gave a sharp, sardonic laugh. "Not exactly," he said. He was a big man with a hearty manner, heavily built but with sufficient height to carry it off without appearing overweight. In contrast, his wife was slender and elegant, with a heart-shaped face and finely moulded features, yet tall enough not to be totally overshadowed by him and with a slightly command-ing air which suggested to Sukey that she might well be the stronger character.

Jim put the brochure on the table without opening it and took a mouthful from his glass. "What's your interest?" he asked.

"I have an elderly relative who spends a lot of time there," said Adrian.

"And a lot of money," Cath put in. "That's what really gets my husband's goat – he thinks she's spending our inheritance!" She caught Sukey's eye as she spoke, inviting womanly sym-pathy, and Sukey gave a little nod and smile of understanding.

31

"It's not that at all," Adrian protested good-humouredly. "I just don't like to think of the old girl being ripped off, that's all."

"What makes you think she's being ripped off?" asked Jim.

"The fees seem extortionate to me for sitting around in a circle chanting gibberish."

"I know someone who goes to what she calls 'chanting week-ends'," Sukey remarked. "She's a teacher and she claims it strengthens the chest and lungs."

"There's nothing wrong with Vera's lungs," Cath remarked with a smile. "You should hear her shout at Bruno when he runs off!" She reached down to pat the golden Labrador stretched out at her feet.

"Just the same, I'm not happy about it," Adrian insisted.

"From what you tell me, there doesn't seem to be anything suspicious about the place," said Jim and added, with what Sukey considered admirable diplomacy, "but if you like, I'll ask around among my colleagues to see if anything's known about it."

"I'd be very much obliged," said Adrian.

He appeared to be on the point of saying something else, but Cath silenced him with a slightly imperious gesture. "Vera says she has a lovely time when she goes there, and she's happier than I've seen her for ages," she said firmly. "I say, if that's how she wants to spend her money, that's her affair." With a glance at her husband that made it clear that the topic was to be dropped immediately, she picked up the jug of iced fruit punch and said, "Would anyone like a refill? Dinner will be in about fifteen minutes."

The spacious dining-room had mullioned windows looking out over sloping lawns bordered by flowerbeds. Gaps in the trees marking the boundary of the property gave glimpses of pasture where black-and-white cattle grazed peacefully in the evening sunlight. Indoors as well as out there was luxury on every side, from the array of silver, crystal and bone china on the gleaming mahogany table to the carefully matched and professionally designed furnishings, yet all was discreet and understated, as if chosen to give pleasure to the owners rather than to impress the visitor. The meal was served by a smiling, ruddy-complexioned woman with stiff iron-grey hair who was treated with courteous charm by her employers and addressed as Nanny. "She looked after Anita when she was a baby and then when she retired she came back to look after Adrian and me," Cath explained affectionately.

When dinner was over, Cath said, "We'll have coffee in the little sitting-room, Nanny." As the four of them stood up, Adrian glanced at his watch and said, "I'll join you in a minute – I'll just go and give Vera a call, make sure the old dear's all right."

"Of course she's all right," said Cath with an indulgent smile as she poured coffee from the cafetière into gold-rimmed porcelain cups. "He's like an old mother hen," she informed Sukey and Jim. "Anyone would think she was a frail old thing in her dotage, but really she's as fit as a flea, still drives around in an ancient Rover, goes off on package holidays and generally enjoys life."

"How long has she been going to RYCE?" asked Sukey.

"Several weeks – I can't remember exactly."

At that moment, Adrian entered the room looking anxious. "There's no reply from her number," he said.

Cath glanced at her watch. "It's only a little after nine o'clock," she said. "She's probably out visiting a friend."

"You know she never stays out this late. She gets up at some ungodly hour in the morning and she's always in bed with her book and her hot milk by nine. I don't like it, Cath . . . I don't like it at all."

Five

"Oh Adrian, do stop fussing and come and have your coffee!" Cath appeared relaxed and her manner was coaxing, but Sukey detected a glint of steel in the look she gave her husband. "And what about a liqueur for our guests?"

"Not for me, thank you," said Jim politely. "It's only a short drive home, but—"

"Wouldn't do for a Detective Inspector to be caught over the odds, would it?" Adrian guffawed, his anxiety momentarily forgotten. "How about you, Sukey?"

"I think, if you don't mind, I'll pass. I drank rather a lot of that lovely wine at dinner."

"I'm glad you enjoyed it."

"It was super, and so was the meal."

With evident reluctance, Adrian sat down and accepted the cup of coffee his wife handed him. He tipped in cream and sugar, stirred it and took a mouthful before glancing at his watch and saying, "I'll call her again at half past."

"Now just relax and enjoy the rest of the evening," said Cath firmly. "Vera's perfectly all right – she's probably visiting friends and has simply forgotten the time."

"Probably. Just the same . . ."

"It's natural to be concerned," said Sukey diplomatically, noting Cath's barely concealed exasperation. "My father used to be like a cat on hot bricks if my mother was five minutes late home from an outing."

There was a brief pause when nobody spoke. Adrian Masters's concern for his elderly relative had cast a noticeable restraint over the gathering, which Cath made a pointed attempt to relieve by saying, "I expect you've heard about Anita's plans for her gap year?"

"A bus trip round Europe in the spring, staying at youth hostels – yes, Fergus did mention it," said Sukey. "Has she booked, or is she still thinking about it?"

"I think she's more or less made up her mind, provided her friend agrees to go with her."

"I'm sure it would be a great experience for them both. And Anita's so good at languages—"

"I can't say I'm very keen on the idea," Adrian broke in. "There have been one or two very nasty incidents lately involving young female students roaming around in foreign countries." He gulped the remains of his coffee, declined a refill with an impatient gesture and stood up. "If you'll excuse me, I'm going to try Vera's number again."

"I'm afraid he's a natural-born worrier," sighed Cath by way of an apology as the door closed behind him. "If Anita does go on this trip, he'll die a thousand deaths until she's safely home."

"That I really can identify with," said Sukey warmly. "Fergus has been muttering about doing the same thing – I know he'd give anything to go with the girls, but he'll be too busy studying for his A levels."

Cath nodded. "Yes, of course, but I'd feel a lot happier if he was with them." She gave a sigh. "Children cause us so much anxiety, don't they?" The two mothers exchanged glances of mutual sympathy.

As if to remind them that he was still there, Jim cleared his throat and remarked, "Fergus mentioned that Vera has no other relatives. I suppose in a way that's why your husband feels so responsible for her."

"He does, and I could understand it if she was in her dotage, but she's only in her mid-sixties and so far as we know she's perfectly fit." Cath picked up the cafetière and said, "Would you like some more coffee?"

Both guests declined, and Sukey glanced at Jim and said, "I think it's time we were thinking of going home – we both have an early start in the morning."

At that moment Adrian re-entered the room. "Our guests are just leaving," Cath informed him, but he appeared not to notice.

"There's still no reply," he said with a frown. He was clearly agitated. "If you'll excuse me, I think I'll pop round and check that she hasn't had a fall or been taken ill."

"Does she live near here?" asked Jim.

"In Churchdown – it's only a few minutes by car. I have a key to the house."

"What about Anita?" Cath protested. "You said you'd fetch her at ten – you know I don't like her walking home along the lanes at night, even with Fergus."

"Can't you do it?"

"I can't drive now, I've had too much to drink."

The situation had all the ingredients of a confrontation and Jim said quickly, "I'll bring Anita back if you like – I've got to take Sukey home so it's no trouble."

"That's awfully kind of you."

At that moment the telephone rang. Adrian hurried from the room; through the open door they heard him say, "Hullo . . . speaking . . . what? Oh, my God!" followed by several minutes' silence while the listeners exchanged fearful glances. At last he said in a low voice, "Thank you, I'll come at once." When he returned his face was ashen. "That was the police," he said shakily. "Vera's car's been found in a lay-by with a woman's body in it. They took her to the hospital – the doctor there thinks she died of a heart attack."

"Oh Adrian, how ghastly!" Cath was on her feet and beside her husband in a moment, one arm linked into his. He leaned against her and put a hand over his eyes. "I suppose there's no doubt that it's Vera?" she said.

He swallowed hard, plainly overcome with emotion. "Her handbag was on the seat beside her and they got our number from that card I made her carry," he said when he had his voice under control. "They've asked me to go and identify her."

"Anita'll be really upset about Vera," Fergus remarked at breakfast the next morning. "She used to make fun of her, but she was really very fond of her – so were Cath and Adrian. I wish you'd told us last night when Jim came to pick her up – I could have stayed with her to comfort her."

"Jim and I agreed on the way home that it was better for her mother to break the news."

"What about her Dad – wasn't he there?"

"He had to go to the hospital to identify the body – that's why Jim took Anita home."

"So the story that he didn't like to drive because he'd had too much to drink was a porky?"

"A white one, told with the best of intentions." Sukey finished her breakfast and took her plates and coffee mug to the sink. "It's time I was leaving for work. What are you planning to do today?"

"Go and see Anita, of course."

"It might be an idea to phone first."

"I'll do that. By the way," Fergus hesitated for a moment before asking in a slightly self-conscious manner, "how did you get on with Cath and Adrian?"

"Very well – they're really nice people. We had a lovely evening until the bad news came through."

The lad's face lit up in obvious relief. "I'm so glad," he said.

When she arrived at Gloucester police station, Sukey knocked on the door of DI Castle's office. He was at his desk examining some papers; as he looked up and beckoned her in, she was struck by how tired he looked. He signalled to her to close the door and sit down. "Morning, Jim. What's new?" she asked.

"Adrian was still there when I got back with Anita last night and he was so badly shaken that I felt I had to offer to drive him to the hospital. I stayed with him while he identified the body and then took him home."

"That was kind of you." *And so typical*, she added mentally before remarking, "You must have been pretty late getting back to the flat."

"Gone midnight." He gave a wan smile. "We've both been notching up Brownie points for our good deeds lately, haven't we?"

"I take it the dead woman was Vera?"

"Oh yes. Almost certainly a heart attack, but there's going to be an autopsy to make sure. The car was properly parked with the handbrake on, which suggests that she felt unwell, pulled off the road to have a rest and just quietly keeled over and died."

"All on her own – poor old thing," said Sukey compassionately. "It doesn't sound as if she suffered much, but it's a shock for the family. Fergus reckons they're all going to be very cut up about it."

"Adrian's not just cut up, he insists there's something suspicious about Vera's death."

"Whatever makes him think that?"

"He swears there was nothing wrong with her heart. I pointed out that these attacks do sometimes come out of the blue without any warning symptoms, but he's not convinced."

"So what's his theory?"

"He's made up his mind that the people at the RYCE Foundation are in some way responsible."

Sukey shook her head in bewilderment. "How does he figure that out?"

"As far as I could tell, it's just a gut reaction. As you know, he's pretty obsessive in his mistrust of that outfit."

"Tell me about it," she said with a wry smile. A sudden thought struck her. "It is an odd coincidence, though . . . that's the second death this week with a link to RYCE."

"You're thinking of Oliver Drew?" She nodded. He considered for a moment before saying, "Yes, it is odd, but I'm sure that's all it is . . . a coincidence." He gave her a puzzled look. "You aren't suggesting there's a connection?"

"No, of course not." She stood up and made for the door. "I

must go and show my face or I'll get a rocket from George Barnes."

The sergeant was seated at his desk drinking coffee from a mug emblazoned with the words "It's not my problem – go away!" in eccentric, spiky capitals. "Holiday souvenir, Sarge?" asked Sukey with a grin.

George grunted. His expression was glum. "The wife found it in a souvenir shop while we were away. She thought it was hilarious."

"And you don't?"

"I would if it was true."

"What have you got for us this morning – where's Mandy, by the way?"

"Rang in two minutes ago to say her mother's not very well and she's called the doctor. She hopes to be able to make it later on, after he's been."

"I hope it's nothing serious." Mandy's widowed mother had come to live with her a few months previously when her health had started to cause problems. "How are we fixed for jobs?"

"Not too bad at the moment – let's hope it stays quiet. Two stone fireplaces nicked from a house under restoration in Cheltenham and one smash and grab from a sports shop, also in Cheltenham. And another power mower taken from a garden shed break-in at Burwell Farm. It's in a village of the same name near Twigworth."

"Sounds as if someone's starting up a business in second-hand power tools."

"Could be."

The traffic was moving freely as Sukey drove out of the city and headed north along the A38. Her thoughts turned briefly back to the house at Marsdean, off the same road but in the opposite direction, where she had been working when Jennifer Drew had learned of her husband's suicide. Despite leaving her home number she had had no further word from the young widow, but the brief conversation with Jim Castle that morning had brought the tragedy back to mind and she resolved to give her a call later on.

She found Burwell without difficulty, a small village with a single main street. She pulled up outside the post office and general store and went inside to ask the way to Burwell Farm. Behind the counter, a morose-looking individual looked up from the copy of the *Sun* that was spread out on the counter and peered at her over the top of his spectacles. "Yes?" he said dourly.

"Good morning. I'm looking for Burwell Farm – can you direct me, please?"

His eyebrows lifted and his mouth twisted in a brief, faintly mocking smile as he replied, "You mean the nut-house? Straight up the road and the first on the left."

"Thank you." Sukey hesitated for a moment before asking, "Why do you call it the nut-house?"

He gave a throaty chuckle and licked a finger to turn a page in the newspaper before saying, "You'll find out."

Two minutes later, Sukey turned through an open gateway into a short gravelled drive leading to a rambling, brick-built house. Just inside the entrance a painted notice bore the legend "Welcome to THE RYCE FOUNDATION".

Six

T he drive ended in a gravelled courtyard. The house, which had the appearance of being over a hundred years old, had a pleasantly welcoming aspect, with the morning sun glinting on mullioned windows and lending a glow to the weathered brick. Swags of scarlet and yellow climbing roses adorned the walls on either side of a heavy oak front door, which opened as Sukey parked her van. A young woman emerged with a filing tray of papers in one hand and a steaming mug in the other. High cheekbones, glossy dark hair and olive skin gave her a slightly gipsyish appearance, accentuated by a colourful, ankle-length dress that clung in soft folds to her rounded hips and full bosom. Her teeth flashed white as she greeted Sukey with a friendly "Good morning" and gave a brief glance at the ID she offered for inspection.

"How good of you to come so promptly," she said. Her voice had a warm, bright quality that complemented her smile. "If you wouldn't mind waiting just a moment . . ."

While speaking, she balanced her drink on top of the contents of the filing tray, fished a key from the pocket of her skirt and unlocked the door to a single-storey building which stood at right angles to the main house and which Sukey guessed had been converted from its original use as part of a working farm. On the door was a notice reading "Reception" and the interior was fitted out as an office, with a steel cupboard and filing cabinet behind a desk on which stood a computer monitor and telephone. There were slatted blinds at the windows and a jardinière containing some well-tended foliage plants in one corner. It was in many respects typical of the offices of small businesses Sukey often visited in the course of her work, except for the exotic note struck by a series of posters on the white-painted walls. One in particular caught her eye. It depicted a human form – whether man or woman was not clear – crouched at the base of a towering mountain. The figure was ringed by the words "internal shackles", each letter slightly distorted to give the appearance of a link in a chain. Immediately above, a second ring spelled out "Inner Wheel", in a similar style but with cracks here and there in the links as if to suggest a partial sundering of the chain. In a third ring, the words "Outer Wheel" carried the theme of liberation a stage further until at the top the shackles disappeared altogether and the single word "Unlimited" appeared in a blaze of bright, bold characters in white, edged with gold. Sukey recalled the shopkeeper's dry comment and suppressed a smile.

The woman put her file and her drink on the desk and glanced round. Seeing Sukey staring at the poster, she assumed a slightly mysterious expression and said in an almost reverential tone, "That is the theme of our work. That is the path along which our initiates are led." She held out a slim, brown hand, the fingers tipped with ruby-red nail varnish to match the full, sensuous lips. "My name's Serena," she added.

"Pleased to meet you," Sukey replied as she took the proffered hand, somewhat taken aback by the style of welcome. In her experience, victims of crime had no time for social niceties, being concerned only with speeding up the process of detection. "Now," she went on tactfully, glancing at the files on the desk, "I can see you're busy so if you could just show me where the missing items were kept . . ."

"Yes, of course. Jarvis will show you – he's the gardener, he discovered the break-in when he arrived at seven o'clock this morning."

"He starts work early," Sukey remarked.

"He has to finish any jobs that call for the use of machinery before morning meditation," Serena explained earnestly. "Complete tranquillity and the absence of any movement is essential if we are to create the right ambience."

"I see," said Sukey, wondering how the meditators managed to cope with the sound of tractors, combine harvesters or aircraft. "Was it Jarvis who called the police?"

"That's right. He went to get out the motor mower to cut the grass and found it had gone, so he called them straight away. They asked for the serial number, but he wasn't able to give them that. I have to phone them and quote an incident number."

"You can let me have the details if you like and I'll pass them on."

"That's very kind, thank you." While she was speaking, Serena took a catalogue of garden machinery from a folder and opened it. "This is what they took." She pointed to an illustration of a ride-on motor mower. "We only bought it a couple of weeks ago – we intended to manage with the old one until the end of the season, but the firm was doing a special offer. They took our old one in part exchange. You can take this if you like – I'll write down the serial number for you." She copied something from a sale docket and handed the catalogue to Sukey. "Now," she went on, pointing through the open doorway and across the yard to a white-painted gate set in a low wooden fence running between the house and a second single-storey building immediately facing the office, "if you go through there you'll find Jarvis somewhere around, either in the garden or the greenhouse."

"Thank you." Sukey went to the van, got out her case of equipment and followed the directions. As she crossed the yard she spotted a notice on the door of the other, more modern and evidently purpose-built block, with the words "Rejuvenation Suite". She speculated briefly on what it might contain as she opened the gate, stepped through and followed a path which led round the corner to the side of the house featured on the cover of the brochure. Double-glazed doors gave on to a paved patio, where dozens of containers of every imaginable shape, size, colour and material overflowed with flowering and foliage plants.

At first sight, the garden appeared to consist solely of a vast expanse of lawn enclosed on three sides by trees and tall hedges and bordered to left and right by flagged paths. The gardener was nowhere to be seen, but she could hear a faint trickle of water nearby and, above it, what sounded like someone using hand-shears. Following the sounds, she took the path on the right-hand side and, to her surprise, after she had walked only a few yards, came to a concealed opening in the hedge. The clipping and the gentle splash of the water became closer and she passed through the gap to find herself in a miniature paved courtyard. Two stone steps led down to a sunken pool where a fountain in the shape of a miniature dolphin played over a bed of coloured pebbles that glistened like jewels in the dappled shade cast by the fronds of a weeping tree. The suddenness of the discovery brought with it a kind of Alice-in-Wonderland sensation, as if she had stepped into another dimension, cut off from day-to-day reality and absorbed into an atmosphere of almost tangible peace and repose. Momentarily forgetting why she was there, she put down her bag, sank on to the stone bench placed invitingly at the water's edge and spontaneously exclaimed, "How absolutely lovely!"

The sound of clipping ceased and a man appeared in front of her, so suddenly that it seemed as if he had sprung out of the ground. She judged him to be about fifty, with a weathered complexion and deeply tanned muscular arms. He wore faded jeans and a checked shirt with the sleeves rolled up to the elbows and he held a pair of shears by both handles. "Morning, Miss," he said politely.

"Gracious! Where did you spring from?" said Sukey with a start.

"Next door!" He gestured behind him with the shears at yet another concealed opening in the far corner of the courtyard. "You're early – they don't start till half-past nine."

Sukey got to her feet. "Are you Mr Jarvis?" she asked.

"That's me. If you want to stay here quietly for a while –" a further movement of the shears invited her to sit down again – "I'll go and work somewhere else."

"Oh, no, I'm not here on a course. I've come about the theft of a power mower," she explained, fishing her ID from her pocket.

"Oh, right. You'll want to see where they broke in. It's this way." He beckoned with the shears and she followed him through the opening by which he had made his unexpected entrance. It led to yet another secluded area where a similar stone bench was surrounded by beds of plants arranged in a wheel. A spicy perfume hung in the air. "You won't need me to tell you that these are aromatic herbs," Jarvis remarked.

"This is the most fascinating garden I've ever seen," said Sukey. "How many of these little green cubby-holes are there – and are they all connected?"

"There's eight in all – six this side and two the other. They were planned like this by a previous owner, but the folks who run this place find them just right to sit and think in." Evidently, "meditate" was not part of his vocabulary. "We can get to the outhouses through here," he went on, leading the way to yet another concealed opening in the far corner, beside which was a small wicket gate. "Course, I can't bring machinery through – I just use it as a short cut when there's no one around."

Beyond the gate, the normal world reappeared in the shape of a patch of uncultivated ground at the back of the "Rejuvenation" building, with a compost heap, several cold frames and sundry terracotta pots stacked neatly in a corner. A lean-to glasshouse took up part of the wall and alongside was a brick-built shed. The door stood open; two heavy padlocks, their hasps cleanly severed, lay on the ground beside it. "That's where the mower was kept. I should have been using it this morning, the grass is due for a cut," Jarvis grumbled. "You can see how the blighters got in – must have used bolt cutters, those padlocks are the strongest I could find. They nicked a hedge-cutter and a strimmer as well, only they weren't new."

Sukey opened her bag and got to work. Jarvis stood by watching as she bagged up samples and searched for clues. "Been doing this job for long?" he asked as she got out her camera and focused on the print of a boot clearly visible in a patch of damp earth.

"Quite a while. How about you?"

"Been a gardener all my life." He fished out a packet of cigarettes and lit one, leaning against the wall of the shed. "Worked for these people since they came here," he added. He seemed disposed to chat, and it occurred to Sukey that he might be a useful source of information.

"I'd never heard of this place until a couple of days ago, and then I came across two people who'd been . . . what do they call them? Initiates?"

"That's right." He lifted his face to the sun and exhaled smoke skywards. "It's a rum set-up on the face of it – all that stuff about wheels and the cosmos – but I must say, a lot of them seem to find it helps. I've seen some of them turn up on their first day looking scared out of their wits but after a while something seems to happen . . . they look sort of peaceful. Mostly, that is. Once in a while it seems to go wrong."

"How do you mean?"

"Hard to say. I never get to talk to them, of course, but now and again I come across them, sitting in one of the gardens doing their thinking. Mostly they sit there with their eyes shut and a smile on their faces, as if they're having a pleasant dream, but once or twice I've had the feeling that the dream wasn't so pleasant." He broke off and inhaled deeply on his cigarette. "Suppose you can't win 'em all," he added philosophically.

Sukey's interest was aroused. "I don't suppose you happen to remember a gentleman recently who appeared disturbed . . . you know, having a bad dream?" she asked.

Jarvis pursed his lips and thought for a moment. He took several deep drags on the cigarette before replying, "Can't say I do. There was a lady, though, only yesterday it was – but she wasn't in the garden, she came running out of what they call the Rejuvenation Suite just as I was packing up."

"Running?"

"Well, hurrying. It was unusual – they mostly come out of there looking half asleep."

"What time would this have been?"

"About five o'clock, I suppose."

"You work a long day."

"I'd been to the dentist in the morning so I started later than usual."

"This lady – was she one of the regular initiates?"

"I've seen her once or twice before and she always seemed happy enough, but this time she looked sort of put out, as if something had upset her. She got in her car and drove off as if she had a train to catch."

"What sort of age was she?"

"Sixtyish I suppose, she had white hair. Why do you ask?"

"I happen to know of a lady who used to come here. She died suddenly last night of a heart attack and I wondered . . . did you happen to notice what car she drove – the lady you were speaking of, I mean?"

"A red one, a Metro I think. Oh dear –" Jarvis's ruddy features registered concern – "I'm sorry to hear about your friend."

"I didn't actually know her, she's a relative of a friend," Sukey explained. "I've finished here now; I'll just go back to the office and have a word with Serena. Thanks for your help."

He dropped the butt of his cigarette on the ground and stamped on it. "A pleasure," he assured her.

She found Serena laying out a selection of slim paperbacks on a table just inside the reception area. She looked up and said, "Did you find anything? Do you think there's any chance of catching the thieves?"

"It's hard to tell at this stage, but we'll do our best. Jarvis tells me there were some other items stolen – do you happen to have their serial numbers as well?"

"The strimmer and the hedge-cutter? Probably." Serena went to the filing cabinet; while she was searching, Sukey glanced idly at some of the books. The titles struck her as distinctly bizarre: *The RYCE Road to the Great Unlimited, Your Cosmic Energy*

47

Released, What Your Cosmic Energy Can Achieve, You and the Cosmos. She picked up the first one and glanced idly at the cover. "They're for sale," Serena told her as she wrote numbers on a piece of paper.

"Er, not for me, I don't get much time for reading," Sukey said hastily and put the book down."

"At least, take a brochure. There's no charge for that." Serena gave another flashing smile as she held one out.

"Thank you," said Sukey politely. She took the brochure and slipped it into her shoulder bag. A thought occurred to her. "By the way, could you tell me where you bought the mower?"

"From an outfit called 'Lawnmowers Unlimited' in Tewkesbury. Why do you ask?"

"It might help the police in their enquiries, that's all. They'll be in touch if they have anything to report."

As Sukey returned to her van, a young girl cycled through the gate, dismounted and parked her bike alongside the wall of the building. She was dressed in blue jeans and a matching T-shirt that set off her long straight blond hair and blue-grey eyes, and she had an air of calm that seemed to reflect the pervading atmosphere of the place. She gave Sukey a friendly smile as she entered the office.

Seven

After dealing with the two jobs in Cheltenham, Sukey drove to Pittville Park and ate her sandwiches beside the lake watching children with their mothers feeding the swans before returning to the van and checking in to central control for further instructions.

"Garden shed broken into and another motor mower gone missing," the officer taking the call informed her.

"Tewesbury area?" Sukey enquired.

"How did you guess?"

"Anything else?"

"No, that's it for the moment."

The detached bungalow on a corner plot about half a mile from the town centre was in sharp contrast to Burwell Farm, but was just as well maintained. The garden was a picture of geometric order, the grass immaculately trimmed, "the edges looking as if they'd been cut with a razor blade, everything clippable clipped into shape and all the plants standing to attention", as she described it to Fergus that evening. It reflected the personality of the owner, an elderly gentleman with a neatly trimmed white moustache and an upright military bearing who introduced himself as Major Hyde, pointed indignantly to the splintered door of his garden shed and barked, "Happened while my wife and I were out visiting friends yesterday evening. Blighters must have watched us leave. Don't know what this country's coming to, in my day you could go out and leave your door open and no one'd steal a farthing. Things are coming to a pretty pass when you can't turn your back for five minutes without being robbed."

He stood watching while Sukey, who had been interposing sympathetic noises during his tirade, began inspecting the damage. An old-fashioned bicycle lay on the floor inside the shed. "Did they have to move that to get at the mower?" she asked.

"As it happens, they would have done. Why do you ask?"

Sukey got out her brushes and began dusting the frame. "They might have left prints when they handled it," she explained. A couple of minutes' work revealed evidence that someone had grasped the bicycle by the crossbar. "Would that be yours?" she asked, pointing to the distinct outline of a thumb shown up by the grey powder.

"Definitely not," the major said flatly. "I always hold it by the saddle and handlebars."

"What about your wife?"

"Not allowed in the shed," he responded without a flicker of a smile.

"Then we might be in luck. I'll need to take your prints for elimination, if you've no objection."

"None whatever. Anything to help catch the blighters." He remained watching without further comment until she had finished her examination and then led her indoors. He sat down at the kitchen table while she took his fingerprints. "I thought criminals wore gloves nowadays," he remarked as she manipulated his fingers.

"Not all of them. You'd be surprised how dim some of them are. It's how a lot get caught, making idiotic mistakes like that."

"They should bring back National Service," he declared with a snort of contempt as he scrubbed his hands at the sink. "That'd teach 'em to behave themselves, give 'em a taste of old-fashioned discipline."

"That's not a bad idea," Sukey agreed diplomatically as she packed her equipment away. "Just one point," she added casually, "Do you mind telling me where you bought the mower?"

"A place just up the road from here – Lawnmowers Unlimited. Not been open long. They offered a good deal in part exchange. Why d'you ask?"

"Only that there's been a spate of thefts of garden machinery in this area and we're trying to establish some sort of pattern, that's all."

"Can't believe they've got anything to do with it. Chap who runs it is ex-army, thoroughly decent sort. Well, good hunting. I take it it's all right to get the door repaired now? That young fellah-me-lad in uniform who came first thing said to leave it till you'd had a look at it."

"Oh yes, that's quite OK." Giving the usual assurances about keeping him informed, Sukey left.

It was only half-past two; having checked in and been told that there were no more jobs for her that afternoon she decided to pay Lawnmowers Unlimited a quick visit before returning to the station, partly out of curiosity and partly because she had decided some time ago that her own lawnmower had had its day. She found it without difficulty, the end unit in a small row of shops comprising a hairdresser, a bakery and a general store. She parked the van on one of the spaces marked out on the forecourt and went to have a closer look. Beside the entrance, a placard announced a special discount on any power-operated machine, coupled with 'generous' part-exchange terms. She studied the display in the window, which was crammed with an assortment of small mowers and other sundry items of garden machinery. A glance through the open door offered a glimpse of some larger pieces of equipment arranged in a neat row, all shiny and new and bearing the names of well-known manufacturers.

At the far end was a counter and behind it a run of metal shelving stacked with spare parts. Above the sound of pop music from a hidden transistor radio, some energetic hammering in the background suggested that the rear of the premises was being used as a workshop. A middle-aged man in dark blue overalls was serving a customer. Above his head was a notice reading "Any Item Not in Stock Obtained to Order", and a further notice propped at the side of the counter offered repairs and servicing at competetive prices.

Sukey waited until the man was free and then said, "Good

afternoon. I'm thinking of buying a new mower and I haven't any idea what's available – can you give me details of some models and prices? Nothing too elaborate, I've only got a small garden . . ."

He was only too ready to offer advice and within minutes she had received a bewildering collection of brochures and price lists. "I'll have to talk this over with my husband," she said. "By the way, I live in Brockworth – do you deliver that far afield?"

"There might be a small charge if it's outside our area." The man glanced over his shoulder. "Brockworth OK for free delivery, Darrell?" The hammering ceased and a cropped head appeared round the end of the row of shelving, glanced briefly in Sukey's direction, nodded and said, "No problem," before disappearing again.

"Has Darrell been working for you long?" Sukey asked casually as she gathered up the brochures and prepared to leave.

"About six months. First class mechanic, he is – does all the deliveries as well, knows the area like the back of his hand. I don't know what I'd do without him. That's what I tell him, anyway – keeps him in a good mood," he added with a wink.

Back at the station, Sukey stopped to have a word with the desk sergeant before going up to the SOCOs' room. "D'you remember a lad called Darrell something who was caught nicking bicycles a while back? I was here when he was brought in – he was kicking up a fuss, claiming police harassment, demanding to see his brief."

The sergeant grinned. "They all do that. What makes this one special?"

"He was called –" Sukey trawled her memory – "Mullin? Marling? No, Millings."

"The name does ring a bell," the sergeant admitted. He scratched his head with his pen. "Yes, I remember now," he said after a moment's reflection. "Scruffy little bugger, hair almost down to his knees. What about him?"

"I think I saw him this afternoon working for an outfit

supplying lawnmowers in Tewkesbury. He's had a David Beckham haircut, but I'm almost sure it was the same bloke."

"Nice to think he's decided to earn an honest living for a change."

"Except that I've a notion he might be doing a little moonlighting. Thanks, Sarge."

Sukey went upstairs to the SOCOs' room to write her reports and pack up her samples for examination. "I've an idea who might be behind the mower thefts," she informed Sergeant Barnes. "A young villain called Darrell Millings. It's only guesswork at the moment, but if his fingerprints match these, we might get lucky. I'll put in a note for a special check."

"Quite the little sleuth, aren't we?" George remarked with mock sarcasm.

"We keep our eyes open," she retorted. "Well, that's my lot for today. See you tomorrow."

On her way out she tapped on the door of DI Jim Castle's office, which was just along the corridor. He was on the phone, but he beckoned her in and she waited until he had finished. "Something to report?" he said.

"I'm not sure. Do you happen to know what car Adrian Masters's aunt drove?"

"I think he said it was a Metro."

"A red one?"

"I don't know about the colour. Why do you ask?"

"It's just that my first job this morning was at a house called Burwell Farm. Only it isn't a farm now, it's the headquarters of the RYCE Foundation." She could tell from the way his eyebrows lifted and his mouth pursed that he was interested in hearing more.

"I got chatting to the gardener." She recounted the conversation. "It occurred to me that the woman he saw driving off in a red Metro might have been Vera. He said she seemed 'put out', was the way he described it. If it was her, maybe she'd had some kind of argument or disagreement with someone that upset her and brought on the heart attack."

"I suppose it's possible," Jim agreed in a tone that suggested he considered it unlikely.

"Do you think I should mention it to Adrian?"

"I wouldn't advise it. He strikes me as the sort who shoots from the hip, and knowing how he feels about the place, he's quite capable of charging round there and throwing accusations around. He could end up in all sorts of trouble."

"You're probably right."

"What was your impression of the RYCE place, by the way?"

"There's a very peaceful, benign sort of atmosphere about it, although of course I didn't see inside the house or meet the proprietors. A girl called Serena who seems to run the office was very pleasant and helpful. Their publications are a bit weird –" Sukey reeled off some of the titles – "but nothing struck me as sinister."

"If I were you, I'd just let it drop."

"Serena gave me a brochure. I'm thinking of becoming an 'initiate'," she said with a provocative twitch of the lips.

"You'll do nothing of the kind."

She sensed that he wasn't joking; a perverse desire to goad him further prompted her to retort, "Why not? I thought releasing my cosmic energy might add a whole new dimension to my personal life." She left the room without giving him a chance to reply.

When she reached home she found Fergus in the kitchen surrounded by textbooks. "Just doing a spot of work on my French assignment," he explained.

"I'm glad you're taking it seriously." She went to the sink to fill the kettle for tea. "Have you seen Anita today?"

"I phoned just after you left and I went over and spent the morning with her."

"How are things there?"

"They're all pretty cut up over Vera, of course. Cath's tearing her hair out because Adrian keeps on about RYCE – he reckons it's all their fault that she had the heart attack." Unconsciously confirming Jim Castle's prediction, Fergus added, "Anita says he's been threatening to go round and 'sort them out', as he calls it."

"How does he figure out it's their fault?"

"Cath says it's a gut reaction. He's been so dead set against the place from the start that he's ready to blame them for everything. He's even predicting that it'll turn out she's changed her will in their favour."

"That would look bad," Sukey admitted. "Still, Cath's right – he should keep well away from the place unless he's got something concrete to go on." She made the tea, poured out two mugs and fetched milk from the refrigerator. "Now, if you wouldn't mind making a bit of room on the table . . ."

"Sure." Fergus pushed his books and papers to one side and pulled out a chair for her. "How was your day, Mum?"

It had been her intention to tell him about the visit to the RYCE headquarters, without referring to the conversation with Jarvis, but in the light of Jim's comments and knowing he would almost certainly mention it to Anita, who would then pass it on to her parents, she decided to say nothing. Instead, she gave him a humorous version of her encounter with Major Hyde, her subsequent visit to Lawnmowers Unlimited and her hopes of solving the case of the missing garden machinery.

"Another brilliant success for super sleuth Sukey Reynolds!" he exclaimed, raising his mug in salute. "You are clever, Mum!"

"Aw, shucks, it was nothing."

"What's for supper?"

"Lamb chops."

"Is Jim coming?"

"Not this evening – he's on late turn."

"He will be free at the weekend, won't he?"

"I'm not sure. Why do you ask?"

"It's just that Dad wants me to spend it with him and I don't want to leave you on your own."

"That's sweet of you." As always, she was touched by his mature consideration for her. "Is there something special happening?"

"I think he wants me to meet his new girlfriend."

Sukey looked up from her tea in surprise. "How long has this been going on?" It had taken Fergus's father, her ex-husband Paul, a long time to recover from the shock of his second wife's horrific murder.

"He's known her quite a while – she works at his office – but I think he's been scared of getting involved."

"That's understandable. You go ahead and make your arrangements – I'll be all right."

The telephone rang and Fergus leapt to his feet. "That might be Anita – I'll get it." He said, "Hullo," listened for a few moments and then said, "Yes, she's here. Hold on, please." He covered the mouthpiece with his hand as he passed the receiver to his mother. "It's a Mrs Drew. She sounds in a bit of a state."

"Sukey, is . . . that . . . you?" Jennifer was hyperventilating, her words coming in jerky, disjointed phrases. "Something's happened . . . I need . . . to talk to someone. Please . . . can you come?"

"What is it? Has there been another break-in, or—"

"No, it isn't that. I've discovered . . . I think I may have found out . . ." There was a pause during which Jennifer seemed to be fighting for breath.

"Do please try and calm down," Sukey urged. "Take some deep breaths," she added as the sounds of distress continued.

It was several moments before Jennifer spoke again. Then she said in a barely audible whisper, "I think I know now why Ollie killed himself."

Eight

It was well after nine o'clock when Sukey turned through the gates of Marsdean Manor. Jennifer Drew must have been looking out for her; the car had barely come to a stop when the front door was flung open and she came stumbling towards it, wrenched open the driver's door and clutched at Sukey as if in terror that she would change her mind and drive away again.

"Thank God you're here! I thought you'd never come!" she gasped. Her body was shaking uncontrollably and her teeth chattered as if with cold, but her hands were hot and her eyes fiery red in her deathly white face.

"I came as quickly as I could." Sukey got out of the car, took her by the arm and guided her back into the house. "Did you take my advice and have a bite to eat?"

"I had a glass of milk – I couldn't face anything solid." At least, she was no longer hyperventilating. The moment the door closed behind them she said, "You had someone with you – a man answered the phone. Who was he? What have you told him?"

"That was my teenage son, Fergus. All I told him was that you're still very upset after your husband's death and you're alone in the house and in need of a bit of company."

"Did you mention RYCE?"

"No, why should I?" Sukey asked in surprise.

"I wondered if perhaps you'd guessed."

"Guessed what?"

"I'll explain in a minute."

Although her breathing was more normal she was still trembling and there was a feverish glitter in her eyes. Sensing that she needed to calm down before she was in any state to tell her story coherently, and deliberately making her voice brisk and matter-of-fact, Sukey said, "Would you like me to make you some coffee?" Jennifer nodded. "Then let's go in the kitchen. You can show me where everything is."

The need to do something practical and the comforting presence of another human being seemed to have the desired effect. By the time the coffee was made and poured out, Jennifer had stopped trembling. "Shall we drink it in here?" Sukey asked.

Jennifer shook her head and put the cups on a tray. "No, we'll go into Oliver's study. That's where I found it."

"Found what?"

"I'll show you in a minute."

It was not long after sunset; the curtains in the study were still open and a pale, almost full moon hovering above the horizon lent a theatrical quality to what remained of the daylight, as if an invisible hand was manipulating it for dramatic effect. Sukey felt a trickle of gooseflesh which vanished as Jennifer switched on the lamps and closed the curtains, destroying the illusion.

From a pile of letters laid out on the desk and secured by a heavy glass paperweight, Sukey surmised that Jennifer had been going through her late husband's correspondence. "All this has arrived since Ollie went missing," she explained. "I decided to open it, just to see if there was anything that could give a clue . . . and this is what I found." She put down her cup of coffee and picked up the single sheet of paper that was lying on top of the heap. "It's his bank statement," she said. "Just look at that."

She had started to tremble again; the hand that held the paper was shaking so violently that Sukey had to take hold of her wrist to steady it. "What is it you want me to see?" she asked.

"That figure there . . . one thousand pounds withdrawn in cash a couple of weeks ago."

"What about it?"

"Don't you understand?" Jennifer's voice, still hoarse with weeping, now betrayed signs of mounting hysteria. "That's about the time when things started to go wrong again . . . they were blackmailing him . . . it was their fault he died . . . they killed him!" She covered her eyes and broke into a storm of crying that, despite Sukey's desperate attempts to calm her, continued uncontrollably for several minutes until, as if a switch had been thrown, it abruptly ceased. Jennifer dried her eyes, sniffed and reached for her cup of coffee. She took a sip, pulled a face and said, "It's cold. Yours must be as well. I'll go and warm it up in the microwave."

She put both cups back on the tray and swept out of the room with what seemed to Sukey a disproportionate show of urgency. Through the open door came a series of beeps; then she was back, handing Sukey her cup of reheated coffee with an artificially bright "Sorry about that." They faced one another in the chairs they had been sitting in on Monday when Jennifer confided her anxiety over her husband's absence. Apart from the apology, she had not uttered a word since remarking on the cold coffee and Sukey felt increasingly uneasy at her sudden change of mood. The sense of unreality she had experienced when entering the study began to return; the tension initiated by Jennifer's extraordinary outburst, followed by the unnatural period of calm, was beginning to mount. She felt like an actor caught in the nightmare of being on stage with no idea of the part she was expected to play.

It seemed an age before Jennifer spoke. Then she said, "You do see, don't you, that they killed him?" The feverish glitter had returned to her eyes. "Oh, I know what you're going to say," she rushed on before Sukey had a chance to respond. "He was the one who put the pipe on the exhaust . . . he put it in the car . . . he shut the windows and switched on the engine to die all alone in those poisonous fumes . . ." Her voice shook, but this time it did not break. "He did all that because they were blackmailing him, so it was their fault he did it. They killed him!" she repeated.

"Jennifer, I don't understand," said Sukey. "Who do you think was blackmailing your husband?" But even as she put the question, she had the feeling that she knew the answer.

59

"The people at RYCE, of course. Who else?"

"Do you have any proof?"

"I don't need any proof. Why else would Oliver have drawn out a thousand pounds in cash, if it wasn't to pay off a blackmailer?"

"I don't know, but there could be a perfectly reasonable explanation."

"Like what?"

"I don't know," Sukey repeated helplessly. "Perhaps he was negotiating some business deal he hadn't told you about, or maybe he just liked to have a lot of cash in the house in case he needed it."

"He talked everything over with me, and he's never drawn out that amount of cash before. I know, I've checked through his bank statements for the past six months. That was hush money paid to those creatures at RYCE. If only I hadn't sent him there!"

"I thought you said things had been so much better since he started going there."

"Things were better, and then they got worse again. Why were they demanding all that money? They must have done something to him."

"What makes you so certain the money was intended for RYCE? In any case, to blackmail someone you have to have a hold over them, know some guilty secret—"

As if Sukey had not spoken, Jennifer repeated, "They must have done something to him."

"What sort of something?"

"That's what I intend to find out."

Sukey was becoming increasingly alarmed. If there was any doubt that Jennifer was in a thoroughly irrational state of mind it was dispelled by her next words. "I've worked out exactly what I'm going to do," she declared. "I'm going to become one of their initiates and find out what tricks they get up to." She took a deep breath and looked Sukey full in the face. Her eyes burned with an almost fanatical glow. "I want to ask you a favour," she said.

"What is it?"

"When I find what I'm looking for, I'll need a witness. Will you come with me?"

Sukey had been listening in growing astonishment and disbelief at the succession of wild accusations and bizarre plans for justifying them, and casting about for some way of persuading Jennifer to take a more balanced view of the situation. *Think it over . . . wait until the first shock has passed . . . have a word with your doctor*, were some of the suggestions that sprang to mind. It took a moment for her to grasp the full significance of the young widow's closing words, and when she did she could only sit and stare with her mouth open.

As if interpreting her silence for refusal, Jennifer grasped Sukey by both hands. "Please!" she begged. "Say you'll do it – you promised to be my friend!"

"I know I did, and it's as your friend that I'm asking you not to go rushing into something that might lead you into serious trouble," Sukey said earnestly.

It dawned on her as she spoke that here, in a more extreme form, was almost a carbon copy of Adrian Masters's reaction to the death of Auntie Vera and his insistence that someone at RYCE was in some unspecified way responsible. It was totally illogical, yet the fact that the two events, occurring in such quick succession, had aroused the same passionate reaction, was uncanny.

"I know what I'm doing, I don't need to think about it," said Jennifer dismissively.

"Well, I do." Sukey found herself regretting having ever become involved in this bizarre scenario. "I'm a single parent with a son who's still at school, I have a full-time job, I can't just drop everything and—"

"If it's the money, don't worry about that – I'll pay for everything."

"It isn't just a question of money. Listen, Jennifer." Sukey gently squeezed the hands that remained clinging to hers. "You've had a terrible shock, you're overwrought and grieving.

It's very difficult to think clearly in those circumstances, and being in the house by yourself doesn't help. Why don't you let me try and arrange for someone—"

"I'm all right, I don't want anyone else in the house, unless you – would you stay with me for a day or two? Just until we can arrange to become initiates? I'll fill in the forms and everything—"

This was becoming more difficult by the minute. "Now listen, Jennifer," said Sukey firmly. "You must get this into your head – I have responsibilities that I can't just drop at a moment's notice, and in any case you're in no fit state to make decisions. Give it a day or two, wait till you've calmed down."

"I don't want to calm down. I want to stay angry." Jennifer spoke through gritted teeth, her mouth set in an obstinate line.

Sukey had a flash of inspiration. "I read somewhere that revenge is a dish best eaten cold," she said.

Jennifer gave a disdainful sniff. "What do you suppose that means?"

"I think it probably means that you stand a better chance of succeeding if you plan things carefully, rather than go rushing off like a bull at a gate."

"You think so?" For the first time, Jennifer showed signs of wavering.

Sukey pressed home her advantage. "It makes sense to me."

"But you will help me?"

"That depends on what you decide to do."

"But you aren't saying no?"

Prevarication seemed to be the only way out of an increasingly tricky situation. "I'm not saying no, but I'm not saying yes either – and I'm certainly not committing myself one way or the other tonight," Sukey said firmly. "And I want you to promise not to do anything precipitate. Think things over for a day or two. And in the meantime, I suggest you have a chat with your doctor – and you'll have to see your solicitor as well." She indicated the stacks of files and correspondence on the desk. "You'll have a lot of business matters to deal with."

And perhaps that'll take your mind off this crazy obsession, she added mentally.

"What do I want to see the doctor for?" Jennifer demanded, a shade belligerently.

"You're still in shock. He'll give you something to help you cope – and make it easier for you to think everything out more clearly," Sukey added by way of an inducement. "And one more thing. I'd be very careful not to go repeating these accusations about RYCE to anyone else. You have absolutely no proof that they've done anything improper and you could lay yourself open to an action for defamation."

Jennifer's features settled into a sullen expression. "All right," she muttered.

"So what was up with Mrs Drew?" asked Fergus. "She sounded pretty worked up on the phone."

Sukey gave a wry grimace. "'Worked up' is the understatement of the week. The shock of her husband's suicide has affected the poor girl's state of mind very badly. In fact, she's quite paranoid at the moment. On the strength of finding from her husband's bank statement that he recently drew out a thousand pounds in cash, she's convinced herself that he was being blackmailed and that was what drove him to suicide."

"What on earth does she suppose he's done to lay himself open to blackmail?"

"You tell me. It can't be ruled out, I suppose, but I tried to persuade her not to jump to conclusions – said there could easily be a perfectly ordinary explanation. She brushed all that aside and went on to allege that it's someone at the RYCE Foundation who's behind it."

Fergus's jaw dropped. "You're kidding!"

"That's not all. She's planning to enrol for one of their courses and go snooping around in an attempt to track down the supposed blackmailer, and she only wants me to go along with her to help with the detective work."

"Did you say you'd do it?" At the word "detective" a familiar gleam dawned in Fergus's eyes. "It might be rather a lark. Seeing what really goes on there, I mean."

"Now you're the one who's kidding." Wearily, Sukey passed a hand over her eyes. "That place is beginning to haunt me," she complained.

"You turned her down, then?" There was no mistaking the lad's disappointment.

"I'm afraid I was a bit ambivalent because I didn't want to cause another wobbly by saying an outright no, but I assure you I've no intention of getting mixed up in any of her half-baked schemes. For goodness' sake, I hardly know the woman." Sukey got up from the couch, where she had collapsed as soon as she reached home. "It's nearly eleven and I've had a gruelling day. I'm going to bed."

Fergus gave a guilty start. "Oh Lord, I almost forgot – Adrian rang not long after you left. He asked if you'd call back when you got home. Said it didn't matter how late it was."

"What did he want?"

"He didn't say, except that it was important."

Sukey gave a resigned sigh. "I suppose I'd better see what he wants or he'll be sitting up half the night." She picked up the phone. "What's their number?"

Adrian answered on the first ring. "Sukey? It's good of you to call back."

"Fergus said you wanted to speak to me urgently."

"Yes. I don't know if he or Anita ever mentioned it, but Vera kept a diary, quite a detailed one."

"No, I don't think so."

"Actually, she had quite a flair for writing. There wasn't anything secret about it – in fact, she used to read bits to us occasionally, usually about people she'd met, places she'd been to and so on. She had a great sense of humour and quite a racy style – some of it was very entertaining." Adrian paused for a moment before continuing. "I've just been reading through the last few entries. I was looking for some reference to her health, any suggestion that she suspected there was anything wrong."

"Did you find anything?"

"Nothing much on that score. I don't think she'd consulted a doctor for years, but there was a recent entry that made me sit up. She'd met this bloke she knew in a pub somewhere – she was a great one for having pub lunches. She writes, 'Met Ollie in the Green Dragon. Hadn't seen him for ages – he used to come to RYCE and they did him a lot of good, but he hasn't been lately. I've quite missed him, he was a real gentleman. He looked very down in the mouth today and I tried to cheer him up. I suggested he come back to RYCE for a booster session. His reaction was extraordinary – he turned the colour of a beetroot and said, "Those bastards – I wish I'd never set foot in the place!" Then he banged his beer mug down on the table and stomped out without even apologising for saying "bastards".' There!" A note of triumph entered Adrian's voice. "What do you think of that? I knew there was something fishy about that place."

At the reference to the man called Ollie, Sukey's mind had been instantly on the alert and she had listened with growing interest. Not wishing at this stage to say anything that Adrian could seize on to reinforce his suspicions, she said cautiously, "It does sound as if something went a bit wrong in that man's case, but it doesn't necessarily mean—"

"They're up to something, I'm sure of it. It's no good going to the police – they won't take it seriously. That's why I'm telling you."

Briefly, he explained his reasons for calling her. "I don't expect you to decide right away," he said. "All I ask is that you think it over."

Anything to get rid of him so that I can go to bed and forget all this crazy nonsense. "All right, I'll do that," she said wearily and hung up.

"So what was that about?" asked Fergus.

"Gus, you aren't going to believe this. He's asking me to do the same as Jennifer Drew – play detective at the RYCE Foundation."

Nine

"It's a very striking coincidence, certainly, but I don't believe it's anything more than that," said Jim.

"Two unexpected deaths with a rather questionable feature in common, and you're saying it's no more than coincidence?" Sukey looked at him in surprise. Recalling the numerous occasions when he had crossed swords with a certain recently retired superintendent in what seemed to her to be comparable circumstances, she added, "You're beginning to sound like Mr Sladden."

"Point taken, but in neither of the cases we're talking about is there anything to suggest that a crime has been committed. It's simply that two highly-strung people have shown a similar reaction to the sudden death of someone close to them. Jennifer Drew is obviously so shattered by her husband's suicide that logical thought has gone out of the window, and as for Adrian Masters . . ." Jim shook his head in exasperation. "He's been so anti the RYCE outfit from day one that he's ready to believe anything against them. I'm sure they're both barking up the wrong tree."

"Adrian'd be even more convinced if he knew about the state she was in when Jarvis saw her leave the house the very day she died," Sukey reminded him.

"Then you'd better not mention it," said Jim sharply. "In any case, you can't be certain it was Vera."

"It would be interesting to know how many elderly women among the RYCE initiates drive red Metros."

"All right, it probably was her, but it still doesn't prove

anything against the people who run it. My advice is to forget all about it."

"But what about Vera's comments in her diary? Doesn't that indicate that Oliver Drew held RYCE responsible for his sudden switch from euphoria to depression? Something must have happened to account for that outburst."

"In the first place, we don't know that it was Drew she was referring to – didn't you say the diary merely mentioned someone called Ollie? And it's more than likely she exaggerated his reactions anyway – the way she apparently took exception to the word 'bastards' shows a pretty old-maidish attitude."

"Maybe, but I still think Adrian may have a point when he—"

"Now look here, Sook." She could tell from his tone that he was beginning to lose patience with the topic. "The mere fact that Oliver Drew and Vera Masters both attended meetings of a somewhat eccentric cult doesn't suggest to me that their deaths are in any way related. It's not as if the cause of death was the same. Vera obviously had a heart condition that no one suspected – the doctor who examined her body is confident that the autopsy will confirm it – and as for Oliver Drew, for all we know he might have been up to his neck in some shady deal that his wife knew nothing about."

"All right, but I'd still like to know a bit more about the background to this outfit." Sukey began unpacking and putting away the supplies they had brought in for the weekend, took two glasses from a cupboard and put them on the table. From the refrigerator she took a can of beer and handed it to him. "You did promise Adrian you'd ask around," she reminded him. "Did you find out anything?"

His frown gave way to a smile as he took the can. "Thanks, I'm ready for that." He pulled off the ring, poured out the contents and took a long draught. "Yes, I did, as a matter of fact. There's nothing about the organisation in our records, but Andy Radcliffe happened to remember reading something about it in the local press a couple of years or so ago." He gestured towards the empty glass. "What are you going to have?"

"A gin and tonic, please. Will you fix it for me while I do the spuds?"

He poured her drink and and took another appreciative swig from his own. "TGI Friday – it's been a long week."

"Hear, hear!" Sukey put potatoes into the sink and turned on the tap. "Well go on, tell me," she said impatiently.

"It's nothing to get excited about. The couple who run the place are Percival and Edith Burrell and Andy said they were in a spot of trouble once for making misleading claims for what they refer to as their 'therapies'. Some unofficial watchdog got hold of one of their brochures and showed it to his doctor, who reported them to the local health authority. As far as Andy remembers, they simply agreed to withdraw their current publicity material and submit a revised version for approval. No, I'm afraid Adrian Masters and your little friend Jennifer will just have to accept that there's absolutely no call for any kind of criminal investigation into the deaths of their dear ones. Come on, love," he coaxed, picking up his beer and Sukey's so far untouched glass. "You look tired as well – let's relax in the sitting-room for half an hour before we start thinking about food."

She was only too ready to accept the suggestion. Throughout the day her mind had been in turmoil as the result of the disturbing requests that she had received the previous evening, first from Jennifer and then from Adrian, to take on what amounted to a private investigation That was something she had omitted to tell Jim when describing her visit to the former and the phone call from the latter, knowing that his reaction would have been to insist without hesitation that she refuse. Her own common sense told her that she should do just that, but at the back of her mind a notion lurked that despite Jim's perfectly rational arguments, there was some justification for suspicion, a notion that refused to be stifled. Her innate curiosity was beginning to make its voice heard as well.

For the moment, however, she was content to relax on the couch with her head on her lover's shoulder and enjoy the prospect of two days of his company. For once, there was no urgent inquiry afoot that threatened to disrupt their plans at short notice, Fergus was spending the weekend with his father and the weather was set fair.

Jim put an arm round her and rested his cheek against hers. "Had a good day?" he asked.

"Fairly routine."

"George Barnes told me about your bit of detective work on the missing garden machinery. I hear it led to a result."

"Oh yes, it was Darrell Millings, as I suspected. He'd been delivering the goods, casing the place at the same time and sneaking back to reclaim them. He must have had an accomplice, though – the ride-on mower that was nicked from Burwell was too big and unwieldy for one person to handle."

"I heard it was recovered, along with most of the other machinery that was nicked. Well done!" He gave her shoulder a squeeze. "A few more satisfied customers to set against the ones we couldn't help."

"I know one person who won't be rejoicing – Darrell's employer. He thought the sun shone out of his ears."

"Ah well, you can't please everyone."

They finished their drinks in a contented silence. Then Sukey said, "I suppose we'd better start thinking about supper."

"If you're tired, why don't I pop out for fish and chips? The steaks will keep till tomorrow."

"Good idea."

As Jim got up and reached for his jacket, which he had thrown over the back of the couch before sitting down, the telephone rang. Sukey's heart sank as without preamble in response to her "Hullo", Jennifer Drew said, "I've been waiting all day to hear from you." Her voice had a sharp, brittle quality, very different from the broken-hearted tones of the previous day.

"I'm sorry, I've not long been home from work." Out of the corner of her eye, Sukey caught sight of Jim in the doorway, his eyebrows forming a question. "You sound better," she went on, thinking as she spoke that "different" might have been a more appropriate word.

"Have you thought about what I asked you?"

"Yes, I've thought about it," Sukey replied cautiously, silently adding, *I've hardly been able to think of anything else.*

"I went to the doctor like you advised me," Jennifer went on. "He gave me some pills called . . ." – there was a pause, during which Sukey envisaged her checking the label on the bottle – ". . . diazepam. I took one right away and another one just now and you were right, it's made me feel absolutely fine."

"What did I tell you? Just keep on taking them for a day or two and—"

"So now I feel ready to go ahead with my plan."

"Your plan?"

"Don't you remember? I'm going to enrol with RYCE and you're going to come with me, aren't you? I've started to fill in the registration forms – that is, I've done mine, but I'll want your full name and address and a few other details."

"Now just a minute . . ." Sukey felt herself losing her grip on the situation. Jim's penetrating green eyes were fixed on her now, their expression no longer one of mild curiosity. "Look, you've caught me at an awkward moment," she said.

"So when shall I call you?" From Jennifer's tone, it was clear that grief and raw emotion had given way to an ice-cold determination.

"I don't know, I'll have to think . . . I'll call you back."

"Well, don't leave it too long." There was a click as Jennifer ended the call. Sukey put down the phone and looked helplessly across the room at Jim. He had put on his jacket and his car key was in his hand, but he clearly had no intention of leaving until she had explained her obvious discomfiture.

"What was that all about?" he demanded.

"Oh dear, I suppose you had to know sooner or later, but I was hoping we'd have the weekend in peace."

He listened in growing disbelief and indignation as she outlined Jennifer's plans for solving the mystery of her husband's suicide and her demand for Sukey's active participation, which had been followed almost immediately by a similar request from

Adrian Masters. "I don't believe it!" he exclaimed. "I never heard anything so outrageous in my life! Why on earth didn't you turn them both down on the spot?"

"I was afraid to do that in Jennifer's case because she was in such a fragile emotional state that I thought she could easily have a total breakdown. I was hoping that when she'd had a chat with her doctor and taken his advice, she'd see things differently, but she seems more determined than ever to go ahead."

"Then she can do it without you."

"I'd already half come to the same conclusion myself when Adrian made exactly the same request. It seemed uncanny, like an omen—"

"Rubbish!" Jim interrupted. His jaw was set, his eyes were hard with anger. She recognised that the anger was on her behalf, yet at the same time partly directed at her for so much as contemplating agreement. "I can confirm what he says about there being no call for a police investigation and he's absolutely no right to expect you to go poking around to satisfy his totally unfounded suspicions. If he wants to pursue them he can do it himself."

"Cath won't hear of his going near the place – she's terrified he'll make a fool of himself throwing wild accusations around. That's why he's asked me to do a spot of sleuthing for him."

"You'll do nothing of the kind, do you hear me? If he wants to make a fool of himself, let him."

Sukey stared at him open-mouthed. Apart from an episode during the Dearley Manor investigation when he had expressly ordered her to stay away from the place, he had never before taken such an authoritative attitude. In that case, he had been acting in his official capacity with every right to issue the command, but this was different. The last thing she wanted was to fall out with him but, feeling her freedom to make her own decisions was under threat, she was impelled to make a stand.

"I don't like being told what I may or may not do in my own time," she said. She was aware that her voice was shaking with indignation and she gave a half smile in an attempt to rob the words of their sting.

There was no answering smile. "Do I take it you're seriously thinking of going along with this wild scheme?" he demanded.

"To be perfectly honest, I'm intrigued. From what I've seen there's nothing in the least sinister about the place – quite the contrary. I can't see that there'd be any harm in going along to one or two sessions, in fact, it might be quite interesting and if I can set two very distressed people's minds at rest—"

"I don't like it," he said stubbornly. "Anyway, how do you plan to fit it in with your job? You're not thinking of taking time off?"

"No, as it happens I'm on late turn next week so I'll have the mornings free."

"I'd be much happier if you'd forget all about it."

She went to him, put her arms round his neck and kissed him. "Let's not talk about it any more now – don't let it spoil our weekend," she said softly.

He responded to her embrace, but he was evidently only partly mollified. "Just remember what I told you," he said.

"I'll remember." If he noticed the irony in her tone, he chose to ignore it.

By tacit consent, the subject was dropped for the rest of the weekend. They spent Saturday morning in the garden, went to an open-air concert in a local park in the afternoon and watched a video in the evening. On Sunday, despite earlier forecasts of sunshine, the weather broke so they cancelled plans for a walk in the Cotswolds and went to an art exhibition instead. And each night they made love, the sheer joy of their shared passion driving away any lingering hint of discord. When it was time for Jim to go home, he drew her close, saying, "Thanks for a wonderful weekend."

"Thank *you*," she whispered back.

She was beginning to think there would be no further reference to RYCE, but with one hand on the latch of the front door, he said, "I hope I'm not going to hear any more about this crazy scheme you told me about earlier?"

"Not another word," she promised.

"That's a good girl."

As she watched him drive away, she told herself that she hadn't been telling a lie. After all, she had no intention of revealing the plan that had been slowly forming in her mind.

Ten

S hortly after Jim's departure Sukey heard the sound of another car pulling up outside the house. The next minute she heard Fergus's key in the door; without closing it behind him he came straight into the kitchen where she was rinsing milk bottles. Omitting his usual hug of greeting he said, a little breathlessly, "Mum, Dad's waiting in the car – he'd like to come in and see you for a moment if that's all right."

"What on earth does he want?" Various possibilities flashed through Sukey's mind, most of them concerned with money. The far from generous allowance he made for Fergus had from time to time been the cause of acrimonious exchanges. Her thoughts must have been reflected in her expression, prompting her son to say, "It's nothing nasty, honest – on the contrary. He wants to tell you himself, though."

Seeing no reason to refuse, she said, "All right, ask him in." *As long as he doesn't stay too long*, she added mentally. The weekend had been enjoyable enough and she was always happy in Jim's company, but the pressure she had been under from three directions was beginning to take its toll. She went to the sink and filled the kettle. "I was just going to make some tea – I suppose I'd better offer him a cup."

"Why not? I'd like one as well. I'll go and tell him it's OK."

"You'd better show him into the sitting-room."

"Right." As Fergus disappeared she began hastily plumping up cushions and tidying away scattered newspapers and magazines – almost, she reflected as she worked, as if she was trying to remove any obvious traces of Jim's presence. Thinking about it later, she realised that it had been an automatic, unthinking reaction born of the desire to avoid giving Paul any reason to refer to the relationship. Even though he was aware of how things were between her and Jim, in her present state of mind she felt instinctively that to hear it referred to by her ex-husband, however casually, would in an indefinable away sully and diminish something precious.

Having set the room to rights, she quickly glanced in the mirror above the mantelpiece. She patted her cheeks and smoothed into place the short curly hair that Jim had playfully ruffled as they said their goodnights, asking herself as she did so why it should matter how she appeared to Paul, yet not wanting him to think she was, as the saying went, "letting herself go". She smiled at her reflection; the radiance that always remained after time spent with Jim was still there, masking the tiredness.

There was a movement in the doorway and she turned to see him standing there, a little awkwardly, with their son beside him.

For a long time their only contact had been by telephone or letter. She had not met him face to face since the occasion when, in response to a frantic telephone call and against Jim's express instructions, she had gone to the holiday cottage on the Dearley Manor estate where he had taken refuge on the night of the brutal stabbing of Myrna, his second wife. Her reaction to his desperate plea for help had at the time been a mixture of contempt, revulsion and disbelief that she could once have been in love with this craven individual whom terror had stripped of all dignity. She recalled his dishevelled appearance, the new lines that the strain of a marriage already on the point of breaking down had etched on a face that was thinner, the skin less healthy, than she remembered. Tonight, the transformation came almost as a shock: he had put on weight, there was colour in his cheeks and a light in his eyes that reminded her for one poignant moment of their early years together.

"Good evening, Susan," he said, and held out his hand. She took it almost reluctantly; it was the first physical contact between them since the day he left the home they had shared for over ten years.

"Good evening, Paul." She gestured towards a chair. "Won't you sit down?" With the politeness he had always shown, he indicated that she should sit before accepting the invitation, but she remained standing. "I was just about to make some tea, I'll be with you in a minute," she said.

"You stay here and talk to Dad, I'll make it," Fergus said and scuttled out of the room.

"He's a good kid," said Paul with a touch of pride and satisfaction.

As if I needed you to tell me that, she thought. Aloud, she said, "I believe there's something you want to tell me."

"Yes." He cleared his throat. "I daresay he's mentioned I've been out a few times with a lady who works in my office?"

"He did say something, yes. I was glad to hear you've started to get out and about a bit, after—" She broke off abruptly; she had intended to avoid any reference to the tragedy, not because he had been mourning the loss of a beloved wife, which had been far from the case, but because it was difficult to forgive him for the strain her involvement in the police investigation that followed the murder had put on her relationship with Jim Castle.

With a perceptiveness which surprised her, he said, "I know what you did to help me must have made things difficult for you."

"It did at the time, but it's all right now."

"So I understand from Fergus. I'm glad."

"So what is it you want to tell me?"

He appeared self-conscious; for a second, he reminded her of her son when, as a child, he had been on the point of confessing to some misdemeanour. Then he took a deep breath and the words came out in a rush. "Margaret and I are getting married in October. We'd like Fergus to be at our wedding. I . . . we hope you've no objection."

"Why should I object? If that's what Fergus wants—"

"He says he does, but he insists he won't do anything to upset you." There was a hint of resentment in Paul's voice, as if he was jealous of the lad's devotion to his mother. Once again, Sukey experienced a stirring of the old bitterness at the callous way he had deserted them. It was only recently, as Fergus had approached manhood, that the father had begun making genuine efforts to build an enduring friendship with his son. Still, she told herself, it was better late than never; this was not the time to resurrect an old grudge.

"I assure you, I won't be the least upset. It's good news – I hope you and Margaret will be very happy," she said sincerely.

"Thank you." There was a pause before he added, "And I want you to know that I'll continue to look after Fergus . . . financially, I mean."

"It didn't occur to me that you'd do anything else." This time, she could not keep a caustic note from her voice. The way his lips tightened at the retort told her the shot had gone home.

An uneasy silence was broken by Fergus appearing with a tray of tea. "What d'you think, Mum? Isn't it brilliant? Aren't you happy for Dad?" His young face glowed with pleasure.

"Of course I am." She handed Paul a cup of tea saying, "I'm afraid we haven't any champagne to drink to you and Margaret, but congratulations anyway!"

"Thank you."

The tea was consumed in what seemed to Sukey an artificial atmosphere of cordiality. She was thankful when Paul took his leave. As the door closed behind him and she locked it, shot the bolts and fastened the safety chain that Jim insisted on, she had an irrational sensation of symbolically erecting a barrier between herself and a period in her life which still had the power to unsettle and disturb her. Since the moment when she and Jim had become lovers it had never occurred to her that she was still in some way a prisoner of those years of struggle and disillusion. The surprising thought flashed into her mind that a few "touchy-feely" sessions with Jennifer at the RYCE Foundation might have a therapeutic effect, despite her being there for a totally different purpose.

Fergus was in the kitchen, rinsing out the tea-cups. "Did you tell Jim about Jennifer and Adrian?" he asked.

"You mean, about their asking me to investigate RYCE? Yes, I told him."

"What did he say?"

"What do you think? He nearly went ballistic, practically forbade me to have anything to do with it."

"Does that mean you're not going to do it?"

"I still haven't quite decided, but his attitude really put my back up. We'd already talked about the situation at some length but I didn't say what I'd been asked to do because I knew how he'd react. Then Jennifer rang at the wrong moment, he heard my end of the conversation and I couldn't get out of telling him."

"So what are you going to do?"

"I'm going to try and stall Jennifer for a day or two while I do a little preliminary nosing around. I don't think Adrian will be a problem – I'll have to tell him anyway, because I need his help."

Fergus listened while she told him what she had in mind. His face lit up in admiration. "Gosh, Mum, that's a brilliant scheme!" he said.

"I know!" she sighed. "It's just natural genius!"

"And so modest," he laughed, and then grew serious again. "You won't let this business screw things up with Jim, will you?"

"Not if I can help it." For the moment, keeping her right to make her own decisions was uppermost in her mind.

They finished tidying up and went upstairs to bed. Sukey, having determinedly dismissed everything to do with RYCE from her thoughts, lay awake for a while reliving some of the rapturous highlights of the weekend before falling into a deep, peaceful sleep.

"Don't tell me you can't make it today, I couldn't bear it," said George Barnes when Sukey called him early the following morning.

"Why, what's up?"

"I'm one short already. Mandy's mother's been rushed to hospital—"

"I'm sorry to hear that, but it's all right, I'll be with you later. I'm just calling to ask who in uniform handled the Millings case – you know, the missing lawnmowers."

"I think it was PC Grey. Why d'you want to know?"

"Just curious. Can you transfer me?"

"I'll try. He might not be on duty this morning."

She was in luck. PC Grey was not only at the station, but he was able to give her the information she sought. Next, she called Adrian Masters. An hour later she was on her way to Burwell Farm. Serena had just opened the office and she looked a shade taken aback as Sukey entered. "I didn't expect to see you again," she said.

"I happened to have a job in the area this morning, so I just popped in to let you know that the police recovered your motor mower—" Sukey began, but Serena interrupted.

"Yes, I know, we had a phone call from the police late yesterday afternoon. They said we couldn't have it back right away, though, they need it as evidence. Jarvis wasn't best pleased to hear that."

"Oh." Sukey was thrown for the moment. Her intention had been to ask if Jarvis was there so that she could break the news to him, in order to give herself the excuse that she needed. Instead, she thought quickly on her feet. "While I'm here, would you mind if I had a word with Mr Jarvis? I've got a clematis that's looking a bit sick and I'd like to ask his advice."

Serena looked slightly surprised, but said, "No problem. You know where to find him."

When Sukey showed the gardener the photograph that Adrian had lent her, he said without hesitation, "That's the lady."

"And you said she came out of the Rejuvenation Suite in a great hurry, looking upset and anxious?"

"That's right. Dunno what goes on in there," he added with a grin. "Can't say the poor lady looked particularly rejuvenated – maybe the treatment just didn't agree with her."

"Perhaps not. Thank you anyway. Oh, by the way" – Sukey suddenly remembered the excuse she had given Serena – "I've got

a clematis that's not doing very well and I wondered . . ."
Clematis were evidently one of Jarvis's favourite plants and it
was a considerable time before she was able to make her escape
without appearing rude.

Before leaving, she paid another visit to the office. Serena was
reaching for the telephone as she entered; her expressive features
registered a momentary hint of impatience before it was replaced
by the familiar professional smile. With her hand still hovering
over the instrument, she said, "Was Jarvis able to help?"

"I'll say he was. I've learned more about clematis than I
realised there was to know – they're obviously one of his
passions." Sukey went to the door as if on the point of leaving
and then, as if she had only just remembered, turned back and
said, "Wasn't it sad about poor Vera Masters?"

"Vera? What about her?"

"She died very suddenly last Wednesday. Hadn't you heard?"

"No, we hadn't." There appeared to be nothing simulated
about Serena's look of concern. "How dreadful – what happened?"

"She had a heart attack. Her body was found in her car a few
miles from here. Her family had no idea there was anything
wrong with her and they think she might have had some kind of
shock or upsetting experience that brought it on. From an entry
in her diary it looks as if she was due here that day."

"Last Wednesday." Serena thought for a moment. "I'm not
sure, I'd have to get Josie to check. I'm so sorry, she was a lovely
lady and she was making splendid progress with us."

"Yes, I understand she was always very enthusiastic about
RYCE and the happiness she found here." Sukey hesitated for
a moment before saying casually, "I don't suppose you or
anyone else noticed anything unusual about her manner – or
whether anything happened while she was here to trouble or
upset her?"

"I don't think I spoke to her that day. I think it's unlikely –
everything that we do is quite the reverse of distressing. It's all
conducive to peace and tranquillity."

"The reason I'm asking is that last time I came, Jarvis happened to say he'd seen a lady who seemed a little agitated coming out of your 'Rejuvenation' department. He only mentioned it in passing because he said it was so unusual to see anyone here looking anything but happy and peaceful."

Sukey had the impression that Serena was not altogether comfortable at the direction the conversation was taking. "We can't be held responsible for any of our initiates' health problems that we haven't been told about," she said with a frown. "One thing I'm quite sure of is that none of the techniques we practise carries any risk of over-exertion." She paused for a moment, frowning. Then she said, "I'm really sorry about Vera, but I'm sure Freya or Xavier would have mentioned if she'd seemed in the least unwell while she was here. Our leaders," she explained in response to Sukey's questioning look. "They direct all the stages of the initiates' search for the Unlimited." A touch of reverence endowed the final words with a hint of mystery.

"I'm sure you're right. I believe," Sukey added, and this time she made a point of looking directly at Serena, "that she was quite upset about what happened to another of your initiates, Oliver Drew."

Serena drew her breath in sharply. Her expression became guarded and she hesitated before saying, in a noticeably altered tone, "His suicide, you mean? Yes, it was a great shock when we read about it in the paper." She gave a sigh that had a hint of the theatrical. "I'm afraid Oliver was one of our few failures. It occasionally happens that a person's problems are so deep-rooted that even with our help they can never achieve the Unlimited."

"Vera said he'd been doing so well, but she happened to meet him shortly before he died and said he seemed very down – quite disturbed, in fact."

"Did she say why?" A hint of anxiety lurked in the dark, glittering eyes.

"Not that I know of, but I didn't know her personally – her family are friends of my son. I could ask, if you like. It might help your leaders in dealing with initiates who have similar problems."

"Please do. I'm sure any information you can give us would be a great help. Now, if you'll excuse me . . ." Once more Serena's hand strayed towards the telephone; there was no mistaking her wish to end the conversation.

Sukey made a point of taking the hint. "Of course. I'm sorry to have taken up so much of your time. As a matter of fact," she added as if the thought had only just occurred to her, "I'm really impressed with this place. I might consider enrolling for a few sessions myself – I'm finding life pretty stressful at the moment."

"You will be very welcome and I can promise you untold benefits. We shall look forward to receiving your application." A certain lack of spontaneity in both the utterance and the smile that accompanied them suggested that it was a form of words learned by heart and used on many such occasions.

Nevertheless, as Sukey said goodbye, she had the feeling that she had handled that rather well. She might, however, have felt a shade less confident had she seen the calculating expression in Serena's eyes as she watched her return to her car and drive away, or been a party to the thoughts running through that colourful young woman's head.

Eleven

"I knew it! I told you there was something dodgy about that place, didn't I, Cath?"

"Yes, dear, several times." The gently indulgent tone in which Cath Masters responded to her husband's question, and her resigned half-smile as she handed Sukey a cup of coffee and offered a plate of chocolate biscuits, indicated that she was still not prepared to treat the situation as seriously as he did.

Adrian turned back to Sukey. His features, highly coloured and on the fleshy side, registered a mixture of triumph and determination as he said, "You agree, don't you, that they need investigating?"

"I'm inclined to think there's something going on there that they'd rather people didn't know about," Sukey replied cautiously, "but it doesn't have to be anything criminal. It's possible that some of their practices might be challenged by the medical profession and bring bad publicity if they became generally known."

"But from what you said about the way this woman Serena reacted—"

"Her shock and sadness when I told her of Vera's death struck me as absolutely genuine. The fact that she seemed a little put out when I mentioned what the gardener said could simply have been because she didn't like the idea of him gossiping to strangers." A pang of guilt struck her. "I hope I haven't got him into trouble."

"Never mind the gardener," said Adrian. He took a gulp from his coffee cup and waved aside Cath's offer of a biscuit. "I'm convinced that something sinister goes on in that building – the one they call Rehabilitation – and I believe it upset Vera so much that it brought on her heart attack."

"Rejuvenation," Sukey corrected. She shook her head. "I'm sorry, but I can't see that there are any grounds for making that assumption. All Jarvis said is that he saw her coming out looking what he called 'put out', but it doesn't mean that anything untoward happened in there. It could have been simply the onset of her illness that was affecting her."

Adrian glowered, but decided to abandon that line of argument for the time being. He drained his cup, declined Cath's offer of a refill and demanded, "What about the other chap – the one called Ollie that she wrote about in her diary? It's obvious those people had done something to turn him against them. And if they've got nothing to hide, why do you suppose Serena got so jumpy when you spoke about him?"

"It's true she reacted much more strongly then, but it doesn't prove that RYCE was in any way involved in his death. As I said before, it could be that they're particularly sensitive on the subject of publicity. Oliver Drew obviously felt he had some sort of grievance against them, but his problem was of a very intimate nature and the emotional effect—" Sukey broke off, flushing in embarrassment; it was the first time she had admitted to the Masters that she had some idea of what lay behind Drew's suicide.

Adrian pounced. "You've been holding out on me!" he accused her. "You never said you knew who Ollie was."

"That's because I wasn't sure at first that it was the same man."

Adrian's naturally high colour deepened. "The same man as who?" he demanded. "What's been going on that you haven't told me about?"

"Do let Sukey tell us the story in her own way," Cath interposed. "You'll put her off if you keep interrupting."

"Sorry." Adrian made an impatient gesture. "Carry on Sukey, I'm listening."

"When you told me what Vera had written, the name rang a bell. Perhaps you didn't see the report in the local paper—"

"Never read the local rag – takes me all my time to—" Catching his wife's steely look of reproof he gave an apologetic grin and left the sentence unfinished.

"A man called Oliver Drew committed suicide a week or so ago by gassing himself in his car," Sukey explained. "By chance, his house had been burgled the night before his body was found and I was checking it out when the police called to break the news to his widow." Cath and Adrian listened in growing amazement as, without mentioning the attempts to enlist her active co-operation, Sukey recounted how Jennifer had confided the history of matrimonial problems that had led to her late husband's association with RYCE, culminating in her wild assertion that someone there was directly responsible for his death and her determination to prove it. "As you can see," she finished, "her suspicions are based on one very flimsy piece of circumstantial evidence."

"You mean the money he drew out without telling her? That surely suggests he was in some kind of trouble."

"Not necessarily, and in any case not the kind you're thinking of. There could have been any number of reasons why he wanted that amount of cash. The Drews collected antiques, which is why they were targeted by burglars. Maybe someone wanted cash for an item he fancied – a surprise present for his wife, for example. Or he could have incurred a gambling debt. He might even have been into drugs – we simply don't know."

"So how do you account for the way he spoke to Vera the minute she mentioned RYCE?"

"Bearing in mind the very sensitive and personal nature of his problem, it could have been acute disappointment at realising that the improvement was only temporary and he'd shelled out quite a lot of money to no purpose," Sukey suggested. "There's no proof that the money was to pay off a blackmailer, and even if it was, there's nothing whatsoever to suggest the blackmailer was anyone at RYCE ." To her surprise, she found herself playing the devil's advocate. Jim's arguments were lining up in her head in opposition to her instinctive feeling that Adrian was right and there was something to be investigated. She was being pulled in two directions; the decision could go either way.

Adrian must have read her doubts. "Are you saying you won't give me any more help, then?" he demanded.

"I didn't say that. It's just that there's so little to go on."

"If it's a question of money, I've already made it clear I'll pay all your expenses."

Sukey shook her head with a smile. "It's nothing to do with money – although, if I wasn't such a shiningly honest person, I could make quite a tidy sum out of this adventure." Adrian's eyebrows shot up in astonishment as she told him about Jennifer Drew's offer. "She's being even more pressing than you are."

Cath spoke for the first time in several minutes. "That girl shouldn't be allowed out alone," she declared. "She sounds thoroughly unbalanced to me."

"She's obsessed with the notion that something that happened at RYCE caused her husband to commit suicide," said Sukey. "Having failed to convince the police that there's any reason to investigate, she's determined to do it herself. How she plans to go about it – apart from getting inside the place by enrolling as a potential 'initiate' – I've absolutely no idea and I'm not sure she has either."

"From what you tell me, she's hardly the temperament to carry it off," said Adrian. "Her cover would probably be blown in the first half hour."

"That's been worrying me," Sukey agreed. "I have to admit, I'm not happy about the thought of her poking around there on her own. She won't have a clue what to look for or how to set about finding it, and if they do have anything to hide, she could find herself in serious trouble."

"Then she needs a minder," Adrian said firmly. "Tell you what," he added with a flash of inspiration that for the first time brought a smile to his face. "I don't know the lady, but I'll pay you to take on the job."

"I've already explained—" Sukey began, but he waved the objection aside.

"No problem – let Jennifer pay your fees. I'll chip in with the same amount to watch her back and keep your own eyes open. Is it a deal?"

The temptation was almost overwhelming and Sukey felt her misgivings melting away. Just in time, she stopped short of committing herself on the spot. "Police employees aren't supposed to do any moonlighting," she protested, but without conviction.

"Who's to know about it?"

"I've already told Jim about Jennifer's offer—"

"She's not paying you, she's simply covering your expenses. My contribution's strictly between you and me."

"I'll think it over," Sukey promised. "No, please don't ask me to decide now," she added as he opened his mouth with the evident intention of pressing for an acceptance of his offer on the spot. A thought occurred to her. "Just how far back in Vera's diary did you go, by the way?"

"Not very far – as I told you, I was looking for any recent reference to her feeling unwell. Then I came across the entry about her chance meeting with Ollie and it set my mind going in a different direction altogether. That was when I phoned you."

"He immediately put two and two together and made half a dozen," said Cath. "He's known as 'Bull-at-a-gate Masters' at the golf club," she added with an ironic twist of her mouth.

"Would you mind if I borrowed it?" Sukey asked. "She may have made earlier references to RYCE that could come in useful when . . . that is if—" she hurriedly corrected herself.

"Of course you can – it's in my study, I'll go and fetch it." Adrian hurried from the room and the house echoed to the sound of his footsteps as he went bounding upstairs.

The minute the door closed behind him, Cath said earnestly, "I do hope you'll agree to do what he asks. It's not that I go along with all his wild assumptions," she went on before Sukey had a chance to speak. "It's just that he'll give us no peace until it's been settled one way or the other. You see," she lowered her voice as a door slammed above their heads, "He's been to see Vera's solicitor and she did leave some money to the RYCE Foundation . . . not a fortune, but enough to fuel his suspicions. He doesn't want that generally known, so please don't let on that I've told you."

"Of course not."

"Here we are," said Adrian as he re-entered the room with a leather bound book in his hand. "It's one of those five-year jobs and she began it getting on for four years ago. I never thought to look any further back . . ." His expression was sheepish as he handed the diary to Sukey; glancing across at Cath she caught her mouthing the word "typical" but managed to keep a straight face.

"I'll take great care of it." Sukey stood up and said politely, "Thank you for the coffee. I have to go now and get ready to start my shift. I'll speak to you later."

When she returned home she found Anita's bicycle propped against the garage door. Fergus and Anita were seated at the table in the kitchen surrounded by prospectuses from half a dozen universities. "Anita's trying to decide what Uni to apply to," Fergus explained. "She's hoping for straight As, so she can go pretty well anywhere she likes," he added proudly with a fond glance at the girl, who responded with a shy smile. She was fair-haired like her father, but she had inherited her mother's slender build and finely chiselled features.

"You're going to read modern languages, aren't you?" Sukey picked up one of the prospectuses and began flipping over the pages. "Have you any preference?"

"Oxford would be my first choice, but competition's pretty keen, so I haven't decided yet."

"My father used to say, 'Always aim a little higher than you expect to reach and you stand a better chance of achieving your goal'," said Sukey. "My advice would be, make what you really want your first choice."

"That's what my dad keeps telling me." Anita glanced at her

watch and began clearing the table. "I'd better be going. Fergus says you're on at two o'clock so you'll be wanting to get lunch."

"Would you like to stay and have something with us?"

"No thank you, I promised Mum I'd go shopping with her this afternoon."

Fergus leapt to his feet. "I'll get out my bike and ride home with you," he said with the air of youthful gallantry that his mother found so endearing.

When he returned twenty minutes later he said eagerly, "Well, how did it go? I didn't tell Anita where you'd been, by the way, that's why I didn't ask before."

"That was very discreet, but her parents are almost certain to tell her."

Sukey opened the refrigerator and began taking out cheese, ham and various salad items. She gave him a brief run-down of the way the conversation had gone, including Adrian's offer of payment, ending with, "I said I'd let him know."

"But you will do it, won't you, Mum? It sounds really cool."

"I'm not sure that 'cool' is the word I'd have chosen, but . . . yes, I think I will, as much for Jennifer's sake as anything."

"Brilliant!" said Fergus enthusiastically. Then his expression of delight changed to one of consternation. "What about Jim – are you going to tell him?"

"I think I'll have to – except for the bit about Adrian's offer to contribute. He's not going to like it, but I don't want him to find out from anyone else. In any case, you never know what dark secrets I might uncover. I might even need police back-up." The remark was not intended to be taken seriously, but Fergus reacted with alarm.

"Are you saying you think there might be danger?" he asked.

"No, of course not, I was only kidding. Whatever they're up to, even if it's something with a whiff of the unethical, it's hardly likely to lead to murder or mayhem. To be honest," Sukey continued as she went to the sink and began washing lettuce, "There are two reasons for agreeing; one is to keep an eye on

Jennifer and the other is curiosity. I'm dying to find out what goes on during these 'touchy-feely' sessions, as you called them."

"What's your feeling about these oddballs at the RYCE Foundation, Andy?"

Sergeant Andy Radcliffe took a long pull from his tankard of beer and considered for several seconds before replying. "You mean the Burrells?" he said thoughtfully. "You're right when you say there's nothing to warrant a police investigation, but just the same, two deaths within a few days of each other, one of them in particularly tragic circumstances – it does make you think, doesn't it?"

"I'm inclined to agree, but I don't like the idea of Sukey getting further involved." DI Jim Castle studied his own half-finished drink with a worried frown. "I keep telling her it's just coincidence and there's nothing anyone can do about it."

Radcliffe raised his eyebrows. "What's her interest? I know she was checking a break-in at Drew's house when Trudy arrived to break the news about the discovery of the body, and then she went to hold the widow's hand during the ID, but—"

"She's only talking about enrolling with this bloody outfit."

"What in the world for? She doesn't strike me as the sort who needs to go in for that kind of hocus-pocus."

"Of course she doesn't. She was just winding me up when she first suggested it, but it's become more serious now." Castle went on to report the combined pressure Sukey was under from Jennifer Drew and Adrian Masters. "I told her to have nothing to do with it," he said. "Trouble is—"

"That girl has a mind of her own, she's quite likely to go ahead anyway, and you're worried there might be something behind it after all."

"That just about sums it up."

Radcliffe considered for a moment. Then he said, "Why don't you have a word with Mr Lord?"

"Why d'you suggest I involve him?"

"In spite of there being no evidence of any kind, we both have our doubts about those freaks. If Sukey intends to go and suss them out under the pretence of joining in the fun, it might be as well for a senior officer to know what's going on, just in case."

"That's not a bad idea. Thanks, Andy, I'll try and catch him when I get back to the station."

Detective Chief Inspector Philip Lord was relaxing with his feet on his desk while munching an apple when Castle entered his office. "Sorry, sir, am I interrupting your lunch?" he began, but Lord shook his head and waved him to a seat.

"I've been forbidden to eat pub food until I've done something about this." He patted his rounded stomach and gave a rueful grin. "The wife's feeding me a calorie-controlled diet for a couple of months." He finished the apple and dropped the core in the waste bin beside his desk before taking out a handkerchief and wiping the small black moustache which had earned him in certain quarters the irreverent nickname of Charlie C. He grunted, lowered his feet and sat up. "What can I do for you, Jim?"

"You'll probably think I'm making something out of nothing, but I'd appreciate your opinion on a rather curious situation."

Lord listened attentively while Castle put him in the picture. "That girl certainly knows how to pick her cases, doesn't she?" he commented with a grin. "I've told her she should be in CID and she said she was thinking of it." Then he grew serious. "You know, I'm always a bit suspicious of these quacks claiming to cure all manner of ills. I don't deny they may bring benefit to some people, but when you get a case like that poor chap Drew—"

"You reckon there's something suspicious about his death?" said Castle in surprise.

"I'm not saying that, but from what you've told me he was on some kind of a high, thinking his problem was solved, and then couldn't take it when the magic wore off. When untrained, unqualified people start probing into other people's minds, it can bring totally unforeseen results." Lord broke off and played thoughtfully with a brass owl anchoring an untidy heap of papers

91

on his desk. "I don't think it would be a bad idea for your SOCO to go ahead and see what goes on in that place," he said at last. "She won't come to any harm – from what I've seen of her, she's got far too much common sense to be spooked by a load of pseudo-psychological clap-trap. It's up to you what you say to her, of course, but I'd be inclined to let her get on with it." He spent several seconds straightening the documents before replacing the paperweight. "Think it over, Jim – and keep me posted."

"Very good, sir."

Twelve

S ukey was about to leave the house when the telephone rang.
Jennifer was on the line. "I've spoken to the woman in the
office at RYCE and there are just two places left on a morning
course beginning next week," she announced. "I've reserved
them both and told them confirmation will be in the post by
tomorrow at the latest." Her tone – terse, businesslike, with an
underlying hint of steel – held no trace of the emotion bordering
on hysteria of their earlier conversations. This was a woman in
control, with a goal in mind and the determination to pursue it.
"Now, if you'd just give me a few personal details I can put us
both on one application form. She said that'd be all right and it'll
save you the trouble. I know how busy you are."

And make sure I don't skive out of it, I suppose, Sukey thought
to herself with a grimace. Aloud she said, "There's no need for
you to do that. I've got a form, it's in the brochure Serena gave
me—"

"Who's Serena?" A sharp ring of suspicion crept into Jennifer's voice.

"She's a young woman who works for RYCE—"

"How do you know? What have you been doing you haven't
told me about? Have you started making enquiries already?" The
tone altered yet again, this time to excited anticipation. "What
have you found out?"

"I haven't found out anything significant." It had only just
dawned on Sukey that Jennifer knew nothing of her two visits to
RYCE. She had no intention of revealing her interest in the
place, which had given rise to the morning's expedition on behalf

of Adrian Masters, but there was no reason to conceal the theft of the mower that had taken her there the first time. She made as little of the episode as she could, but Jennifer was not easily put off.

"What was your impression of the place? This Serena person – I suppose she was the one I spoke to. What's she like?"

"Fairly young, a little exotic-looking but very pleasant. I didn't spend much time with her, I was speaking to the gardener. I was there to do a job, not to enquire into their business activities."

"Then why did you ask for a brochure?"

"I didn't ask for it, Serena gave it to me. Just a bit of sales promotion, I suppose – she probably dishes them out to all and sundry."

"Anyway, you've got an application form." Jennifer switched back to the purpose of her call. "Please, don't waste any more time, and remember when you send it off to mention my name or they might tell you there isn't a vacancy. Oh, and by the way, I've told them I'm Jennifer Newlyn. It's my maiden name – I don't want them to know I'm Ollie's widow or that I have any connection with him."

"That makes sense, I'll make a note of it," Sukey promised. Evidently, the possibility that she might decline to have any part in the adventure had no place in Jennifer's scheme of things. Her assumption that everything would be arranged in accordance with her wishes betrayed an obsession that Sukey found disturbing. It was difficult to reconcile this iron-willed character with the vulnerable young widow who, in the shock and distress of bereavement, had poured out her most intimate secrets to a total stranger. She recalled Cath's use of the word "unbalanced" to describe her. A vague premonition of dangerous shoals ahead made her wonder whether after all she should fall in with Jim's wishes and decline to have any more to do with the proposed adventure. She had given no firm commitment to either Jennifer or Adrian; there was still time to back out.

"They want a fifty pound deposit. Give me your address and

I'll send it to you," Jennifer rattled on. "The rest of the money is payable on the first day of the course. I'll give them one cheque—"

Sukey thought quickly. Her instinct warned her that it would be unwise to let this highly volatile woman know where she lived. "It's all right, I can manage the deposit," she said. "We can sort out the rest another time."

"I'll give it to you when we meet to plan our strategy."

Sukey looked at her watch. She should have been out of the house ten minutes ago. "Er, yes, I suppose we'd better do that. I'll call you tomorrow to fix a date," she said hurriedly.

"Come now if you like." In Jennifer's present single-minded state, the possibility that Sukey had other demands on her time did not seem to have occurred to her.

"I was on the point of leaving for work when you phoned and if I talk any longer I'll be late for my shift," Sukey said firmly. "I'll call you tomorrow," she repeated and hung up.

The traffic was unusually heavy during the short drive to Gloucester. Roadworks caused a number of diversions and it was nearly ten past two when she reached the SOCOs' office, to be greeted with relief by Sergeant George Barnes. "What kept you? I was beginning to think you were going to let me down as well," he grumbled, running a hand through his thinning hair with an unusually irritable gesture.

"Sorry Sarge, the water company's digging up the ring road."

"Tell me about it," he said wearily. "And the minute they've put it all back together, the gas company will dig it all up again."

"Never mind, I made it. What news of Mandy's mum?"

"She collapsed in the street and was carted off to hospital, that's all I know. Mandy said she'd call when the medics were able to tell her a bit more."

"Have things been busy this morning?"

"Fairly quiet, as it happens. Three burglaries in the Barnwood area – Dave Stevens has been covering those. Says the hand-writing looks the same, but he hasn't been able to connect them with any known villains."

"So what have you got for me?"

"A couple of walk-ins in Tuffley. Similarities there as well – householder in the front garden mowing the lawn, villain enters by the back door and makes off with handbag and credit cards."

"Doors left unlocked, of course?"

"In one case, yes. In the other, the woman had the sense to lock it, but left the key on the windowsill in full view from outside and the window itself unfastened." George handed over the printouts. "Like stealing candy from a baby," he commented.

"Not much chance of finding any evidence there, I suppose," said Sukey as she scanned the details.

"You never know your luck. He could have left a trace or two. Anyway, go along and do your stuff – it gives some reassurance to the victims that we're taking their problems seriously even if the prospects of nailing the villain are thinner than fag paper."

"Is that the lot?"

"For the moment. We'll let you know if anything else comes in."

"Right, I'll get started."

On her way along the corridor Sukey almost bumped into DI Castle as he emerged from his office. Somewhat to her consternation, he beckoned her inside and closed the door. "Remember what we were talking about over the weekend?" he said.

"You mean, about RYCE?" she replied guardedly.

"Yes. I've been having a chat about it with DCI Lord."

Sukey's eyes popped as he recounted the gist of the conversation. Then she burst out laughing. "Do I understand Mr Lord wants me to carry out an undercover operation?"

It was plain that the funny side of the situation was entirely lost on DI Castle. "Certainly not," he said severely. "There's no question of an official investigation. All I'm saying is, if you were still thinking of going along to that place with Jennifer Drew in spite of what I told you, I feel bound to withdraw my objections." He had adopted an officious tone, indicating that he was taking it for granted that she would in any event have made no commitment without consulting him first. It was all that was needed to sweep aside the remaining shreds of indecision.

"I've thought it over and I've already decided to go ahead anyway, but it's very comforting to know that I have a senior officer's approval," she said pertly. "Now, if you'll excuse me, I've got work to do . . . sir."

As the door closed behind her, DI Castle was left with the vivid impression of a defiantly lifted chin and a cheeky smile that aroused an almost irresistible desire to call her back, take her in his arms, cover her elfin face with kisses . . . and plead with her to change her mind. Despite Lord's pragmatic view of the proposed enterprise, he had a bad feeling about it.

Very few new cases were reported for the rest of the day, which meant that Sukey was able to spend some time with each of the two victims of the walk-in thefts, both elderly women living alone who plied her with tea and biscuits while describing in detail how they had discovered that their homes had been so callously violated and their property stolen. Touched by their distress, Sukey undertook before leaving on her next assignment to arrange for a visit from a police officer who would advise them on security precautions.

A short time after she arrived home, Fergus returned from his shift at the supermarket, where he worked a few hours on weekday evenings replenishing shelves. He entered the kitchen carrying several brown-paper carrier bags, which he deposited on the table with an air of triumph.

"Two portions of Indian dinner for one," he announced. "Today's the use-by date and they let us have them at half price. You have a choice – chicken tikka or lamb rogan josh."

"Oh, super," said his mother gratefully. "I didn't have time to prepare anything this morning after that session with the Masterses and the last thing I wanted to do tonight was start cooking. I'll be better organised tomorrow."

"You don't really enjoy the late shift, do you?"

"Not normally, but it's come at a convenient time if I'm to go ahead with this RYCE lark."

"You haven't had second thoughts, have you?" Fergus asked anxiously. "I'm dying to know what goes on there."

"No, I haven't had second thoughts. On the contrary." While putting the food into dishes for heating in the microwave, she told him of Jim's conversation with DCI Lord.

"Gosh, Mum, it'll be like going undercover!" he exclaimed excitedly.

"That's what I said to Jim, and you should have seen his face!" Sukey giggled at the recollection. "Even though I don't believe that either Jennifer or Adrian has any grounds for their suspicions, there is a serious side to it." She told Fergus about Lord's misgivings. "So now, in addition to keeping an eye on Jennifer, I'm expected to watch out for any practices that might lead to adverse reactions from the weak and vulnerable."

"That's quite a challenge," he said thoughtfully. "Any idea how you're going to tackle it?"

"For a start, I'm going to read very carefully through Vera's diary. With any luck, it'll throw up some useful background information."

By the time they had finished their supper and cleared away, it was almost ten o'clock. "I'm for an early night and some preliminary research," Sukey announced. "If you want to stay up and watch telly for a bit, keep the volume down, there's a good lad."

"Will do."

The diary made absorbing reading. Adrian's description of Vera's style – racy, humorous and entertaining – was wholly accurate, but he had given the impression that the contents, although highly readable, were a touch superficial. Instead, it quickly became clear to Sukey that his cousin had been a woman of considerable perception in her observations of people and situations. There were vivid descriptions of fellow members of groups she had encountered on her many package holidays. They seemed to leap off the page to play roles Vera had imagined, based on their reactions to everything from the conduct of guides to the service in hotels. Odd remarks they had made either to her or to one another were recorded in detail, accompanied by speculation of what lay behind them. She seemed to have been a woman in whom strangers naturally confided; it occurred to Sukey that, had she wished, she could have been a successful, even a brilliant novelist. There were references as well to her own family; in one, she described Adrian as "my heir-in-waiting". In another entry she had written, "Got told off again for 'squandering' so much on foreign travel. Methinks he's worried there'll be nothing left in the coffers when I pop my clogs!"

The first mention of RYCE was in an entry dated in early June. Having already referred with compassion and sensitivity to the problems of a friend grappling with sudden and entirely unexpected widowhood, Vera had written:

> I've been reading about a place that claims to help people cope with stress. Their slogan is "Release Your Cosmic Energy". It sounds very way-out to me, but I showed it to Miriam as I thought it might help her come to terms with Tommy's death. The trouble is, she's afraid to go on her own and wants me to go with her, says I'm the only person she has to turn to. That isn't true, of course, she has her daughter, but I suspect she doesn't want Joyce to know what she's planning in case she thinks her father's death has affected her mentally. I suppose I'd better go along, for the first few sessions at least. It'll be something to do, now poor Angie's past it.

As what appeared to have been an afterthought, being written with a different pen, Vera had commented, "It's quite pricey – Adrian will be furious with me!!!"

Sukey skimmed through the next few entries, which were concerned chiefly with such weighty matters as her window-cleaner's problems with a teenage son and her dismay at an accident to her gardener, which meant she would have to cut her own lawns for the next fortnight. Sukey had been reading for over an hour and was beginning to feel sleepy, when she came to an entry which jerked her awake again.

> Our first session at RYCE. Quite bizarre, I could hardly believe sane, grown-up people could bring themselves to take part in such mummery. There we were, all six of us, sitting in a circle in a darkened room, staring up at this strange creature calling herself Freya who was standing on a kind of platform under a spotlight. She was dressed in a dark robe with a wreath of leaves (which I suspect were plastic) round her head, as if she was pretending to be a pagan goddess. Then some oriental-sounding so-called music began playing softly in the background while she began chanting gibberish about energy and the cosmos; after ten minutes or so of that she majestically descended from her pedestal and touched each of us on the forehead with icy-cold fingers. I wanted to laugh, but I could hear the others giving little sighs – rapture? boredom? – so I kept quiet. Then another character calling himself Xavier appeared and told us to close our eyes and think about our shackles – we'd been told earlier about our shackles during what Freya described as our first steps to becoming initiates, while we sat drinking some herbal concoction that tasted as if it had been brewed from dried grass. When it was all over we were sent out into the garden to meditate. It's a lovely garden, laid out with small enclosed areas like outdoor rooms and we were each assigned to a different one. My meditation consisted of admiring the plants and pulling up a few weeds the gardener had missed.

The entry concluded with the comment, "I referred to Xavier as 'the mad monk'. M not amused. I can't imagine what she expects to get out of all that rubbish, but she seems determined to press on."

Well, Sukey said to herself. *It's obvious she wasn't particularly impressed on Day One, but—*

There was a tap on her bedroom door. It opened a fraction and

Fergus popped his head round. "I saw the light was still on and thought you might have fallen asleep," he said. His glance fell on the open diary. "Anything interesting?"

"I've just come to Vera's description of her first experience of RYCE. It's quite a hoot. Listen to this." They chuckled over the tongue-in-cheek style as she read the passage aloud. "Some of the earlier stuff is fascinating too – she must have been quite a character."

"I thought she was a super old dear," said Fergus, "and she had a great sense of humour. I wouldn't be surprised if half the time she was enthusing about RYCE she was just doing it to wind Adrian up."

"She must have ended up being impressed by them, though," Sukey pointed out. "I mean, she wouldn't have advised Ollie to go back for a top-up treatment if she hadn't had faith in what they do. I can't wait to read the next instalment."

Fergus slid off the edge of his mother's bed where he had been sitting whilst they chatted. "You can tell me the interesting bits tomorrow," he said, stifling a yawn. "Goodnight, Mum."

"Goodnight, Gus." Sukey settled down to continue her study of the diary. As she traced the account of Vera's gradual change of attitude from that of mocking sceptic to ardent disciple, she felt her skin prickle. She sensed that she was letting herself in for a very strange, potentially exciting and possibly disturbing experience.

Thirteen

O n Friday afternoon, after the departure of the last of the day's initiates, Percy Burrell followed his normal custom and retreated to his private sanctum in order to replenish by a prolonged spell of yoga and meditation the well of healing on which he had drawn during an exhausting week. Meanwhile his wife Edith retired to the office with her daughter Serena to assess results and consider the candidates for the following Monday's intake. Before they settled down to their task, Serena poured two stiff vodka and tonics which they sipped for a few moments in a contented silence.

From her extravagantly ornamented midnight-blue robe and the circlet of artificial foliage on her long dark hair, Sukey would immediately have identified Edith as the *alter ego* of Freya, so vividly described in Vera's diary. There was no obvious likeness between Edith and Serena – Edith's pallid complexion and classically oval face were in striking contrast to her daughter's warm colouring and the gipsyish cast of feature inherited from her Spanish father, but there was a certain similarity in the shape and set of their eyes – Serena's almost black, Edith's a striking blue – together with an occasional watchful, calculating expression and a slight sideways tilt of the head that to an astute observer would have suggested a blood tie. This they took care to conceal; Serena was presented at the start of each course as an acolyte who had proceeded through the various stages of enlightenment to become a handmaiden to the leaders. Since the "initiates" were invariably too preoccu-pied with their own reasons for being there in the first place to bother about anyone else's, this explanation had never been called into question.

"It's been quite a good week," Edith observed as she savoured her drink. It was one occasion when they could safely indulge in anything stronger than herbal tea since her husband, a dedicated teetotaller naively convinced that the women in his life shared his belief in abstinence from all forms of alcohol, could be relied on to be safely out of the way. "Everyone went off practically singing for joy at their progress," she went on. "Especially Patricia."

"She the one suffering from agoraphobia?"

"That's right. Remember her first day when she had to be cajoled out of the car by her son and for the whole week wouldn't set foot in the house without him? He and his wife are taking her to London for a weekend at the Ritz. They're so delighted they've made her a member of the Circle of Lifelong Initiation and coughed up a very handsome donation."

"Well done, Mum." Serena took a long swig from her drink and put the glass down with a sigh of satisfaction.

"I don't think I can claim much of the credit, it was more Percy's influence. I think she rather fancies him."

"So do a lot of the women, especially the older ones. Haven't you noticed how they always seem more responsive than the men to start with? I think it's probably because they spend more time studying our literature before they get here."

"Well, that's really the basis of the system, isn't it? His books and the stuff he writes for the brochures are what tempt the punters in. After that it's up to us."

"It's the way he puts it across when they're face to face with him that keeps them coming. He fairly mesmerises them – once he's put the 'fluence on them, they're putty in our hands." A wicked gleam appeared in Serena's dark eyes as she studied the contents of her glass before savouring another mouthful. "It's a shame we can't get him to offer 'special treatments' as well, isn't it?"

"Perish the thought – he'd die of shock at the idea!" Edith

giggled. Then her expression changed and she gave her daughter a sharp glance. "Are you saying he does a better job than I do?" she demanded with a touch of resentment.

"No, of course not," said Serena soothingly. "As I said, I'm thinking mainly of the women – there's something about him that has them hanging on every word. I suppose it's because he totally and utterly believes in it himself that they lap it up, whereas—"

"I'm just play-acting? Go on, say it."

"You do it awfully well," Serena assured her, seeing her mother was on the verge of becoming seriously offended. "No one would ever guess. And besides, you have plenty of the men eating out of your hand."

"I didn't do a drama course for nothing." Edith slowly sipped her drink with a dreamy expression. "I had ambition in those days. I always fancied myself in the really dark, dramatic rôles like Electra or Lady Macbeth, but somehow I never quite made it beyond a few undistinguished TV ads. Then I met Percy. I was completely carried away, I thought there was something magical about him, he seemed like someone from another world—"

"He's a fruit-cake," said her daughter flatly.

"Yes I know, I realised that later – but he had me under his spell for quite a long time with all his guff about shackles and wheels and the unlimited. It wasn't long before I started to get bored with it, but it was obvious I wasn't going anywhere with my acting career and I could see there was money in it if I could handle him right."

"So you pretended to be converted."

"I was converted at first – almost, anyway. I just never let on that I'd lost faith."

"I'm amazed he's never rumbled you."

"I haven't forgotten everything I learned at drama school, I'd have you know," Edith said huffily. "He still adores me and trusts me utterly."

"It's always surprised me how you managed to persuade him to go commercial." The conversation was taking a familiar turn but, knowing her mother never tired of telling the story and to compensate for having ruffled her feathers, Serena gave her the opening she wanted.

Edith sat back in her chair, smoothed the folds of her dress, adopted the relaxed, gracious attitude of a celebrity being interviewed on television and launched into the many times retold account of her husband's return from his years in the East burning with what she described, with a dramatic throb in her voice, as a completely altruistic desire to guide the whole of mankind along the path to spiritual enlightenment. There was, she solemnly declared, never any thought in his head of personal gain, but it had soon become clear that his health would not stand up to the ascetic existence of the mystics from whom he learned so much during his travels.

At this point in her narrative Edith gave a sentimental sigh, finished her drink in one final gulp and held out her glass for a refill. Serena shook her head and put the bottle of vodka back in its locked cupboard. "One's enough," she said firmly. "You don't want to give the game away by getting pissed. Top up with plain tonic if you're still thirsty."

Edith pulled a face. "It tastes vile on its own," she said pettishly.

"You're not having another vodka. It was a double I gave you the first time." Edith pushed her glass away and sank into a sulky silence. "Please, Mum, do go on with the story," Serena coaxed.

"You've heard it all before."

"Never mind. Tell me again – I never get tired of hearing it."

"Really?" Edith brightened. "Well, it went like this." She composed herself once more in the attitude of interviewee as she recounted their early struggles working from a small house in north London until Percy's wealthy father died and left them enough capital to buy and convert a larger property. It was Edith, whose shrewdness in commercial matters far outstripped her thespian talents, who found Burwell Farm, recognised its potential for accommodating a much larger number of the sad and struggling souls her husband had dedicated his life to helping and persuaded him that provision of such an idyllic environment more than justified any consequent increase in fees. "It's just as well he doesn't realise just how high some of them are," she finished, with a sly glance at her daughter. "You came back from your wanderings just in time to take over the business side of things."

At the word "business", Serena gave a knowing smirk. She finished her own drink, glanced at her watch and reached for a folder. "Time's getting on, we'd better get down to some work."

The RYCE system was simple and straightforward. Initiates enrolled for five two-hour sessions from Monday to Friday, either for mornings or afternoons. At the end of their first week they were asked, during searching private discussions with one or other of their leaders – whom they knew as Freya and Xavier – to assess their own progress along the path to the Unlimited. They were then asked, with many an encouraging reference to Inner and Outer Wheels, if they wished to sign on for further stages, with the offer of concessionary fees for block bookings. It was a tribute to the influences to which they had been subjected that there were plenty of takers.

At the same time their attention was drawn to a range of complementary, so-called "rejuvenation" therapies, available for a supplementary fee. Charges for these were comparatively modest – unless the participants happened to have any special requirements which were never mentioned at the time of booking, but negotiated directly and in secret with the "therapist" – either Serena or Edith – before the start of treatment.

"I see there have been three requests for rejuvenation," Edith observed. "Any prospects there, d'you reckon?"

"Not with Mollie and Sheila – all they want is aromatherapy—"

"You mean, Oriental Spiritual Stimulation," Edith said reproachfully as she made a note in her diary. "Or OSS if you can't be bothered to give it its full name. You really should use the right terminology, dear, even in private. One of these days you'll slip up in front of an initiate and that would be embarrassing, to say the least."

"Sorry, Mum. Anyway, Josie's booked them with you for next Tuesday. You can sort out with her which goes first."

Josie Garrard was the young woman who had arrived on a bicycle the day of Sukey's first visit to Burwell Farm. She ran the office with a calm, unflappable efficiency which, coupled with an apparent total lack of awareness of or curiosity concerning the actual proceedings during the courses offered by the RYCE Foundation, made her the perfect employee. She welcomed the initiates (whom she privately thought of as "the punters") on their first day, handed out their information packs and dealt with such practical matters as the booking of additional courses and appointments for supplementary therapies.

Edith continued her perusal of the list of bookings. "What about Henry?" she asked. "What's his problem?"

"Ah, he's a bit more promising." Serena passed her tongue over her full, sensuous lips as if anticipating a particularly tasty morsel of food. "He's been complaining of stabbing pains in his head so I've booked him for Indian head massage – I mean, Oriental Cranial Healing – but from the look in his eye I'm pretty confident it's not only his head that he wants massaged."

"Good. Make sure you give him plenty of encouragement – but not too much healing at first. We want him to come back for more, don't we? Now, what about next week's intake?"

"All newcomers for the morning sessions – three men, three women. Ages range from thirty plus to early fifties. One of the women –" Serena flipped through a sheaf of forms held together with a paper clip until she came to the right one – "name of Jennifer Newlyn, sounds quite tense and neurotic. Josie says she's been on the phone several times, desperate for a place and at the same time making a provisional booking for her friend Susan Reynolds."

"Provisional?" Edith frowned. "We can't afford to take chances on people failing to take up their places," she said sharply.

"Don't worry, it's been confirmed and the deposit paid. We had one cancellation, but that was filled almost immediately."

"That's all right then." Edith thought for a moment. "Susan Reynolds – that name rings a bell. Isn't she the woman who came about the garden machinery that was stolen?"

"That's right. She works for the police, calls herself a scenes of crime officer. I've got my doubts about her."

"Oh – why?"

"I've got a hunch she's here to snoop."

Edith raised an eyebrow. "Whatever gives you that idea?"

"She came back a second time, to tell us our stuff had been recovered."

"So what's odd about that?"

"The police had already told us. Besides, she made out she just happened to be doing another job in this area, but I don't think she was telling the truth."

"Why?"

"The first time, she came in a van with her equipment in it – I could see all sorts of stuff in the back when she opened it to take something out. The second time, she came by car, so it seemed to me that she couldn't have been on a job."

Edith shrugged. "Maybe her van was off the road for some reason."

"She couldn't possibly have packed everything into a small car like the one she turned up in. Besides," Serena went on, frowning into her glass, "after she'd told her story about the missing mower having been recovered, she made some excuse to go and chat to Jarvis and then hung about asking me questions about Oliver Drew and Vera Masters."

"Did she now?!" For the first time, Edith appeared perturbed.

"So I think it would be a good idea to keep an eye on her."

"Will do." Edith made a note.

"Should we mention it to Percy?"

"Certainly not. We don't want to let him think the police might be taking an interest in us – remember the trouble we had with the medics a while back? Besides, if he gets the notion that we find the possibility disturbing he might start asking awkward questions. We don't want that, do we?"

"No way!" The two women exchanged conspiratorial glances.

Edith turned her attention back to the matters in hand. "About this request for OCH – Percy would be so pleased to hear someone's asked for that, it's his new baby and he's convinced it has special rejuvenative powers, but I suppose if what Henry's really after is one of your specials . . ."

"There was definitely that look about him when he discussed it with me. He mumbled something about being prepared to pay extra for a longer session and I told him to make a booking in the normal way and we'd talk about it before beginning the treatment. I think he understood me perfectly."

"Excellent." Edith gave a satisfied nod. "In that case, we'll make sure everything's prepared – and we certainly won't mention it to Percy. It's a good job he's such a trusting soul." She glanced at the clock on the office wall. "Let's run through the afternoon punters and then go back to the house – he finishes his meditation in half an hour and he likes me to be there when he rejoins the real world."

"Isn't it a good thing your husband has such regular habits?" said Serena with a mischievous smile as, having checked the final details, they began putting their papers away.

"Isn't it just?" Again, they exchanged glances of mutual understanding. Edith stood up, saying, "You lock up here and I'll go and see about supper – oh, and by the way, make me a new one of these, will you?" She removed the circlet from her head and dumped it in the waste bin. "This one's getting distinctly tatty – I'd hate any of the initiates to see it close to."

A quarter of an hour after his wife and stepdaughter returned to their private quarters and were to all intents and purposes engaged in purely domestic functions, Percy Burrell rejoined them in the room which had been the kitchen of the original farmhouse and now served as their dining and living-room as well. He was a tall, lean figure with hollow cheeks and brooding, deep-set eyes and he was still clad in the monkish robe and sandals that he wore during the day.

"Are you both well and in tune with the Cosmos, my dears?"

he enquired in a slightly abstracted manner as he sipped his regular preprandial glass of cider vinegar and water, in which they perforce joined him with apparent relish. He naively believed Serena and Edith shared his teetotal as well as his vegetarian convictions. As it happened, their eating habits presented no problems; from purely financial constraints, Edith had brought her daughter up on a meatless diet and they had so far managed to keep their occasional tipple a secret.

Percy took as little part as possible in the running of the business, preferring to leave practical matters in the capable hands of his wife and stepdaughter. He was a man totally absorbed in and dedicated to the purpose for which he sincerely believed he had been sent into the world, namely to guide as many people as possible along the path to the state of enlightenment which he called the Unlimited. If he had had his way, he would have spread his message freely without thought of gain and he had taken a personal vow of celibacy, but he had met Edith almost immediately on his return from his wanderings in the East and after a long period of abstinence from the pleasures of the flesh had found her charms irresistible. During one of their nights of passion, prompted by an overweening sense of guilt at his weakness, he poured into her sympathetic and calculating ear his desire to spread enlightenment to all mankind. He was at heart a simple soul; despite his initial misgivings about accepting money for the gift that he passionately wished to share without worldly reward, tributes from delighted "initiates" and a growing band of members of the Circle of Lifelong Initiation soon convinced him that his message was being dissipated far and wide and that his consent, reluctantly given, to "going commercial" had been the right one. Since Edith and Serena took all the sordid business side of things off his shoulders he had nothing to do but devote all his waking hours to spreading his gospel and, in his spare time, surrendering his mind to the boundless bliss of the Unlimited.

Percy Burrell was a fulfilled and happy man.

Fourteen

"So you're still determined to go ahead with this—" Jim Castle began, then broke off as Sukey reacted to his uncharacteristically belligerent attitude with a sharp look that combined amusement and provocativeness and had him momentarily wrong-footed.

"Crazy scheme? Wilful disregard of your feelings?" she taunted him. "Go on, say it, you're just miffed because DCI Lord approves of what I'm planning to do."

"I didn't say he approves, he just expressed some doubts about quacks meddling with the minds of vulnerable people—"

"—and that even though there was no evidence of wrongdoing at RYCE, there'd be no harm in someone carrying out a little quiet investigation. That sounds like approval to me."

"He specifically ruled out an investigation. All he said was—"

"That I, being of eminently sound mind and far from vulnerable, would be the ideal person to do a spot of nosing around," Sukey interrupted with an air of triumph as once again he found himself on the defensive.

"Well, more or less," he said reluctantly. "All the same, I'm not happy about it and I wish you'd drop the whole thing."

"You're not suggesting that I'm likely to be influenced by some weird system of mind games, are you?"

"I didn't say that, but you never know what goes on there—"

"Which is precisely the reason why I'm interested. I really can't understand why—"

As if she had not spoken, Jim continued in the same hectoring tone. "Some of these people are up to all sorts of tricks to make

111

you believe you're undergoing some miraculous form of enlightenment that can change your life. It's just a money-making racket and you've allowed yourself to be sucked into it by two people you hardly know harbouring totally unfounded suspicions."

"You're not being very logical," Sukey pointed out patiently. "If their suspicions are totally unfounded, then there's nothing for you to worry about."

"You're just being driven by curiosity."

"That's partly true," she admitted, "but after thinking about it, and after—" She was on the point of saying, "after reading what Vera wrote," when she remembered that she had not mentioned having borrowed the diary from Adrian to anyone except Fergus and checked herself just in time.

"After what?" Jim demanded.

"After learning that someone like Vera Masters, who according to Cath wasn't nearly so scatty as Adrian likes to make out, came to be so strongly influenced by the RYCE—"

Once more, he refused to let her finish. "You're so bloody inquisitive you felt you had to go poking your nose in," he said with a touch of scorn.

"I'm not poking my nose in, I was asked if I could help." Sukey kept her voice level but she could feel her colour rising from suppressed anger. "Besides, having been to the place, I don't deny I'm curious . . . and I do have a mind of my own, in case you hadn't noticed."

"I've noticed that you don't give a toss what I feel about it."

"That's not fair," she protested. "You said you'd withdrawn your objections."

"I felt bound to tell you what DCI Lord's reaction was, but I'd hoped on reflection you'd have some consideration for my feelings in the matter."

"Oh, stop being so pompous!"

They faced one another angrily across the table in Sukey's kitchen. Two glasses, a corkscrew, a bottle of wine and a can of beer stood unopened between them. With an irritable gesture,

Jim picked up the beer can, tugged at the ring and poured the contents into his glass. Foam rose to the surface and overflowed on to the table.

"Serves you right for pouring your own first." Sukey mopped up the spillage with the dishcloth. "Thanks, I'll see to my own," she snapped, snatching the bottle of wine and corkscrew away as, with a muttered apology, he reached for them. She pulled the seal from the bottle and scowled. "Damn, it's one of those beastly plastic corks."

"Here, let me." He took the bottle from her; their hands touched, their eyes met and the anger melted away. He moved round the table and pulled her into his arms. "Don't let's quarrel, love," he pleaded with his cheek against hers. "It's only because I care for you so much that I'm concerned for you."

"I know." She closed her eyes and relaxed in his embrace. "There's no need to worry, honestly," she assured him after a moment. "There really isn't anything sinister about the place – on the contrary, it has a lovely tranquil atmosphere and the literature is full of references to inner peace and finding yourself and realising your potential. They call it releasing your cosmic energy, but that's probably a phrase they've coined to make it sound as if they've reinvented the spiritual wheel. In fact, they talk about inner and outer wheels. It's all in their brochure—"

"You've got their brochure? I only gave it a cursory glance at the Masterses' – I'd like to have a closer look at it."

"Of course. I'll run upstairs and get it. There's a reference to stress-related problems as well; you might even like to think about going on a course yourself," she added over her shoulder as she hurried from the room.

When she returned a few moments later he had uncorked the wine bottle and filled her glass. "Sit down and drink that before you start getting the supper," he said.

"That sounds as if I'm going to be slaving over a hot stove without your valuable help."

"You said we were eating cold this evening. Besides, I've

something important to read, remember?" He jabbed a finger at the brochure. "I'm sure you wouldn't want me to give it anything but my undivided attention."

"Of course not." Their eyes met and they broke into spontaneous laughter. Thankful that the conflict was over, Sukey put potatoes to bake in the oven and took an assortment of cold meats and salad ingredients from the refrigerator before sitting down with her glass of wine. "There are four of us this evening," she informed him. "Fergus has invited Anita."

There was no reply. Jim was already absorbed in a study of the RYCE brochure.

"Well, what do you make of it?" Sukey asked.

The pair were temporarily alone in the sitting-room after the evening meal. Anita and Fergus were in the kitchen, the former having volunteered to do the washing-up. In normal circumstances this would have occasioned a considerable amount of lively and uninhibited chatter, but this time their abnormally muted voices were barely audible through the closed door. Since Sukey had earlier impressed on Fergus the need to avoid any reference whatsoever in Jim's presence to the subject of her impending attendance at RYCE, she guessed that they were speculating on the possible outcome.

Jim thought for a moment or two before replying to her question. At length he said, "In my opinion, the people running this place are either eccentrics or out-and-out charlatans – probably both. I can understand sad, lonely or inadequate people going for this kind of thing and I suppose if they get comfort from it then Freya and Xavier, as they call themselves, could be said to be doing some good." He gave a sardonic chuckle. "Where on earth did they dream up those names, I wonder? I can see that Percy and Edith don't exactly fit in with grand visions of the mystery of the cosmos, but—"

"I've looked into that. Freya is unusual, but not all that uncommon – remember Freya Stark, the travel writer? It's the

name of a Norse goddess of love, according to a dictionary of
first names I found in the library."

"What about Xavier? Wasn't he some saint or other?"

"Yes, Spanish, seventeenth century I think. It's a Basque word
meaning 'new house'."

"I suppose it's the nearest he could get to the new state of mind
he's promising his so-called initiates." Jim picked up the brochure, opened it and studied the portraits inside the front cover.
"Love in a new house, eh? They're like something left over from
the days of flower-power, him with his beard and brooding eyes
looking half-stoned, Freya with that daisy-chain on her head and
Serena looking as if she'd be more at home at the Stowe horse
fair."

Sukey giggled. "I have a notion that you don't take them very
seriously."

"I have to admit that I haven't found anything disturbing in
what's written in here. Reading between the lines, I suspect that
they're peddling some fairly well-known principles like auto-
suggestion dressed up in a load of fancy new language."

"That's been my impression."

"Well, just keep your feet on the ground and your eyes open
while you're there, that's all."

"That's why I'm going, remember?"

Six people sat self-consciously on low, cushioned chairs arranged
in a horseshoe, sipping a herbal concoction served in fragile
porcelain cups from a round brass tray offered to each in turn by
Serena, bare-foot and clad in a long, colourful garment similar to
the one she had been wearing when Sukey first saw her. Apart
from the single word "Welcome" with which she had greeted
them as they entered, escorted by a young blonde woman who
introduced herself as Josie and checked their paperwork on
arrival, she maintained a calm, aloof silence, directing them to
their seats solely by gesture and acknowledging the polite thanks
of each recipient with a brief smile and a nod of her dark head as
she moved among them with her tray. Covertly watching her,

Sukey noted that she made eye contact with everyone; when it came to her own turn she was subjected to a gaze of such intensity that she experienced an unexpected tingle of gooseflesh. Just part of the technique, she told herself as she sipped at the contents of her cup, which tasted like camomile tea with some additional, slightly scented ingredient.

Sukey and Jennifer had been the last to arrive and there had been no opportunity for contact with the four other members of the group, three men and one woman. It was impossible to assess their ages in the subdued light from several lamps dotted around the walls, diffused by parchment shades decorated with outlines of what were evidently intended to suggest natural objects: foliage, flowers, birds, clouds, moons and stars. The air was perfumed; music of a vaguely oriental character played softly in the background and from some invisible source came the soft gurgle of running water. Classic techniques to encourage relaxation and a receptive mind.

The seats were so arranged that the spaces between them made it impossible for anyone to so much as touch the person on either side or speak to them without being overheard. Conscious of a movement at her side, Sukey glanced at Jennifer and saw her lips moving. Unable to make out the words, she shrugged, shook her head and looked away.

After a few minutes Serena, who had retreated into a shadowy corner, re-emerged and once more moved round the circle, wordlessly holding out the tray to each person in turn. All obediently returned their cups and, as if responding to an unspoken instruction, sat back in their seats with their hands in their laps. There had been no direction to remain silent, yet no one spoke. A few throats were cleared, a few sounds of movement as people settled themselves comfortably, then all was still. Amid an atmosphere of highly charged expectancy, the lights began to dim until the room was in total darkness.

Several seconds passed. Sukey, seated at one end of the horseshoe, was suddenly conscious of a faint rustle and a light draught on her cheek as if the air had been momentarily disturbed. Her eyes were drawn upward by a faint glow from the ceiling which grew in intensity until it fell like a spotlight on the figure of a woman standing immediately beneath it. She wore an ankle-length dress of dark green and and a circlet of small evergreen leaves on the long, straight black hair which fell loosely round her shoulders. Her eyes, fringed with dark lashes, were of a striking blue, her skin was milk-white and her mouth a soft rose pink. She stood for a moment with bowed head, her perfectly shaped hands pressed together in an oriental gesture of greeting. Then she looked up, faced her audience and opened her arms like a priest about to bless a congregation. A slow, mysterious smile spread over her face.

"I am Freya," she announced in a rich contralto. "In the name of the Unlimited, I welcome you to our ever-widening body of initiates." The words were greeted with a ripple of polite murmurs which died away in response to Freya's raised hand. The smile faded, her expression became gravely earnest. "Your time to speak will come later, when you have taken the first steps to coming face to face with your inner selves," she informed them. Her opening announcement had been made in the style of a professional actor, dramatic and attention-demanding but not exaggeratedly so. As she listened to what followed, Sukey was aware of a subtle change of tempo. She was on the alert for any obvious gimmicks, but it took her several seconds to realise that Freya was timing her words to fit the rhythm of the background music. The effect was almost mesmerising. "For the moment," Freya continued in slow, measured tones, "all we ask of you is your silence . . . your silence and your total concentration."

And your money. The words popped unbidden into Sukey's mind and she was startled by the next utterance, which seemed to indicate that the woman had read her thoughts.

"Some of you will have thought long and hard before committing your money to what your common sense, or possibly your friends and families, may have told you is an impossible dream," Freya continued. "They will have told you to see your doctor, take pills, pull yourselves together. Yet such is your need

117

that you have swept aside such negative thoughts and futile advice and come to seek our help. We shall not fail you. We do not ask you to reveal to us the needs or the pain that bring you here. Difficulties at work, problems with relationships, perhaps a bereavement – everyone is different, yet deep down all are the same." At the mention of bereveament, Sukey heard Jennifer utter a faint gasp that was almost a sob, quickly stifled.

"Be still! Be still!" Freya's voice fell to a sibilant whisper. Sukey felt the words inducing a pleasant feeling of drowsiness; momentarily forgetting the need to remain on the alert, she closed her eyes and relaxed with a sigh of contentment. She became aware of a faint movement, followed by the touch of cold fingers on her forehead. An entry in Vera's diary flashed into her mind; with an effort she shook off an increasing sense of lethargy as, through half-closed lids, she watched Freya move swiftly round the rest of the group, uttering the same words and touching the forehead of each person before resuming her place. It was noticeable that one after the other they all appeared to fall into an even deeper state of relaxation.

There was an interval of several seconds before Freya spoke again and this time the rhythmic effect was brought back into play. She placed the palms of her hands together in front of her face and began swaying almost imperceptibly from side to side as she spoke. Covertly watching her, fascinated in spite of herself, Sukey found herself imitating the movement and sensed that the others were doing the same. "Our task is to help you to see your needs and your pain for what they are," Freya intoned. "Internal shackles that keep you in thrall. We will show you how you can throw off those shackles and direct you along the path that leads to the Unlimited." After another dramatic pause she said in a reverential tone, "And now, I will pass you into the hands of our leader."

She moved aside to make room for the white-robed figure who had materialised noiselessly out of the shadows behind her and now stepped forward into the spotlight. "I am Xavier," he announced.

*   *   *

"It really was a most extraordinary experience," Sukey told Jim that evening. "Looked at objectively, it was all so cleverly stage-managed that several times I found myself on the point of being carried away. The combination of subdued lighting, perfume, music and Freya's histrionics was quite hypnotic."

"That's what's been worrying me." Jim took her hand and looked earnestly into her eyes. "Promise me you'll pull out at once if you feel any signs of getting spooked."

"I'm quite sure I won't. I have to admit that Xavier was very impressive—"

"Xavier? I thought you said that Freya woman was the prime mover."

"Oh no, she was just the warm-up act. It wouldn't surprise me to learn that she's had some drama training; she has an impressive range of tone and expressions and gestures to match. No, Xavier's the king-pin, 'our leader' as she described him. After her introductory spiel he uttered some kind of incantation before urging us all to look deep into our innermost souls and silently confront the demons who had forged our internal shackles. We had to face the demons down and imagine ourselves breaking free of our shackles."

"I don't recall anything about demons in the brochure."

"That's probably because it might scare off punters of a nervous disposition," said Sukey with a giggle.

"Is that all that happened? It doesn't seem much for the money—"

"Oh no, there were all sorts of chanting and mental exercises. One of them was to give our demon a name and order it to break our shackles so that we could climb on to the Inner Wheel. Then we had to sit in a closed circle, hold hands and feel the cosmic energy circulating and drawing us up to it. After that we were all sent off to meditate in private in one of the little garden rooms I told you about. Then we went back indoors for a sort of recap, and that was it."

"What a load of old poppycock!"

"It's amazing how plausible it seemed at the time."

"What did the others make of it?"

"I've no idea. We were told to leave in total silence and to – I can't remember the exact words, but the idea was to keep our minds focused on what Xavier called 'eternal truths' for as long as possible before being sucked back into the routine of our ordinary lives."

"Sounds like a good way of discouraging any sort of exchange of views or adverse comment."

"Looked at objectively, that's probably the idea, but everyone accepted it as perfectly reasonable. You know," Sukey continued reflectively, "there's something about Xavier that I can't define. I'm prepared to believe that Freya, and probably Serena, are play-acting and simply in it for the money, but something shines out of Xavier like a beacon. Sincerity, integrity, utter conviction – they're all part of it, but there's another, indefinable quality . . . I can't think of the right word."

"How about 'barking'?" Jim suggested. Sukey burst out laughing, then grew serious again as she said, "I'm a bit worried about Jennifer. I asked her – more as a joke really – what name she'd given her demon and she said, 'Revenge.' I thought at first that was good, that she'd taken the first step towards ridding herself of the fixation that those three were responsible for Ollie's suicide, but then she said, 'I've become quite fond of my demon, we're going to be good friends.'"

"What d'you suppose she meant by that?"

"I asked her, but she wouldn't say any more."

"Well, better keep an eye on her."

"I can't keep an eye on her all the time – not while we're meditating. Besides, it's Xavier and Co I'm supposed to be watching."

"True." Jim stood up. "I'd better be off, I'm on early turn tomorrow. I'll look forward to hearing what happens on Day Two."

"It'll probably be more of the same – with variations, no doubt – for the rest of the week."

At the door he asked casually, "By the way, what do you call your demon?"

She twined her arms round his neck and gazed with mock solemnity into his eyes. "Jim, of course," she said softly, "and I've become quite fond of him!"

"Then you won't want to escape from his shackles, will you?"

"Definitely not."

As Sukey had predicted, Day Two produced few surprises. By the end of Day Three, while still managing to maintain a degree of detachment, she was aware of an increasing sense of wellbeing and inner calm.

"It's quite amazing," she reported to Jim that evening over a drink in a pub near her home. "I can see it in the others as well – not that we have much contact during the sessions, except the touchy-feely interlude, but it shows in their faces as they leave to go home. The first day they seemed bemused, anxious even, but today there was more of a peaceful look about them. They must be starting to shake off their shackles, I suppose."

"What sort of people are they?"

She thought for a moment. "It's hard to say. There's one other woman besides Jennifer and me. I'd put her age at about sixty and she wears a wedding ring so presumably she's either married or widowed. Two of the men look like business types, although they wear casual clothes. The third has a slightly bookish look – a teacher, maybe, or a scientist."

"Ages?"

"Mid forties to fifties, I suppose. It's hard to tell."

"It doesn't sound as if you've been observing them very closely."

"There isn't a lot of opportunity for that. We're either in this semi-darkened room chanting mantras or listening out for cosmic vibrations. Otherwise we're sitting in our private space in the garden quietly meditating until we're summoned back by bells for more of the same. We finish up on the floor doing a few yoga-like exercises before a period of total relaxation and then we're given a few words of profound wisdom to speed us on our way. Today's was something about there being no blame and we all do the best we can according to our awareness of the way things are."

"Surprised I haven't heard that one from any of my villains," Jim commented with a wry smile. "Sounds like a handy cop-out for someone who's just robbed a bank. I suppose," he went on, "there's somewhere indoors to do your meditating if the weather's bad. It wouldn't be much fun in the pouring rain or a blizzard."

Sukey grinned back at him. "Trust you to be practical – yes, I imagine so. We've been lucky this week to have such perfect weather."

"So that's it? Still no group discussions or opportunities to ask questions?"

"Not so far. It says in our welcome pack that there'll be an in-depth personal assessment with one of the leaders on Day Five."

"And you haven't found anything adverse to report?"

Sukey shook her head and nibbled an olive. "On the contrary, I'm beginning to understand why Vera Masters waxed so enthusiastic about the place. I know I didn't start off with any hang-ups – at least none that I was aware of – but I am beginning to feel a sense of inner peace that I haven't known before. On my way home today I suddenly began to have charitable thoughts towards Paul. I suppose it was that talk about blame," she added reflectively.

It was the first time in a long while that she had made any reference to her feelings towards her ex-husband. Jim gave her a searching look. "You aren't getting spooked, are you?" he said anxiously.

"Of course not." She reached across and touched his hand. "Just the same, I'm sure it's having a therapeutic effect. You ought to give it a try some time – it might make you less uptight."

"I'm not uptight!" he retorted indignantly, then gave a slightly embarrassed laugh. "Well, now and again, maybe."

Sukey helped herself to another olive. "One thing worries me a little though," she said after a pause.

"What's that?"

"Will any improvement stand the test of time, or are the so-called demons lurking in the shadows, waiting to pounce on their victims once they finish the course? I suppose they can always go back for a refresher." She fingered the stem of her glass, frowning.

"You said Serena admitted to the occasional failure?"

"Oh yes, she was quite open about it."

"What about the so-called rejuvenation treaments?"

"They're extra – quite expensive, too. Therapies and massages with fancy-sounding oriental names. I understand they're only available in the afternoons or evenings, but we're going to be shown round the therapy rooms and given more details on Friday."

"Perhaps that's where RYCE makes its real money."

"Could be." Sukey's eyes sparkled as she took a mouthful of wine. "That's an idea – if Xavier gives any of the treaments I'm tempted to have a go at one of them – all in the cause of the investigation, naturally."

"You'll do no such thing!" he said indignantly.

She leaned towards him. "Only kidding," she said softly. "I'm more than happy with your, er, treatments."

"So you're still on good terms with your demon?" he whispered back.

"Excellent! Here's to Day Four!" She raised her glass, drained it and put it down.

"Would you like a refill?"

"No thanks, it's getting late and I have to be up early. You know," she added, as she stood up and reached for her jacket, "I'll be almost sorry when the week's over – it's been an interesting experience in a lovely tranquil environment."

But on Day Four the tranquillity was to be shattered.

Fifteen

When Sukey arrived at Burwell Farm the following morning she was immediately conscious of a subtle difference in the atmosphere. She was the last to take her place in the horseshoe and was surprised when, instead of maintaining their usual passive, withdrawn attitude whilst awaiting their cup of herbal tea, two of her fellow "initiates" nodded across the room and smiled at her. She smiled back before turning to Jennifer with the intention of making a whispered comment, but the young widow showed no sign of awareness of anything unusual. She was sitting with her eyes closed; her lids were fluttering as if she was in a light sleep and her hands were pressed firmly together in an attitude suggestive of prayer.

The level of lighting was marginally higher that it had been during the first three days; although it was still low, it had been increased sufficiently to illuminate parts of the room which had hitherto been in shadow. On the walls, which were covered in dark material, Sukey was able to make out framed prints of mystic designs, some of which appeared vaguely oriental in origin; among them she recognised enlarged versions of the posters and book jackets on display in the office. Against one wall was a table with an open display cabinet above it. Various items were set out there: a brass bell, some candles in a variety of shapes and sizes, bottles which Sukey guessed contained essential oils, jars of what looked like pot pourri, books and postcards. No doubt, she thought, there would be an invitation to browse – and buy – before the end of the course.

The air in the room was still perfumed, but with a lighter, more

124

delicate fragrance than before. The music had taken on a new quality as well. Previously it had been exclusively instrumental, soothing and somnolent in tempo but lacking a regular rhythm or sustained melodic theme; now it had acquired a quickening pulse suggestive of an awakening from sleep. Another instrument had been subtly woven into the tapestry of sound – an instrument with a haunting, compelling quality that made Sukey's skin tingle. It took her several seconds to identify it as a human voice; high-pitched, almost religious in character, it sang a counterpoint with no discernible words yet managing to convey a sense of hopeful anticipation.

Serena's manner, too, hinted at a change of mood. She was clad as usual in one of her brilliantly coloured dresses – orange today, with bold splashes of scarlet and vermilion – but instead of her customary silence, accompanied by an enigmatic, penetrating gaze as she offered her tray to each individual, she nodded, smiled and softly said, "Welcome" to each. Yet for some reason, as she took her cup with a whispered "Thank you", Sukey had a feeling that beneath the surface calm lay a hint of watchfulness, almost of disquiet. There seemed to be no particular reason why this should be so. To all outward appearances the week was progressing according to plan; as she had told Jim the previous evening, everyone showed signs of an increasing sense of wellbeing. She herself was feeling the benefit of the strangely effective rituals in which she had taken part. Even Jennifer had seemed more at peace. Although she, like the others, had obeyed Xavier's injunction to depart in silence, she had – surprisingly in view of her declared motive for being there at all – shown no inclination to talk things over on the telephone later. On the other hand there had been no more talk of revenge.

Serena went round with her tray to gather the empty cups and then disappeared through a curtained alcove which, like many other features in the room, had previously been almost invisible. A moment later the curtains parted again and Freya emerged. She took her place as usual beneath the spotlight, but this time there was no dramatic reduction in the general level of lighting.

She stood perfectly still for several seconds, her eyes fixed in a steady gaze that appeared to be focused on infinity rather than her audience, her hands raised and a mysterious smile on her face. Sukey had an eerie sensation that a subliminal message was being transmitted; she found words springing unbidden into her head. *Come out of the shadows,* she seemed to be hearing. *Shake off your crumbling internal shackles, banish your demons, see the Inner Wheel within your grasp. Today, under the guidance of your leader, you will accomplish the first stage of your journey to the Unlimited.*

A low murmur that was almost a sigh of pleasure travelled round the room – a murmur in which Sukey, somewhat to her consternation, found herself quite spontaneously joining. She gave herself a mental shake. Although, as she had assured Jim the previous evening, she was reasonably satisfied that no malign influences were at work, nevertheless she felt in honour bound to keep her senses on the alert for the remainder of the week in order to fulfil her promise to Adrian Masters. She had not yet had an opportunity to bank the cheque he had insisted on giving her; he was hardly getting value for his money and she was seriously thinking of offering to return it.

Freya was wearing a dress of rich midnight blue. In contrast to the dark, unadorned garments she had worn during the first three days it was scattered with fragments of some metallic material which made shifting, glittering patterns of light as she moved. Until now she had worn no jewellery, but this morning a crystal hung from a silver chain round her throat and rings sparkled on her fingers. A few white flowers had been added to the circlet of foliage on her head.

At last she began to speak. "Already," she intoned in a throbbing contralto, "I sense that you are emerging from the shadows. The air is alive with cosmic vibrations. They are all around us, destroying your demons with their divine power. Your internal shackles are crumbling, the Inner Wheel is within your grasp. Picture it, see it, reach out for it, ride on it with thankfulness. Drink from the sacred wellspring of cosmic energy and feel it bearing you towards the Great Un-limited!"

Even as she was assuring herself that this was pure clap-trap, the words had echoed so closely the thoughts running through Sukey's brain a few moments earlier that they caused a sharp twinge in the pit of her stomach. Was she under a light form of hypnosis? Were they all? There had been no mention of hypnotherapy in the brochure, but . . . her pulse quickened; she began to experience a feeling that something unexpected was about to happen and renewed her efforts to keep her mind and her senses firmly under her own control.

Freya moved into the centre of the horseshoe. "Rise and link hands!" she commanded. Everyone obeyed, forming a circle around her. She began rotating slowly, gazing into the eyes of each in turn. It was part of an exercise she had put them through every day during which Sukey had so far managed without difficulty to remain detached while covertly watching the others. This time she felt herself struggling against the influence of Freya's mind. It was a frightening sensation; in an effort to resist, she began mentally reciting the words of "Ring-a-ring-o-roses", which induced an almost hysterical urge to burst out laughing. It was a relief when the silence was broken by the sound of another voice.

"I feel it . . . I feel it!" One of the men – the one Sukey had described to Jim as "bookish" – was gazing at Freya with an expression of bemused wonderment, as if in response to a revelation.

Freya stretched out both hands to him and said softly, "You have reached it . . . the Inner Wheel?"

"Yes . . . yes," he replied eagerly. He broke the circle and came towards her, his own hands extended. Their fingers touched for a second; then, like a man in a dream, he took a pace backwards and sank into his seat.

"We rejoice in your achievement," said Freya earnestly. "Has anyone else reached the Inner Wheel?" Her glance travelled round the other members of the group, who had instinctively

127

moved closer together and reformed the chain. "If so, raise your right hand." Once more, the circle was broken; this time two hands were hesitantly raised and the finger-touching gesture was peformed on each in turn so that only one man, Jennifer and Sukey remained standing. Freya gestured to them to sit down; as they complied, she resumed her place under the spotlight and said, "To the remaining three who have still to take this momentous upward leap I say, The day is not yet over. Place yourselves in the hands of your leader and have faith in his wisdom. See, he comes before you now!"

She turned and flung out a hand in a wide, sweeping gesture. An almost rapturous smile lit up her colourless features. "Xavier!" she cried. "Your initiates await your guidance!" There was a breathless, expectant hush as all eyes were fixed on the curtains behind her.

Seconds passed, but nothing happened. The curtains failed to part. Freya remained motionless, frozen in the attitude she had struck as she uttered her summons. Her eyes seemed to glaze over; her smile became fixed and then faded like snow in the sun. Someone coughed, others fidgeted.

Freya called again, with no result. She called a third time, and now there was a hint of something close to desperation in her voice. "Xavier, come! Your initiates await you with impatience!" Still no response. She turned back to the group, who were now showing distinct signs of restiveness. "Knowing how much strength he will need for this momentous day, he must have fallen into a deeper level of meditation than usual at this time," she said. Her voice had risen in pitch to something that Sukey guessed was close to her normal manner of speaking and it was evident that she was totally unprepared for such a contingency. "Please," she urged them, "compose yourselves and wait quietly while I go and rouse him."

"Well, that was a bit of a let-down," muttered one of the men.

There was a reproving "Sshh!" from the woman sitting next to him.

Everyone lapsed into silence. Nothing could be heard in the

room but the sound of quiet breathing. Sukey found herself counting off the seconds; she had reached thirty when, from somewhere not far distant, came an unearthly wail like that of a trapped animal. It rose to a crescendo and died away before being repeated, closer this time. The inarticulate sound became human; it crystallised into words and became recognisable as the voice of a woman screaming, "Help! Murder! Please . . . someone . . . come quickly!"

As Sukey instinctively leapt to her feet with the intention of going to investigate, she shot a keen glance round the group in an attempt to gauge their reactions. For a moment, everyone remained in their seats, motionless and open-mouthed, wearing the stunned, bewildered look of sleepwalkers jerked violently into wakefulness. Beside her, Jennifer sat with her eyes still closed, her hands tightly clenched. Then, like statues come suddenly to life, the rest sat up and exchanged horrified glances as the cries for help were renewed. One of the men – the one who had commented audibly on Xavier's non-appearance – stood up.

"I suppose we'd better investigate," he said and began making for the door, but Sukey was there before him. She stood in front of it, barring his way.

"Everyone is to stay here!" she commanded. "If there has been a murder, no one is to leave this room until the police arrive to take charge."

The others turned in their seats and gaped at her in astonishment. Jennifer, who had emerged from her apparent trance, was staring first at Sukey and then at the man who had spoken, her hand over her mouth and her eyes wide with alarm.

"Who says so?" the man demanded, glaring at Sukey.

Sukey took her ID from her pocket and held it up for them all to see. "I'm a scenes of crime officer and I work for the police," she said crisply. "If there has been a murder, I'm taking charge until they get here. Please, all of you, stay in your seats while I go and find out what's happened." She was as shaken as the rest of them, but she had evidently managed to inject sufficient authority into her voice to convince them and they all complied but one.

"You as well please, Mr . . . ?"

"Foster. Dan Foster. Why don't I come with you?"

At that moment the woman who had told him to be quiet suddenly burst into tears. "It's horrible, horrible," she wailed. "Just when I was reaching out to grasp the Inner Wheel! If Xavier's been murdered I'll never reach it now! Oh dear God, what will become of me?" She began rocking to and fro in her chair, weeping like a child. Jennifer went over to her and began patting her on the shoulder.

Sukey had a flash of inspiration. "If you don't mind, Mr Foster, it would be very helpful if you'd kindly wait here and keep everyone as calm as possible—"

"—and make sure they all stay put," he interjected, with a marked change of attitude. As she had hoped and anticipated, he was quick to grasp the chance to exercise some degree of command. "Leave it to me."

"Thank you very much. I'll be as quick as I can."

As she emerged from the house she saw Serena and Josie, who she guessed had been in the office when they heard the screams, standing in the middle of the courtyard attempting to calm Freya, who was now alternately gasping, gagging and babbling incoherently, her eyes rolling and her hands tearing at her hair. Serena turned to Sukey and said desperately, "She says Xavier's been stabbed. What shall we do?"

"Has she told you where he is?"

"I assume he's in his private cell in the garden – that's where he does his morning meditation when it's fine."

"Will you show me, Serena? And Josie, will you take Freya somewhere quiet and try to calm her down."

Josie glanced at Serena as if seeking her approval. Serena nodded. She was visibly shaken; her eyes were wide with shock and apprehension and her hands were trembling. "Do as she says," she told the girl. "She works for the police." She beckoned to Sukey. "This way." She darted across the courtyard and through the gate leading to the garden, crossed the wide central expanse of lawn and raced along the dense hedge that formed the left-hand boundary, the skirt of her voluminous, brightly coloured dress billowing about her legs. Following at her heels, Sukey noticed that, unlike the similar hedge on the right, this one appeared at first to have no access to "rooms" similar to those used each day by the initiates for meditation. It was not until they had almost reached the far end of the garden that Serena pulled up short and pointed. "This is Xavier's private cell," she said in a hoarse whisper.

Sukey looked through the gap, but all she could see could see was a wall of dense greenery rather than a view of the interior. A rope was strung across the entrance, suspended between two invisible supports. From it hung a small rectangle of varnished wood on which was painted the single word, "Private". Serena reached out to grasp it but Sukey caught at her wrist.

"Don't touch it – don't touch anything for the moment," she said urgently. "Everything must be left exactly as it is. There may be fingerprints."

"Don't we have to go in there and look?" Serena whispered. She was trembling more violently than ever and appeared appalled at the prospect.

"I'm afraid so." Sukey said gently. She took the girl's hand; it was as cold as ice. "I'll go first, if you like."

"Please."

"OK, you wait here." Sukey was surprised at how calm she felt; previous encounters with murder in the course of her work had shaken her to the core, but this time her pulse was steady and her breathing regular. Just the same, she hesitated for a moment before stepping carefully over the painted notice and taking four short paces to the left – all that were needed to bring her into the open and in sight of Xavier's body.

He was lying face downwards in a crouching position, as if he had been attacked while sitting cross-legged, with his back to the entrance, at the top of the shallow flight of steps leading down to the pool that formed the central feature of the enclosure. He had toppled forward on his knees with his arms folded beneath him, the upper part of his head overhanging the water and his backside in the air. A casual observer might have assumed he was contemplating the water plants – or possibly, seeing his white robes and sandals, have taken him for an oriental monk at prayer. His posture might even have struck them as slightly ridiculous – but for the dagger that someone had plunged up to the hilt in his back.

Sukey swallowed hard before stepping forward, picking her way carefully to avoid disturbing possible evidence. Her gorge rose at the sight of the reflection of the man's face in the still water and she had to steel herself to place her fingers on his neck, knowing instinctively that it was hopeless yet harbouring the faint hope that she might find a pulse, however weak. There was none. There was blood on the white garment where the weapon had entered, but surprisingly little. Then she realised where most of it had gone. The dagger must have passed clean through the body and gravity had done the rest, sending a scarlet tide flowing over the stone rim of the pool to form a slowly spreading stain in the still water.

She stood up and made a swift survey of the scene. The space had been laid out in the style of a miniature Japanese garden, with dwarf trees in strange, convoluted shapes planted here and there among variegated stones and gravel. Her first thought was to check whether there was any other means of access to the enclosure; so far as she could see there was none.

From behind her came a horrified gasp and the sound of retching. Serena had followed her and was staring at Xavier's body with her hand over her mouth. Her eyes were glazed and her face had taken on the yellowish tinge of beeswax. Sukey put an arm round her shoulders and drew her gently away.

"There's nothing we can do for him now," she whispered. "We must call the police at once – and no one must leave before they arrive and take over. They'll want statements from everyone."

As she led the unresisting Serena back to the house, it crossed

Sukey's mind that she knew nothing, absolutely nothing, about the background of any of the so-called initiates except Jennifer – and apart from the man who had introduced himself as Dan Foster, not even their names.

Sixteen

T hey were halfway back to the house when Jarvis emerged through one of the gaps in the hedge on the opposite side of the garden and hurried across the lawn to intercept them, his ruddy features registering concern.

"What's up?" he asked. "I heard someone yelling – has there been an accident?"

"No accident," said Sukey grimly without stopping. "Xavier's been attacked in his . . ." She hesitated for a moment before rejecting the word "cell" that Serena had used first and opting for ". . . his private retreat. I'm about to call the police and an ambulance."

"Attacked? Is he badly hurt?" Jarvis fell into a shambling trot alongside them. "Is there anything I can do? I learned first aid when I was a Boy Scout—"

"I'm afraid he needs more than first aid."

"I could maybe do something to help until the paramedics arrive." Jarvis pulled up short. He was already out of breath; Sukey had not slackened her pace and Serena passively allowed herself to be led along, but it had plainly been an effort for him to keep up with them. "Why don't I just go and see?" he panted, turning on his heel with the apparent intention of going to investigate, but Sukey called him back.

"He's best left alone till the experts get here," she said sharply. "You'd better come with us while I contact them. No one is to go near him or touch him until they arrive and take charge."

Jarvis swung round and glowered. "Who says so?" he demanded with a hint of truculence. Then he recognised her. "I remember you, you came about the stolen mower—"

"That's right, I'm a scenes of crime officer working for the police and—"

"That doesn't give you the right to order the likes of me about," he interrupted rudely.

"Don't argue, Jarvis, just do as she says." Serena's voice was weak, but firm.

"If you say so, miss." With evident reluctance he trailed after them, grumbling under his breath.

When they reached the front door, with Jarvis still trailing a few paces behind them, Sukey said in a low voice, "Serena, I want to keep things as calm as possible until the police get here, so will you please leave the talking to me?" The girl nodded dumbly, apparently still dazed with shock. "I'm simply going to say Xavier's been hurt and I'm calling for help, but nothing about murder. I suggest we join the others in the meeting-room," Sukey went on in her normal voice. "You too, Mr Jarvis," she added as the gardener hung back. After a moment's hesitation he dropped the half-smoked cigarette he had been holding, ground it into the gravel with the heel of his boot and followed them into the house, still muttering.

Sukey blinked as she entered the room. Someone – presumably Dan Foster, who had summarily taken charge – had evidently found the dimmer switches and turned the lights full on. He had pulled his chair to the spot where Freya and Xavier normally stood and now sat facing the group, who were sitting before him like students at a tutorial. He stood up when Sukey and her charges entered and the others turned to stare at them, their faces pale under the unfamiliar glare. A chorus of questions broke out, quickly stilled as their self-appointed leader raised a hand. Like submissive children they lapsed once more into silence, their expressions reflecting varying degrees of shock and bewilderment.

"All present and correct – no one's left their seats since you went out," he said, in the slightly smug manner of a prefect reporting to the headmaster.

"Thank you, Mr Foster, I appreciate your help."

"No problem. What's your name, by the way?"

"Sukey Reynolds."

"Well, Ms Reynolds, can you tell us what's happened? Is it true that someone's been murdered?"

"It's a bit previous to talk about murder, but it's true that Xavier has been attacked and he appears quite seriously wounded. I'm afraid I can't give you any more details at this stage," she added in response to the questions that everyone began firing at her simultaneously. The woman who had earlier collapsed in tears once again began sobbing hysterically. Jennifer, who had moved across and was kneeling on the floor beside her, put a comforting arm round her shoulders.

"Shouldn't we send for a doctor?" said Foster.

"That's exactly what I'm about to do." While she was speaking, Sukey had taken her mobile phone from her shoulder bag which was still lying on the floor beside her seat. She began punching buttons. "I have to notify the police as well and ask them to send an officer here as soon as possible," she went on. "Meanwhile, I'd appreciate it if you'd all sit tight a little longer. Yes, hang on a second," she said as her call was answered by an officer in the control centre. To ensure that she was not overheard, she left the room to make her report, adding at the end, "Please make sure that DI Castle is informed immediately."

On her return she almost bumped into Jarvis who had apparently made up his mind to be unco-operative and was about to leave. Foster marched across and took him by the arm.

"Where d'you think you're going?" he said angrily.

Jarvis rounded on him and jerked his arm away. "Don't you lay hands on me!" he snarled. "I can't waste time hanging around here, I've got work to do."

"That will have to wait. You heard what the lady said – we all stay here."

In an attempt to avert what threatened to be an ugly confrontation, Sukey patted the back of her own empty chair and said coaxingly, "Why don't you just sit here and relax for a few minutes, Mr Jarvis? It'll make things so much easier for the police to do their job if we all remain together until they arrive." His scowl indicated that he had no interest in easing the lot of the police, but after a moment's hesitation he complied.

"Is it all right if I go and see how Freya is?" asked Serena.

Sukey gave her an appraising glance, noting that her colour was returning to normal and her breathing becoming steadier, although her hands were still trembling. "Yes, of course – and perhaps you'd like to stay with her while Josie joins us here. And by the way, will you give me the number of Freya's GP? She must be pretty shaken up and she could probably do with a sedative."

Serena shook her head. "She won't take drugs – none of us does, it's against our beliefs. Leave her to me – I'll make her a calming herbal infusion if she needs one." She disappeared through the curtained alcove.

"I reckon we could all do with a calming infusion, but my choice wouldn't be one of her concoctions," muttered one of the men.

"Maybe Josie could organise some coffee," said Sukey. From the bark of sardonic laughter that greeted the suggestion, it was evident that the speaker had something stronger in mind.

"It shouldn't take more than twenty minutes or so for the emergency services to get here," said Sukey. "I'm afraid I have to ask you not to leave this room until they arrive and take charge. Till then, I'll be outside in the courtyard keeping an eye open for them."

"Suppose we refuse?" The man who had expressed the need for a drink stood up. He was short and heavily built with a hard look about him; his attitude held a trace of belligerence. Like Foster, he appeared to have shaken off to some extent the state of shock and confusion still plainly affecting the others. "You can't force us to stay if we insist on leaving. My name's Loveridge," he added as if this somehow gave him the right to challenge her. "I'm a very busy man and I have an important appointment later on. If it's going to mean overstaying our time here—"

"It's only half-past ten and we're normally here until twelve,"

Sukey reminded him. "Of course, I have no power to detain you, but the police will want to take statements from everyone sooner or later."

"What use can I be? What use can any of us be?" He glanced round the room as if inviting support for his show of defiance, but no one spoke. Foster merely shrugged. Jennifer was staring at him with her mouth open, as if aghast at his effrontery. The weeping woman had fallen silent and was sitting back in her seat with her eyes closed, as was the third man in the group, who had not uttered a word since his ecstatic claim to have come within reach of the Inner Wheel. "We've all been in here together since we arrived," Loveridge went on, "so it can't possibly be one of us who attacked Xavier."

"We've no idea at the moment what time the attack took place," Sukey pointed out. "Until that has been established, none of us can be eliminated."

He began to bluster. "Here, what are you suggesting?" he demanded. "What possible motive—?"

"I'm not suggesting anything, it's simply a matter of the way these things are handled."

"You mean, we're all suspects?" His nostrils flared in indignation, as if he had suffered a personal insult. "That's a positively outrageous—"

"Oh, sit down, man!" Foster interrupted impatiently. "Can't you see, she's doing her best to deal with a ghastly situation."

"Thank you." Sukey gave her champion a grateful glance as Loveridge, his face sullen, resumed his seat. There was a movement behind her; the curtains parted and Josie appeared. "How's Freya?"

"She's calmed down a bit, but she's obviously still very distressed. Serena's given her some herbal tea and she's going to stay with her until the police arrive." The girl put a hand to her forehead. "It's terrible, terrible. Xavier was such a good person . . . almost saint-like . . . who would want to hurt a wonderful man like him?" Her voice cracked and her eyes filled.

"Try not to upset yourself," said Sukey gently. She glanced round the room. "Let's see if we can find you a chair."

"This will do." Josie crossed the room and stooped to pick up a three-legged stool which stood beside the table with its assortment of bric-a-brac. As she straightened up, she froze and uttered a faint gasp that was almost a sob.

Sukey moved quickly to her side and saw that she was staring fixedly at the display cabinet on the wall, her eyes dilated with fear. "What is it?"

"It's gone," Josie said in a shaky whisper. "The knife . . . it's gone." The colour had drained from her face.

"What knife?"

Josie pointed to a tooled leather sheath lying on the bottom shelf. "It was in there. Do you suppose . . . ?" Her voice trailed away.

"Are you saying that sheath contained a knife . . . a dagger?"

"Yes."

"Rum sort of thing for a peaceful chap like Xavier to have lying around," observed Foster, who had crossed the room to have a closer look. He reached out as if to pick up the sheath to examine it.

"Don't touch it!" said Sukey sharply and he hastily withdrew his hand.

"Sorry, should have known better," he mumbled, looking slightly foolish. "Fingerprints and all that."

"Xavier brought it back from his travels in the East," Josie explained. Her tone was slightly defensive as if she resented the criticism implied in Foster's comment. "He calls it the Sword of Truth."

"When did you last see it?" Sukey asked.

Josie shook her head in bewilderment. Her blue eyes were awash with tears. "Last Friday afternoon Serena asked me to help the initiates choose books and things – she normally does it herself when she isn't giving a treatment."

"And the knife was in its sheath then?"

"I can't say I noticed it particularly, but I'm sure I would have done if it wasn't."

"Just a minute," Foster interposed. "Are you saying that whoever attacked Xavier used a knife . . . that knife?"

Sukey shook her head. "I'm not saying anything of the kind, but nothing can be ruled out at this stage. You'll have to wait until the police and the doctor get here and carry out their examination. They'll be in a better position than I am to answer your questions."

"I wish they'd get a move on," said Loveridge impatiently.

"Perhaps you could put the waiting time to good use," Sukey suggested. She fished her notebook from her bag, tore out half a dozen sheets and passed them round. "If you'd all write down your full name and address and a phone number where you can be contacted, it will help to speed things up when the police get here."

"Won't that information be available in the office?" asked Foster.

Josie, who had been standing as if transfixed during the discussion with the stool in her hands, put it back in its place saying, "Of course it is – I'll go and get it."

"Sorry, the office is out of bounds as well for the time being," said Sukey. "Josie, if there aren't any more comfortable chairs I'm afraid you'll have to sit on that stool for the time being . . . unless one of the gentlemen—"

"Here, have my seat," said Jarvis grudgingly.

"Thank you, Mr Jarvis." Sukey gave him a smile of appreciation, which was not returned. The gardener stood up, moved to one side and pulled a packet of cigarettes from his pocket, then put it back in response to a sharp reproof from Foster.

"I'll be outside keeping an eye on things until the police get here," Sukey repeated. "Meanwhile, no one is to touch anything on that table or on the shelves – or even go near them. Mr Foster, will you kindly see to it?"

He sprang to attention and saluted. "Ay ay, skipper!" The frivolous response evoked a tutting noise from the tearful lady and he made an apologetic gesture. "No offence meant," he said hastily.

Feeling that she had had as much as she could handle at the moment, and praying that the action she had taken to deal with the emergency would meet with official approval, Sukey left them to it. It was a relief to be outside and away from the oppressive atmosphere indoors. Although she had no reason to expect the killer to return to the scene of the murder, she made a point of taking up a position which gave her a view of both the garden and the main entrance. From the time of Xavier's non-appearance, followed seconds later by Freya's screams indicating that something was seriously amiss, her professional training had taken over. Now that she had a moment to reflect – and knowing that, more than the average witness, she would be expected to give a detailed account of everyone's movements and reactions including her own – she began a mental reconstruction of the sequence of events from that moment of anti-climax. She pictured herself taking immediate charge of the situation before going outside to investigate; saw once more the agitated group of women in the courtyard; did her best to recall the exact exchange of words before rushing down the garden in Serena's wake.

The police would want to know as far as possible the exact route they had taken so that they could eliminate it in their examination of footprints, but there was no paved path alongside the left-hand hedge and in any case Serena had led the way diagonally across the lawn. Studying the scene, Sukey did her best to visualise the track they had taken across the grass as they ran and mentally kicked herself at her failure because of her haste to get the distressed girl away from the murder scene as soon as possible.

Breathing deeply of the fresh air on this pleasant but unseasonally cool July morning, Sukey detected a hint of freshly cut grass. Jarvis had mentioned on her first visit that he always carried out any task involving machinery early in the morning, "to avoid disturbing the folks at their meditation." The mower would have picked up most of the cuttings, but . . . glancing down at her feet, she noticed scraps of green clinging to her trainers. Which meant that anyone else who had walked over the lawn that morning would probably have some on their shoes. Which meant that probably included the killer.

Then something else occurred to her. Somewhere in Vera's diary had been a slightly flippant reference to a "Sword of Truth", which suggested that the missing dagger had played some part in one of Xavier's rituals. Another thing to include in her report to the police.

She had reached this stage in her deliberations when the first police car arrived.

Seventeen

The first to arrive was a solitary uniformed constable whose face was unfamiliar. Sukey went to meet him as he got out of his patrol car; he was young, evidently nervous and, she guessed, fairly inexperienced.

"PC Douglas Irving," he announced. "I've had a report of an incident here – a suspicious death."

"That's right, a man's been stabbed. I'm pretty sure he's dead, but we have to wait for a doctor to confirm it. The body's in the garden."

He looked at her doubtfully and then glanced round at the cars parked in the yard. "I was told a SOCO was already at the scene but I don't see a van."

"That's me – I'm Sukey Reynolds from Gloucester, but I'm not on duty, I just happened to be here at the time so I took charge and called for assistance. I've managed to contain everyone indoors in the same room, except the woman who found the body – she's the victim's wife, by the way – and another woman who works here and is looking after her. She's pretty distressed, as you can imagine."

"Only natural."

"I assume you'll want to take a look at the murder scene and report back."

"I suppose I'd better." Irving appeared far from happy at the prospect. "A rapid response team is on the way along with CID and a local doctor," he added. "Should be here pretty soon." The hopeful glance that he cast in the direction of the main entrance suggested that he would welcome their immediate arrival, thus sparing him an unpleasant duty.

143

Sukey, who was already feeling the strain of the past half-hour, was in no mood to make allowances. "It's this way – and let's not hang about," she said briskly. She set off with Irving at her heels. "We'll need to mark out an access route before the mob gets here and starts tramping all over the place, so please take exactly the same path as I do. It won't be as accurate as I'd like, but . . ." Glancing back over her shoulder she noticed that the young officer had taken out a handkerchief and was dabbing beads of sweat from his forehead and upper lip. She felt a pang of sympathy and said, "Not dealt with many murders, have you?"

He shook his head, looking slightly shamefaced. "This is my first. I only joined the force a year ago and there isn't much in the way of violence round here apart from domestics and punch-ups after the pubs close. I suppose everyone feels a bit groggy the first time."

"Not just the first time." She made an effort to sound encouraging. "I don't think any of us ever quite gets used to it – except the forensic pathologist, of course. I think he quite enjoys it. This one isn't as messy as some I've encountered."

While she was speaking they had reached the entrance to Xavier's private retreat. Sukey pointed to the notice strung across the gap in the hedge. "He's in there – and whatever you do, avoid coming into contact with that board. Ready?"

Irving licked his lips and nodded. "Might as well get it over with," he said shakily.

"Good lad." She gave him an encouraging pat on the shoulder. "I find deep breathing helps. There's no need to approach him too closely. Just walk to the end of this hedge and take a good look, but please don't go tramping around. The less disturbance before the SOCOs arrive and begin their examination of the scene, the better."

"Won't you be dealing with it?"

Sukey grinned. "Not me – I'm a witness. In fact, you could say a possible suspect."

Irving managed a weak smile in return before moving forward and disappearing from view behind the enclosing hedge. When he returned a couple of minutes later he had turned a sickly green and was holding the handkerchief to his mouth. "Come on now, some good deep breaths and you'll be fine," Sukey encouraged him. "Well done, you managed without actually puking," she went on as he complied with a series of shuddering gasps.

"Not a pretty sight, is he?" Irving said shakily. "What was he doing there – some kind of yoga? Is he a monk or something? What sort of place is this anyway?"

"I suppose you could call it a kind of healing centre, but there's no time to go into that now. It's run by a trio of oddballs – at least, there were three of them until . . ." She gave a meaningful glance over her shoulder. "Come on, let's get busy on that access route." They worked fast to mark out a corridor across the lawn and seal the entrance to the murder scene with lengths of blue-and-white tape. When they had finished, Sukey felt able to relax for the first time since the drama began. She closed her eyes for a moment, listening to the hum of bees and the twittering of birds as Nature went about her business, indifferent to human tragedy.

Moments later the peace was shattered by the sound of wailing sirens and the courtyard became a confusion of cars and flashing blue lights as the first of the rapid response teams arrived and figures in blue uniforms tumbled out. Irving hurried across to report to the sergeant in charge, leaving Sukey standing alone beside the entrance to the garden. She became aware of a strange sensation, as if the earth was tilting beneath her feet, and she grabbed at the gate for support. Someone took her by the arm and half led, half carried her into the office, lowered her on to a seat and gently pressed her head towards her knees. A familiar voice said, "It's OK, you'll be fine in a moment." She looked up; through a blur of totally unexpected tears, she saw the concerned face of DS Andy Radcliffe.

"I can't believe it . . . I can't believe it." Edith Burrell had cast off her robe and was lying prone on a couch in the family's private sitting-room, mopping her swollen eyes with a handful of pulpy paper tissues while Serena massaged her back and shoulders.

"Who would want to kill Percy?" she moaned. "He's never harmed anyone . . . he spent his whole life helping other people . . . he didn't have an enemy in the world."

"That's what we've always thought, but there must be some-one. Maybe someone who's never managed to shake off their internal shackles has been nursing a grudge against him. We've had the occasional drop-out, as you know."

"But not for a long time – and as far as we know none of them blamed Percy. Can you think of anyone?"

"Not offhand."

"Do you suppose it was one of this week's new initiates?"

"Mum, I simply don't know."

"I remember once or twice catching that Susan Reynolds casting furtive looks at the others when she should have been giving Percy – Xavier, I mean – all her attention."

"You never said."

"I kept an eye on her because you warned me about her. It was only the first day – I haven't noticed anything since. You said she works for the police . . . maybe they suspected something was going to happen." Edith's voice rose in a hysterical wail. "Why didn't they warn us?"

"Hush! Lie still now – we'll talk about it later."

Little by little, under her daughter's skilled hands, Edith grew quieter. "We know so little about the initiates," she said after a while. "That's Percy's doing, of course – he always insisted on not asking them a lot of questions." She blew her nose, discarded the sodden mass of paper and reached for a fresh supply from a box on a low table beside the couch. "He said they were here to discover in secret their true nature and the hidden strengths that lie within them, not shout their weaknesses to the house-tops like drunks at a meeting of Alcoholics Anonymous."

"Well, they'll have to be a bit more forthcoming when the police get here and start asking them questions."

This further reference to the police induced a fresh gush of tears as the consequences of her husband's murder began to dawn on Edith. "Oh God, they'll want to question us as well."

Her voice rose to an even higher pitch. "They'll say I did it, they always think it's the wife."

"Now you're talking nonsense."

"But that's what they always say – I've read it in the papers. They might even say we planned it together. Serena, what can we do?" Edith flung off the ministering hands, sat up on the edge of the couch and grabbed her daughter's wrists. "They'll put us in prison! We're ruined!"

"Hush! Come and sit over here while I give you some OCH." After an initial resistance, Edith allowed herself to be settled in a low-backed chair where Serena began massaging fragrant oil over her forehead, neck and temples. "Just be still, be still." She adopted the vibrant, hypnotic tones that she used when giving treatments to the initiates. "We'll manage, you'll see."

Once more, the gentle but purposeful movements had the desired effect. "Oh, that's wonderful, dear," Edith said dreamily. "You have a natural gift. Percy was always so proud of you." Speaking the name sent the tears flowing afresh and she reached for more tissues. "What in the world are we going to do without him? We can't possibly carry on—"

"Yes we can – we must. He'd want us to. His spirit will live on and be our guide."

Edith paused in the act of wiping her eyes, sat up and looked at her daughter in astonishment. "What are you talking about?" she exclaimed. "You don't really believe in all that?"

Serena gave a sly smile. "I'm a disciple, remember – one of his earliest converts. Think about it, Mum. We can do it between us – I know your spiel backwards, you know his and everything else is set out in detail in his books."

Edith shook her head in bewilderment. "Are you suggesting I can step into his shoes – become the leader?"

"Of course you can, if I back you up. In time, we'll recruit someone else to join the team. That man who grasped the Inner Wheel this morning for example; from the way he reacted he could be very promising material, but if not there'll be others." Serena broke off to pour a fresh supply of oil into her palm.

"After all," she went on as she resumed her task, "we've managed to fool Percy all this time, so all we have to do is persuade the punters that we've inherited his powers. We have to or the business will fold and we'll lose everything."

"You're right." Edith felt some of the tension beginning to ease under the combined influence of her daughter's ministrations and harsh, inescapable reality. "This morning's a write-off, but perhaps there'll be a chance to have a word with the group before they leave and give them some words of encouragement, tell them Xavier's power is reaching out to them through the cosmos and the sacred wells of energy are still there within them, waiting to be tapped."

"That's the idea."

"And the Inner and Outer Wheels and the Unlimited?" Edith's enthusiasm waxed more strongly as the idea took hold of her mind. "I know it all by heart and I have Percy's writings to refer to if I need fresh inspiration. I'd better start reading them again." As if anxious to get down to work without delay, she stood up and reached for her clothes. "You're absolutely right, dear – we aren't going to let Percy's death destroy our business, are we?"

"Not on your life."

There was a timid knock on the door. "Who is it?" Edith called.

"It's Josie. The police are here and they want to know if Mrs Burrell is feeling up to answering a few questions."

"Tell them I'll be ready in ten minutes." Edith slipped back into the midnight blue dress and studied herself critically in the mirror. "God, what a fright I look! I'll have to put on a bit of make-up before I face them."

"I wouldn't – you're a grieving widow, don't forget. Just bathe your eyes in some cold water and tidy your hair and you'll be perfect."

"I suppose you're right. Should I put on a different dress? Maybe this one's a bit too gaudy with all these shiny bits?"

Serena considered for a moment. "I wouldn't have said so. It's got a bit rumpled and damp with your tears, which all adds to the effect. I think I'd better put on something a bit more subdued, though," she added, glancing down at her own flamboyant outfit. "Something dark and sombre would be more the thing. I'll slip upstairs and change."

"Well done Sukey, you did a great job in a very difficult situation and I'll make sure it gets known in the right quarters," said Radcliffe.

"Thanks, Sarge. It looked like getting tricky once or twice. Jarvis, the gardener, and one of the punters, who calls himself Loveridge, started to get stroppy, but a chap named Dan Foster was very supportive and helped to maintain order."

Radcliffe made a note of the names. "You say one of them 'calls himself' Loveridge? Why d'you say that?"

"Because I've a feeling it might not be his real name."

"Any particular reason?"

"Just a thought. We know that Jennifer Newlyn is really Jennifer Drew – she told me quite openly that she didn't want it to be known that she had any connection with someone who'd killed himself after attending courses here."

"Because her motive in enrolling was to uncover what she'd convinced herself was some sort of scam? Yes, I take your point. You're suggesting that at least one other member of the group had an ulterior motive as well."

"I think it's a strong possibility. It doesn't have to be an intention to murder, of course, but—"

"You're absolutely right, that's something to bear in mind. Look, Sukey, as soon as you feel up to it, I'd like you to give me a detailed account of everything that happened this morning from the moment you arrived, and any observations about the others' behaviour that might occur to you."

"I feel up to it now, if you're ready."

"Good girl. No need to write anything down – we'll tape it. If you'd just be giving it some thought while I go and organise things in the house." Radcliffe, who had been seated at Josie's desk in the office after helping Sukey to a chair, stood up and went to the door. "By the way, the SOCOs are here – they might want a word with you – and the doctor's been and declared the victim dead—"

Sukey put a hand to her forehead. "The SOCOs! That reminds me, I'm supposed to be on duty at two."

"We should be through in time, but . . ." Radcliffe gave her a keen glance, noticing her pallor and the signs of strain round her eyes. "Would you like me to call George Barnes and say you're not up to it?"

Sukey shook her head. "He's short-handed already, what with one being on holiday and Mandy still at her mother's bedside. It might be an idea to let him know I might be late signing on, but I'll be OK, honest, Sarge."

"If you say so. I'll be back as soon as I can."

He returned ten minutes later carrying two steaming mugs on a tray. "I asked a girl called Josie if there was any chance of some coffee and she produced this. It looks a bit weak, but at least it's hot."

"Thanks." Sukey took her cup and sipped from it gratefully, then pulled a face. "It doesn't taste much like coffee," she complained. "It's probably dandelion root or some other concoction."

"Is that the sort of thing they're into here?"

"If the cups of herbal tea they offer us when we arrive are anything to go by, it wouldn't surprise me to learn that they're total food freaks, although we're never offered anything to eat. We're not expected to give any thought to our physical needs while we're here."

"All to do with the spirit, eh?"

"That's the general idea."

"Right." Radcliffe put a tape recorder on the desk, found a spare socket in the wall and plugged it in. "Are you ready?"

"Sure."

For the next fifteen minutes Sukey related the events of the morning in chronological order and in as much detail as she could remember. Radcliffe listened without interruption until she came to the moment when Jarvis appeared with his offer of first aid.

"So you didn't let on at that point that the victim was dead?" he asked.

"Not to him. I simply said Xavier was best left until the paramedics or a doctor got here. Serena knew, of course, because we were together when we found the body, but I warned her not to say anything to the others until the police arrived. She was obviously in a state of shock, but on the whole she kept her head very well."

"And you say Jarvis was difficult both then and later on?"

"He didn't like me telling him what to do – which was understandable, I suppose. He became particularly stroppy later, when I insisted that everyone had to stay in the meeting-room until the police got here. One thing strikes me as odd, now I come to think of it, is that when he came rushing out to ask us what was going on, he gave the impression that he'd been attracted by the sound of screaming and come to investigate."

"That would be the wife, I suppose, throwing a wobbly after she discovered Xavier's body? What's odd about that?"

"Only that several minutes must have elapsed after Freya came rushing back to the house in hysterics and everyone else, including Freya, was inside and well out of earshot."

"Hmm." Radcliffe made a note. "We'll see how he accounts for his delayed reaction. Any other thoughts about him?"

"He was very resentful at being confined with the others. He claimed he had a lot of work to do, yet I didn't get the impression during my earlier encounters with him that he was exactly a ball of fire – for example, he was quite happy to stop for a fairly prolonged chat about clematis. It occurs to me that he might have something to hide – although I doubt if he had anything to do with the murder."

"No?"

"It doesn't seem likely. For one thing, assuming the dagger used to kill Xavier is the one normally kept in the place Josie pointed out to me, it's unlikely that Jarvis even knew it was there.

151

Come to think of it, I'm wondering how many of the others did – I certainly didn't. The lighting level was so low for the first three days that you'd have needed to be having a good snoop round to notice it – or any of the other stuff on that table or the shelves."

"Would there have been opportunities for any of the group to do that?"

"I'm sure there would – either when they first arrive, or possibly as they were leaving. Not that I ever spotted anyone doing it."

"What normally happens when you arrive?"

"As soon as we're all settled, Serena appears with her tray of drinks."

"Does everyone arrive at the same time, or—"

"I can't answer that, I'm afraid. I was always the last."

"And there's no pre-session conversation?"

"Absolutely none. It's actively discouraged, but as I explained earlier, today was going to be different."

"Right, I think I've got the picture so far. Let's turn to the rest of the witnesses. Tell me something about their reactions."

"I've been thinking about that. Remember that of the six people in the group, four were completely unknown to me until news of the murder broke and it was only then that two of the men identified themselves. Up to that point –" Sukey closed her eyes and tried to relive the scene in her imagination – "we'd all been doing exactly as we were told. Not a single question was asked, or any kind of objection raised . . . we were all like . . . like clay in the hands of a potter. There were quite long periods when I felt completely won over. Then I'd pull myself together and remind myself why I was there. I couldn't help being affected, though." For a moment, the horror of what had happened seemed to fade from Sukey's mind; a strange feeling of calm stole over her and her eyelids drooped.

Radcliffe gave her shoulder a gentle shake. "Here, don't go falling asleep!"

"Sorry." Sukey blinked and raised her head. "I must be still under the 'fluence!"

"More likely you're completely knackered," he said sympathetically. "Just a few more points. These two men who identified themselves. You say Foster was helpful, but Loveridge less so."

"That's right. From the way they reacted to the situation, it occurs to me that they might not have been genuinely convinced by all the rituals and exercises and so on that we were put through. In other words," Sukey went on reflectively, "of the six members of that group, I'd say that only two were genuinely won over by it all."

"And they are . . . ?

"The other woman and the third man."

Eighteen

"Ah, Jim. Come in and have a seat." Detective Chief Inspector Philip Lord took a bite from a digestive biscuit held in one hand, washed it down with a noisy gulp from a mug of coffee, swung his neatly shod size seven feet back to the floor and laid on the desk in front of him the open file which had been reposing in the angle between his plump thighs and ample stomach. "I've been going through Radcliffe's preliminary report and witness statements on the RYCE Foundation stabbing," he went on as DI Castle pulled up a chair and sat down. "Never bargained for this when we let your favourite SOCO loose among the crackpots, did we?" he added with a sardonic chuckle.

"No, sir, we didn't, and to be honest I wish we hadn't."

"Nonsense man, it was the best thing that could have happened. I'm really impressed with the way she kept her head and did a first-class, professional job. You must admit that if she hadn't been there and taken charge from the moment the killing was discovered, all hell would have been let loose and our task would have been a hundred times more difficult. You should be feeling very proud of her."

"I am sir, of course," Castle said warmly. "It's only that—"

"And without her observations, evidence would be even thinner on the ground than it is already," Lord continued.

"That's quite true, sir. Just the same, I'm not happy about it."

"Give me one good reason."

Castle frowned and ran his fingers through his thick brown hair. "It's hard to be precise. I just have a feeling the notions

154

she's been picking up at that place have had an effect on her."

"What sort of effect? Are you saying her assessment of the situation may have been distorted in some way?"

"No sir, nothing like that. I had a quick word with Radcliffe before I came to see you and he said that although she was a bit shaky when he first got there, once she'd pulled herself together he was amazed at how cool and collected she seemed and how accurately she recalled everything."

"So what's the problem?"

"It's just that she seems to have fallen under the spell of the place. As you know, she went there under a certain amount of pressure."

"I thought you said she was keen to go." Lord gave Castle a searching glance; a hint of a smile lurked beneath the Chaplinesque moustache.

"Her curiosity was aroused. I made it clear to her that I wasn't keen on the idea, but—"

"But Sukey, being an independent-minded young woman, resented being told what to do," Lord interrupted shrewdly.

"I suppose that might have had something to do with it," Castle admitted. "The thing is, she went." He was on the point of adding, "with your blessing," but wisely refrained. "At first, she seemed to be taking it all with a good pinch of salt," he continued, "but by the end of the third day she was stressing how peaceful and relaxing it was and how at the same time it was giving her a fresh outlook, helping her come to terms with certain past events in her life that still trouble her from time to time – that sort of thing."

"So what's wrong with that?"

"It's the weird things they preach there that bother me – all that stuff about getting to know one's inner being and breaking free from internal shackles and jumping on imaginary wheels. And the chanting and meditating and so on. When she tells it she makes it all sound as if it's a bit of a laugh, but . . ." Jim cleared his throat in embarrassment before going on. "And then yesterday evening she said . . . she suggested I might benefit from attending one of their courses."

Lord threw back his head and emitted a hearty gust of laughter that ended in a bout of coughing as a piece of biscuit went the wrong way. He pulled out a handkerchief, wiped his mouth and brushed the residual crumbs from his moustache. "You shouldn't take yourself so seriously, man," he admonished Castle. "Can't you see she was having you on?"

"I don't think she was, I think she meant it. She said something about it helping me to be less uptight."

Lord shrugged. " 'Uptight' isn't a word I'd have associated with you, Jim – not so far as your work is concerned. I can't answer for your private life, of course. Perhaps you should think about taking her advice," he added with an impish grin. "Have you spoken to her since the murder, by the way?"

"No, sir, I haven't had a chance. I understand Radcliffe took her statement, but I've only managed a brief word with him because I've been out of town most of the day. She'd already reported for duty and left the office – she's on late turn this week and next."

Lord frowned. "She should have gone straight home to get some rest. Couldn't Barnes have brought in a relief?"

"I asked him about that, but he said she insisted on carrying on as normal because he's short-staffed at present."

Lord gave a nod of approval. "She's a real tough little cookie, isn't she? Well, back to this case. The first thing that strikes me from this report – I'll let you have it when I've run through one or two points with you – is that from the time the witnesses arrived at the house there doesn't seem to be any means of verifying their statements. It's as if everyone was making a point of not noticing what was going on around them."

"That ties in with what Sukey remarked on from the beginning. It's part of the underlying RYCE philosophy – you don't go there to exchange ideas or talk about your problems, you go to 'discover your inner self and release your cosmic energy', as they claim in their brochure. Apart from Day One, when the so-called initiates receive their welcome packs and are given an outline of the programme, told where to find the toilets and so on, they simply go along with everything the two people who run the establishment – Freya and Xavier, aka Percy and Edith Burrell – tell them to do. When they aren't listening with rapt attention to words of wisdom they're chanting mantras, doing yoga or sitting in little secret hideaways in the garden contemplating their navels. Any interpersonal communication either before, during or after the sessions is actively discouraged."

Lord frowned. "Hmm – that's not going to make our task any easier," he commented. "Now, have a look at this." He took a sheet of paper from the file and pushed it across the desk. "Radcliffe's sketched out this plan of the garden. As you can see, it's almost completely encircled by hedges. Anyone using this route –" with a stubby, manicured forefinger Lord traced a path which began at the point where Sukey had encountered Jarvis on her first visit and ran behind the network of garden rooms and the far end of the lawn – "could get this far without being seen. There's a gate in the lower left-hand corner which gives access to a kitchen garden and a small orchard – it seems they're into growing their own organic fruit and veg. From there, a quick dash would bring the killer to Burrell's private hideaway, which is here. Whoever designed the garden unwittingly created ideal conditions for anyone out to get him to strike unobserved."

Castle studied the plan for a minute or two. "I see all the mini-enclosures on the right-hand side of the garden are inter-connected, but not the two on the left, with Burrell's the one nearest the house. Who uses the other, by the way?"

"The wife shares it with a third member of the establishment – a woman called Serena Elford. According to their statements, they arrange their meditation periods to fit in with their other duties."

"So our killer would have to show himself for the few seconds it would take to get from the gate to Burrell's cubby-hole," Castle observed. "Unless he was prepared to take a chance on being spotted, he knew enough about the set-up to be pretty sure no one was likely to be looking out at the time. He'd also have to be reasonably sure of finding his victim there. Who else besides his wife and Serena Elford knew about his morning routine?"

"Pretty well everyone. According to Sukey, they were told at the end of the first day that from then on they were free to arrive early and do a spot of pre-session meditation in the garden rooms – they were each assigned to a particular one, by the way – but were specifically asked not to wander around or go near Burrell's private sanctum."

"Has the time of death been established, by the way?"

"Not precisely. All the pathologist would say is that it was probably somewhere between seven and nine o'clock. According to the widow, the three of them – that is, Mr and Mrs B and Serena – had breakfast together about half-past seven as usual. Burrell went out to start his meditating at about eight o'clock, which was his normal time, so that narrows it down quite a lot. Mrs B says she spent the next half-hour or so preparing the meeting-room while Serena went over to the office to check on some admin. The windows in the meeting-room are blacked out and there's no view of the garden from the office, so there was no chance of either of them spotting the killer. Josie, the girl who runs the office, got there soon after nine o'clock. She's not a hundred per cent sure, but she thinks everyone had arrived by then. The sessions normally begin at half past."

"What about the gardener?"

"He claims he was in his potting shed from the time he arrived at about half-past eight until he heard all the kerfuffle when the body was discovered. There's no confirmation of that, of course, and I see Radcliffe's made a note that Sukey thinks he might be hiding something on account of the fuss he kicked up when she insisted he stay with the others until our troops arrived. She's also suggested we try and get more background information on the other four members of the group. Any idea why that should be?"

"None whatever, sir. As I said, I haven't seen or spoken to her since the killing, and so far she's never referred individually to any of the other people in the group. I doubt if she even knew their names, except Jennifer Drew. As you know, it was partly through her that Sukey was there in the first place."

"Ah yes, Jennifer Drew," repeated Lord. He fondled his moustache reflectively. "She registered as Jennifer Newlyn, her maiden name. She was quite open about it – said it was because she didn't want them to know she was the widow of Oliver Drew. Now that's interesting." A sudden gleam appeared in Lord's sloe-black eyes. "According to her statement, she went there with her mind full of suspicion, convinced that her late husband was the victim of some form of blackmail that drove him to suicide, but that in a very short time she felt nothing but good, benign influences which persuaded her that even if that was the case, it had nothing to do with RYCE. Radcliffe says here that when DC Lisa Crombie interviewed her she was in, quote, 'a highly charged emotional state, probably readily susceptible to new ideas'."

"Now you come to mention it, sir, Sukey said something that might bear that out. At the end of the first day she had a brief word with Jennifer and said she was still going on about revenge, but after that she appeared to become more relaxed and peaceful and avoided any further contact."

"Hmm, interesting," Lord repeated. "I take it no evidence has ever been found to connect Drew's suicide with the fact that he used to attend sessions at RYCE?"

"None at all, sir. I suspect that poor girl is going to need some professional counselling after this."

"That could well apply to the other four. They must all have personal hang-ups of some kind or they'd never have been there in the first place. And it's more than likely," Lord went on as he closed the file and pushed it across the desk in Castle's direction, "that the solution to this case may depend on our being able to get them to talk about those hang-ups. I'd like you to read through that, Jim, and also have a good chat with Sukey at the earliest possible moment. Get her impressions on the reactions of everyone involved. They may in the end prove just as important as her observations." Lord suppressed a yawn, glanced at his watch, stood up and reached for his jacket. "I'm going home. You know," he said morosely, "I have a feeling it's going to take us a long time to get to the bottom of this case."

"Mum, I thought you'd never get home! What's the latest on the RYCE murder? The radio report gave hardly any details and Adrian's been on the phone every five minutes wanting to talk to you. I promised I'd ask you to—" Fergus broke off as the phone starting ringing. "That'll be him again. Will you take it while I make some tea?"

"I suppose I'd better." With a weary sigh, Sukey put down her bag and reached for the receiver. "He needn't think I'm going to add anything to the official statement, though."

She barely had time to say, "Hello," when Adrian's agitated voice exclaimed, "Sukey, at last! What the hell's this about a murder at RYCE? Were you there? Who was it? I got on to the police as soon as I heard the announcement on the local news this evening, but all they would say was that they were called to the house this morning and found the body of a man. A murder enquiry has begun and they'll be issuing a further statement later."

"Then I'm afraid you'll have to wait until they do, Adrian."

"Oh come on, Sukey, you were there, you must have picked up some information when you were doing your SOCO stuff—"

"I wasn't on duty at the time, and in any case—"

"But you must know who the victim is, and have some idea—"

"Yes, I know that, but if the police won't release his name I'm not prepared to either."

"But I do have a personal interest—"

"As far as that's concerned, all I can say is that I can see no reason to think there's any connection whatsoever between this murder and the death of your aunt."

"But you can't be sure of that?"

"It's impossible to be sure of anything at this stage, but it seems highly unlikely."

"Didn't you find a single clue in Vera's diary to give you a lead?"

"Adrian, I've read every entry since the one where she wrote about her first visit to RYCE. As it happens, her impressions are very much the same as mine – that is, we were both very sceptical at first but we soon came to recognise the value and the beneficial effect of the RYCE teaching, despite their somewhat eccentric methods. I'm not saying I'm as euphoric as Vera," Sukey added in response to an exasperated groan at the other end of the wire. "I'm merely saying that I've detected nothing but benign influences—"

Adrian gave a harsh, mirthless laugh. "You can't tell me it was benign influences that caused Vera to keel over the way she did."

"No, of course not. She had a heart condition that no one suspected – you have to accept that. Look, Adrian, I'm sorry if you feel I've let you down in any way. If it'll make you feel any better, I haven't banked your cheque—"

"Oh, for heaven's sake, it's not the money. But please, Sukey, don't write Vera out of the frame altogether. I still think there's a link – Cath and Anita think I'm crazy, but I can't help it. Just say you'll keep an open mind."

"All right, I promise you I'll do that and I'll let you know immediately if I come across anything."

"Thank you."

Sukey put down the phone and turned back to Fergus, who was pouring out the tea. "Gosh, he's like a dog with a bone, isn't he?" the lad remarked as his mother sank wearily into a chair and gratefully accepted the full mug he handed her.

"He's obsessed. He's still on about finding clues in Vera's diary. That reminds me, I should return it."

"You obviously didn't find anything useful."

"Apart from the fact that she made a passing reference to a bout of indigestion, which might or might not have been a symptom of the heart condition that killed her, nothing at all."

"I heard you telling Adrian you weren't going to tell him anything that hasn't been officially released, but . . ." Fergus

161

fixed his mother with a look that plainly said, *You're going to tell me, aren't you?* Sukey folded her lips and shook her head, but he put a hand on her arm. "Come on, Mum, you know you can trust me. You've told me everything that goes on at RYCE so far and asked me to keep it to myself – I haven't even told Anita. Just think" – his voice took on a familiar, wheedling tone that Sukey had always found difficult to resist – "I might even remember something you've mentioned that could help you solve the case."

"I'm nothing to do with the case now, except as a witness."

"But you were there when it happened, weren't you? Was it you who found the body?"

"No, his wife found it—"

Fergus pounced. "Freya?" Sukey, realising she had slipped up, gave a resigned nod. "So it was Xavier?"

"Please, Gus, don't let on I told you."

"Hand on heart!" said Fergus solemnly. "How did it happen?"

"He was stabbed in the back while meditating."

"Gosh!" Her son's eyes saucered. "Why on earth would anyone want to top him, though? I thought you said he was a good guy."

"That's the impression he gave, but it's obvious there's someone out there with a grudge – maybe a former initiate for whom things went wrong and who held Xavier to blame. No therapy can work for everyone; even Serena admitted that they have their occasional failure, like poor Oliver Drew."

"What are they going to do now, I wonder? About their courses, I mean. Tomorrow's the last day for you – what's going to happen?"

"I've had a message from Sergeant Radcliffe that we're to attend as usual – if we want to, that is; some people may be too shocked to go near the place again. Presumably there'll be some kind of announcement – that's all I know at the moment. It's hard to see how they can carry on without Xavier – he's been the linchpin of the place."

The telephone rang again; this time it was Jim Castle. "Sook, I guess you must be exhausted so I won't bother you this evening, but DCI Lord asked me to have a word with you about the RYCE killing. Can we meet tomorrow – say for a bite of lunch?"

"That'd be lovely."

"You're OK, aren't you?"

"Yes, I'm fine."

"Lord was full of praise for the way you handled things, by the way." There was a brief pause before Jim added softly, "I'm so proud of you, Sook."

"Thank you." She felt a warm glow of pleasure at his words. "See you tomorrow then."

"About one?"

"Fine."

"Love you."

Sukey looked round for Fergus, but he had slipped quietly out of the room. "Love you too," she whispered. "Goodnight."

When Fergus reappeared a moment after she replaced the receiver, she said casually, "By the way, when are Dad and Margaret getting married?"

"In October – why?"

"I thought I'd get them a present, just to show there's no ill-feeling. Any idea what they'd like?"

A slow smile of sheer delight spread over the lad's features. "I could find out. Gosh, Mum, RYCE has done something for you, hasn't it?"

"Yes, I think it has." Sukey yawned, finished her tea and rinsed out her mug. "I'm tired, I'm turning in. Will you lock up, Gus?"

"Sure. Goodnight, Mum."

For some reason that she could never explain, the word "therapy" that she had used during her conversation with Fergus came back into Sukey's head as she got into bed and settled down under the covers. It reminded her of the final entry in Vera's diary; something about a session in the "Rejuvenation Suite" that she was eagerly looking forward to. The recollection prompted a vague question, but Sukey's tired brain could pursue it no further. Moments later she was fast asleep.

Nineteen

S hortly before nine o'clock on the evening of the murder of
Percy Burrell, his widow Edith appeared in the kitchen. Her
daughter Serena was staring out of the window across the fields
where sheep and cattle had grazed during the years when Burwell
was a working farm. The sun was on the point of setting, turning
a bank of cloud on the western horizon into a blazing inferno
that lent a ruddy glow to the girl's naturally warm colouring.

When her mother entered, she swung round and exclaimed,
"Where in the world have you been? I've been looking every-
where for you – everywhere the police haven't sealed off, that is.
We still can't go out in the garden because they haven't finished
their so-called fingertip search; Josie couldn't use the office until
that detective sergeant had finished carrying out interviews and
the Rejuvenation Suite's out of bounds until they've done poking
about in the therapy rooms. Don't worry," she added, "they
won't find anything. I stashed it all away as usual after Henry's
OCH yesterday. We're on to a winner there, by the way. He's
booked a double session for next week."

"That's good," said Edith absently.

"And the police say we should be able to have the garden back
by about midday tomorrow. I'm a bit worried about next week
though – there could be cancellations when the news gets out."

"They will return." Edith joined her daughter at the window,
her gaze fixed on infinity. The sky was changing by the minute,
fading from flaming orange and vermilion to the pale flush of a
ripe apricot as the sun finally sank from view. "They will return,"
she repeated softly, "or others will take their place."

"Sure they will." Serena took her mother's hand and squeezed it gently. "It's going to be tough for the next few weeks, but we'll win through. You did brilliantly this afternoon, Mum. I was worried at first that the shock would have been too much for you and the session would simply fold, but the way you handled it was inspired."

"I was inspired." Edith's voice had a faraway quality, as if her mind was in another dimension. "His spirit was working through me." She closed her eyes, raised her arms above her head and began to speak in the exultant tones of an evangelist addressing a prayer meeting. "I will keep faith, Xavier. I, Freya, will be your mouthpiece and carry on with your mission. In the name of the Unlimited, I pledge you my word." She reopened her eyes and let her arms fall to her sides, but continued to gaze out of the window with an expression of near ecstasy.

Serena eyed her uneasily. "Snap out of it, Mum – you're not talking to the punters now," she said. Edith gave no sign of having heard her. "You haven't told me yet where you've been hiding yourself all this time," she went on. There was still no response. She waved a hand in front of her mother's face. "Planet earth calling Edith Burrell, are you receiving?"

Edith started as if awakened from sleep and turned wide, questioning eyes on her daughter. "What was that, dear?" she asked languidly.

"Where did you go when the afternoon punters had gone home?"

"The initiates," Edith corrected mechanically.

"All right, the initiates. Where were you?"

"In Xavier's room, of course."

"The attic room where he used to meditate when the weather was too bad to use the garden?"

"Where else? "

"That's one place I never thought of looking. What on earth were you doing there?"

"Tuning in to the cosmic vibrations. Serena, they were every-where, so clear, so powerful. Through them I could feel his spirit calling to me. The wellspring of his inspiration was flowing into me, releasing my cosmic energy, giving me the strength to carry on with his work.''

''Mum!'' There was a sharp note of anxiety in Serena's voice. ''What are you on about? You know you don't take all that stuff seriously.''

Edith looked at her aghast. ''How can you say such a terrible thing? After all these years of serving Xavier, are you saying that you're rejecting the eternal truths that he revealed to us? Have you lost touch with the Unlimited?''

''Mum, for goodness' sake . . .''

Edith took both the girl's hands in her own and gazed earnestly into her eyes. ''It's the shock, of course, the terrible loss we've endured that has shaken your faith. Don't despair, my dearest child, just remember those four vital words that he taught us: Release Your Cosmic Energy. Repeat the mantra over and over again whenever doubt assails you. The power is still there within you. We'll meditate together before we go to bed. I promised Xavier.'' The large eyes were swimming in tears that slowly overflowed and slid down the pallid cheeks. In that moment, mystic inspiration dissolved in the reality of physical loss and Edith became the grieving widow weeping in her daughter's arms. ''I'm going to miss him so badly,'' she sobbed.

''Oh Mum! Are you saying you were still in love with him? I've always thought . . . you've been saying for years . . .''

With an effort, Edith controlled her sobs. ''I know,'' she said brokenly. ''I thought so too, but now he's gone . . . all this time we've been deceiving him, letting him think we were true believers while playing our own game. But now I know . . . it's taken his death to make me realise the truth.'' At this point, the light of fanaticism rekindled in Edith's eyes as she continued, ''He's been taken from my sight, but he will continue to be my spiritual guide and yours too, while together we continue his great mission.''

Serena opened her mouth as if about to challenge the assumption, but quickly recognised that this was not the time for rational discussion. ''Yes, he's out of sight,'' she said gently, "but of course he's still out there in the Unlimited. You – we, that is – will remain forever united with him there."

Edith gave a deep sigh of relief. "I knew I'd make you understand," she whispered.

"Of course I understand." Serena took her mother by the arm and led her to a chair. "You need rest and something to eat. Sit there and relax while I prepare our supper."

"Was it you?" The woman's voice was shrill, panic-stricken. "Was it you who killed him?"

The man glared at her. "Are you out of your mind? What possible reason would I have to kill him? I'd nothing to gain from his death. In any case, I didn't even know the knife was there."

"That's easy to say – how do I know you're telling the truth?" She clutched at his arm. "You haven't got an alibi . . ."

He shook himself free. "That doesn't make me a murderer. The way that lot of crackpots run the place probably means none of the others have alibis either. It also means that any of us could have done it with only a chance in a million of being spotted. You, for instance."

"That's a dreadful thing to say."

"It's no more dreadful than for you to suspect me. You were there before me; if you'd been snooping around at any time during the first three days you could have seen that knife, you knew where he'd be at that time, that he'd be alone and off his guard doing his meditation thing—"

"All the others knew that as well." He shrugged, but made no reply. "I didn't do it, I swear it!" Her voice rose to a thin shriek. "How can you possibly believe I'm capable of sticking a knife in someone?" She swallowed, struggling for self-control. "Please," she implored brokenly, "please say you don't believe it!"

"Why should I believe you?" he said. His face was stony, his voice cold. "I feel I hardly know you at all. You could be capable of anything."

She gazed at him in horror. "You won't . . . you didn't say that to the police, did you?" she faltered.

"What do you take me for? The last thing I want is for them to get wind of our relationship."

She put a hand to her mouth, her eyes wide with alarm. "Oh dear God, why did we start this?"

"You mean, why did *you* start it. I had my reservations all along, but you were so insistent . . . and now we could be in all sorts of trouble."

"So now it's all my fault," she said resentfully. He shrugged, but did not answer. "Who was to know such a terrible thing would happen?" she went on. "Haven't you any idea who might have done it?"

"I reckon any one of the people who were there at the time is capable of murder, given the provocation. If you ask me, they're all barking mad – they wouldn't be there otherwise."

"We were there and we're not—"

"All right, we had our reasons, didn't we?" Just for a second, the grim expression softened a fraction.

"What did the police ask you?" she said after a moment.

"Just the usual questions – what time did I arrive, who was there already, did I see any strangers or anyone acting suspiciously. They made it pretty clear that it was only a preliminary statement, of course – they'll want to question us all more closely later – 'when we've recovered from the trauma' as that detective sergeant so delicately put it," he added with a trace of a sneer. "Then I had to fetch a change of clothes and hand over what I'd been wearing, 'for forensic tests' they said. I thought that was a bit of liberty, but it would have looked bad to object. How about you?"

She gave a weary shrug. "The same."

"Well, let's hope they don't probe too deeply into my background. That would be a total disaster. I think it would be better if we didn't see one another again for the time being – after tomorrow, that is."

"You think we should go tomorrow?"

"Don't you want to?"

She shuddered. "I feel as if I never want to go near that place again."

168

"I think we should, after the statement Serena issued on Freya's behalf. It might look fishy if we stay away."

She gave a resigned nod. "I suppose you're right."

"But after that, we mustn't risk being seen together."

"If you say so." She grasped his arm, her mouth working, her eyes half blinded by tears. "You will keep in touch, won't you?"

He jerked his arm away. "Only insofar as is absolutely necessary."

When Sukey arrived at the pub in Brockworth where they had arranged to meet, she found Jim already seated at a table for two in one corner, a half-pint glass of beer in one hand. As it was Friday, the place was fairly busy and the level of chatter was high enough to ensure that no one was likely to overhear their conversation.

He got to his feet as she slid into the chair opposite his. "I've taken a chance and ordered coronation chicken sandwiches for us both," he said. "I thought it would save time, but if you want something different—"

"Coronation chicken will be fine. Did you ask for wholemeal bread?"

"Of course. What would you like to drink?"

"Something long, cool and non-alcoholic, please."

"Elderflower cordial?"

"That'll do nicely."

He returned with her drink just as a waiter appeared with their sandwiches. When they were settled, Jim said, "So, how did it go this morning? Did all the punters show up?"

"Surprisingly, yes. The atmosphere was pretty subdued at first, which was only natural, but—" Suddenly aware that she was hungry, Sukey broke off to take a hearty bite from her sandwich. When she was free to speak again, she said, "Freya was amazingly composed – you really have to hand it to her. She started off with a short, obviously prepared address, beginning with a sort of lament for Xavier's death followed by an assurance that his spirit was reaching out to each and every one of us from the Unlimited. She ended with an impassioned plea for our support in carrying on his work. It was awesome, mesmerising. I might never achieve the famous Inner Wheel, let alone the Unlimited, but I couldn't help being affected by it." Sukey gave an involuntary giggle. "All this talk about wheels makes us sound like a load of hamsters, doesn't it?"

Jim responded with a wry smile, then grew serious again. "It sounds as if they'd already established a pretty powerful hold over everyone's mind – yours included." He looked at Sukey with a troubled expression in his greenish eyes. "I've noticed a change in you, Sook, and it bothers me."

"You don't have to worry. I'm not spooked, as you call it, although I'm sure what I learned over the past few days has helped me cope. At the same time, I find I'm taking a more philosophical view of things that have troubled me over the years. As for the present, and the future –" she raised her glass and leaned towards him – "as far as you and I are concerned, there's been no change at all," she whispered.

He put out a hand and gently brushed her cheek with his fingers. "That's a mighty big relief," he said huskily. After a moment, he sat back and continued in a more matter-of-fact tone, "Well, I suppose we'd better get down to business. Tell me about the rest of the morning. There must have been some changes in the programme – isn't Friday the day when you're supposed to get your one-to-one assessments and be shown the therapy department?"

"You mean, the Rejuvenation Suite!" Sukey corrected him, unconsciously echoing Edith's air of reproach. "Yes, we saw that shortly before we left, after the police had finished checking in there. It's just a series of small rooms with couches where they do various treatments – they call them by fancy names but I'm pretty sure they're things like aromatherapy or reflexology dressed up to make them appear different. The set-up is very much like a natural healing centre I once had to attend in Gloucester after a break-in."

"What about the interviews? I suppose Freya did those?"

"I had mine with Serena. She explained that normally I'd have seen Freya or Xavier and that she'd stepped into the breach because of the tragedy, but if I wanted to discuss anything 'deeply personal' as she put it, she'd arrange for me to speak to Freya. I can't answer for what she said to the others, but as far as I was concerned it wasn't so much a chat as an opportunity to 'assess my progress towards the Inner Wheel', bearing in mind that I wasn't one of the enlightened souls who claimed to have already reached it."

"And what did you say to that?"

"I said – quite sincerely – that I felt I'd derived considerable benefit from their teaching and went on to express my condolences, said how much I admired Freya's courage and wished them well for the future. She thanked me and that was more or less it."

"No sales talk about signing on for a further course?"

"No. Come to think of it, that's a little surprising," Sukey added after a moment's thought. "You may recall my saying I had the impression at first that Xavier was the true believer, as it were, and that Freya and Serena were in it solely for the money. Maybe I was doing them an injustice."

"Maybe. Anyway, it's your impressions that I'm after now. You're in the unique position of having been able to observe everyone's reactions from the time the body was discovered." Jim sat back and renewed his attack on his sandwiches. "Take your time."

Sukey glanced at her watch. "I haven't got all that much time. I'm supposed to start work at two."

"It's all right, I've told George Barnes you're likely to be late. Mandy's mother's out of danger so she's back."

"That's good." Sukey finished her own sandwiches, picked at the side salad and took a few mouthfuls from her glass of cordial. "Reactions," she said reflectively. "Well, Freya went to pieces completely, which was only natural. Serena had left earlier through the alcove at the back of the meeting-room where the cast make their entrances and the next time I saw her she was in the courtyard with Freya. The others sat sort of mesmerised. Then one of the men who gave his name as Dan Foster said something about going to investigate."

"And I noted from the statement you gave Radcliffe that you said everyone was to wait there while you went to see what was going on. How did they take that?"

"Foster was a bit stroppy at first. No one else objected at the time and as soon as I showed my ID his attitude changed and he offered to come with me."

"And you asked him to stay and keep an eye on the other four. How did he react then?"

"He seemed quite chuffed at the suggestion, as if he welcomed the chance to show off his leadership qualities."

"And the others?"

Sukey contemplated her glass, trying to recreate the scene in her mind's eye. "Pretty much as you'd expect, I suppose. I mean, they all looked shocked and apprehensive. Jennifer particularly so," she went on, as a flash of memory recalled the closed eyes and the clenched hands, followed by the look of sheer terror. "Then the other lady broke down and started wailing about losing her grip on the Inner Wheel and Jennifer went over to comfort her. That was when I had the idea of asking Foster to stay and keep an eye on everyone. He rose to the bait immediately. You know," Sukey went on reflectively, "I have my doubts about him."

Jim raised an eyebrow. "Why do you say that?"

"I think it's because he reacted so quickly when we heard Freya yelling. The others sat there looking gob-smacked for several seconds as if they couldn't believe what they were hearing, but he was on his feet straight away."

"So were you."

"Yes, but I've had police training."

"You're implying that Foster wasn't quite so carried away as the rest of them?"

"I'd say not, although" – once again, a flash of memory – "he was one of the two who claimed to be approaching the Inner

Wheel; I remember seeing him put a hand up when Freya asked. In the light of what happened next, I'm seriously wondering whether that was genuine. It might be worth a bit of probing into his real motive for being there."

"I'll pass that on to Radcliffe. Anything else you recall that might be significant?"

"Well, Loveridge certainly kicked up a great fuss about having to stay put until the police arrived – carried on about having a business to attend to, even though he'd have been there till midday if things had been normal."

"And the others?"

"The man who was the first to say he'd reached the Inner Wheel – I've no clear impression of him . . ."

"Let's call him the Hamster," Jim suggested slyly.

"Yes, why not? Well, as far as I remember he stayed in his seat with his eyes shut the whole time. The weepy lady had calmed down and was sitting there beside him."

"What about Jennifer?"

"She was looking at Loveridge as if she couldn't believe her ears. She seemed really shocked at the way he was going on. No," Sukey said after a moment's thought. "Not so much shocked as terrified. Up to that point, she'd kept her cool pretty well, all things considered."

"That could be a kind of delayed shock, but I'll mention it anyway."

"Then there's Jarvis, of course – the gardener. I'm surprised you haven't asked about him. He got very stroppy about being made to stay with the others."

"That doesn't surprise me," said Jim with a chuckle.

Sukey eyed him suspiciously. "You've been holding out on me," she accused him. "What's Jarvis been up to?"

"There's quite a large greenhouse tucked away behind the Rejuvenation Suite. He uses it to raise plants for the garden and the house. He's also raising a very healthy crop of cannabis – far too much for his own use. We suspect he's been supplying quite a sizeable clientele."

"And I suppose his first thought was to try and hide his merchandise before the police began poking around."

"It seems likely."

"Do you reckon Xavier found out and threatened to shop him, or burn his plants or something?"

"That's one possibility we're considering. You probably recall mentioning in your statement that he didn't turn up to ask what the fuss was about until several minutes after Freya began screaming. What does that suggest to you?"

Sukey thought for a moment. "That he already knew Xavier was dead?"

"Exactly."

Twenty

" **S** ukey?" Jennifer's voice sounded thin, nervous. "I'm sorry to be calling you so late. I spoke to your son earlier and he told me it would be all right."

"No problem – I've only just got in. How are you feeling? I was hoping to have a word with you before you went home today, but by the time I'd finished talking to Serena you'd left."

"I couldn't get away fast enough after what happened yesterday. Such a terrible thing to happen . . . I just wanted to say . . . that is . . . I thought it was splendid the way you coped."

"Thank you."

"And to thank you for agreeing to come with me. You must think me an awful fool to have got so worked up, imagining all that nonsense about blackmail, but at the time I—" Jennifer broke off with a faint, humourless laugh.

"There's no need to apologise. Until the tragedy, I was finding it a most enlightening experience, something I wouldn't have missed for the world."

"Really?"

"Really. It seemed to be doing you some good as well. I thought you seemed much more at peace with yourself until—"

"Oh, I was, I am. Much more at peace." Jennifer broke in with another high-pitched laugh that did not sound quite natural. "Or at least I was until that dreadful attack on poor Xavier – I can't imagine who would want to kill a kind, gentle soul like him. Just the same, I'm sure his teaching is helping me . . . will help us all get over the trauma much more quickly. And I'm *quite* convinced now," she hurried on, "that no one at RYCE had *anything* to do with my husband's death. Just the same, I don't think I'll be taking up Serena's offer. I couldn't *bear* to go there again. I didn't really want to go this morning, but he said, that is, I . . ."

"Who said what?" asked Sukey, after Jennifer failed to continue after an interval of several seconds.

"Why, Xavier, of course." There was another feeble attempt at a laugh. "That might sound crazy," Jennifer huried on, "but I'm sure *you'll* understand. Do you know, I really felt he was calling me from the Unlimited, like Freya said. Didn't you feel that too?"

Had she been strictly truthful, Sukey would have admitted to feeling nothing of the kind, but having no intention of being sidetracked into a discussion of metaphysics she said, "I suppose I did, in a way." Either Jennifer's mind had been seriously disturbed, or she was hiding something. Suspecting from her manner that the latter explanation was the more likely, Sukey determined to glean as much information as possible. "This offer from Serena you spoke about a moment ago," she said. "What was that?"

"She said if I ring the office one day next week Josie will arrange for me to have a free treatment. Didn't she say that to you?"

"No, she didn't."

"How strange. I'm sure it was an oversight. It's not surprising, really. The poor girl must still be in a state of shock, even more than the rest of us."

"I expect that's the reason," said Sukey mechanically while mentally searching for a possible alternative explanation.

"She'll probably get Josie to call you when she realises. Will you accept?"

"I might."

There was another silence. Sukey was trying to think of a polite way of ending the call when Jennifer said, "Do you know if the police have any idea yet who killed Xavier?"

"Not really. I don't know much more than what they say in their official statements."

"But I thought . . . I mean, you work for them."

"Yes, but in this case I'm only a witness. I'm not involved in the actual investigation."

"Oh, I see. I hope you didn't mind me asking."

"No, of course not. Take care, and don't hesitate to call me if you want a chat."

"Thank you." Jennifer's voice had fallen to a whisper. "Goodbye."

Sukey frowned as she replaced the handset, asking herself if she had imagined the artificial quality in the apparently casual question about the progress of the police inquiry.

"Was that Jennifer?" Fergus, who had been watching a football match on the television, entered the kitchen and went straight to the sink to fill the kettle.

"It was."

"She phoned earlier. She sounded pretty uptight – what did she want?"

"The excuse was to give me a pat on the back for the way I handled the situation after the murder and to thank me for agreeing to go with her."

"Why do you call it an excuse?"

"I think the real reason was to pump me over the police investigation. She sounded disappointed when I explained I wasn't part of it and couldn't tell her more than had already been made public, yet earlier she'd been at great pains to say that she was sure her suspicions about blackmail were unfounded."

"So why the questions?"

"Exactly. She also referred to a mysterious 'he' who I gather insisted that she went along to this morning's session even though she didn't really want to. She broke off at that point as if she realised she'd slipped up, and then tried to turn it into a reference to Xavier calling from the Unlimited."

Fergus, busy with the tea-things, cocked an eyebrow. "Did you tell her to pull the other one?"

"I was tempted, but I thought it best to let her think I'd swallowed it. She could be in quite a delicate mental state or—"

"Or she was on a fishing expedition," Fergus remarked shrewdly. "Any idea who 'he' might really be?"

"Possibly." He eyed her expectantly, but she shook her head. "My ideas are pretty nebulous at the moment. I need to think. Tomorrow, perhaps, when I'm less tired."

"By the way, I forgot to mention – Jim phoned earlier to say he's probably going to be tied up most of tomorrow and he'll give you a call as soon as he has a spare moment."

"Thanks. What are your plans for the weekend, by the way?"

"I'm going to watch Anita play tennis tomorrow afternoon. She's reached the final of her club tournament."

"Good for her – wish her luck from me."

Fergus glanced up in the act of pouring out the tea. "Perhaps you'd like to come along as well, as you won't be seeing Jim," he suggested.

"That sounds like a nice idea, I might just do that. Thanks, love," she added with a grateful smile as she took the cup he handed her. "Just what I needed. Do you fancy a pizza for supper? There's one in the freezer."

"Sounds fine. With chips and salad?"

"Sure. There's some apple pie left from yesterday. We could have that with ice cream."

There was no further reference to the murder of Percy Burrell that evening, but several unresolved questions were buzzing away in Sukey's head and she made several notes before settling down for a much-needed night's sleep.

Early on Saturday morning Sukey called Jim in the hope of catching him before he left home. There was no reply, so she tried police headquarters in Gloucester. On being told he was in the building but unavailable, she asked to be put through to DS Radcliffe. He greeted her request with some surprise, appeared doubtful that Serena's "oversight" had any particular significance, but agreed to check with the other witnesses. "It'll take a while to get through all the follow-up interviews, but I'll let you know as soon as I can," he promised. She was about to go on to refer to Jennifer's reference to an unidentified "he", but as he indicated politely but firmly that he was pressed for time she thanked him, put down the phone and turned her attention to breakfast.

The day was fine and warm with a light breeze, ideal for tennis. Anita won her match amid ecstatic applause from her friends and parents, who invited Fergus and Sukey to join the celebratory barbecue in the evening. Fergus accepted immediately, but Sukey declined on the pretext of having domestic chores to attend to. After congratulating Anita and admiring the trophy, she said her goodbyes and was on her way back to her car when she felt a touch on her arm. Turning, she came face to face with Adrian Masters.

"You won't forget your promise, will you?" he said in a low voice. "About Vera," he went on, glancing over his shoulder as if suspecting an eavesdropper although there was no one within sight. "I'm sorry to keep banging on about it, but worrying about the poor old dear is keeping me awake at night. I daren't mention it to Cath again, she'd hit the roof," he added with a rueful half-smile, "It's just that the thought of her dying alone in her car like that haunts me. I can't rest until I know the whole story."

Seeing the signs of strain round his eyes, Sukey was tempted to drop a hint that she might have the germ of an idea, but swiftly decided against it. To raise his hopes over something that might turn out to have no connection whatsoever with Vera's death seemed pointless at this stage. So she repeated her undertaking to remain on the alert and to let him know immediately if anything relevant emerged during the police enquiry, and then thankfully made her escape.

It was almost eight o'clock that evening before she had any word from Jim. He sounded tired and dispirited. "Is there any chance you might be able to feed a weary DI?" he asked.

"I've had my supper, but I could rustle up some sausages and chips from the freezer. Will that do?"

"Perfect. I'll be with you in half an hour."

He was there within twenty minutes. "God, what a day!" he

groaned as he sank on to the couch in Sukey's cosy little sitting-room and closed his eyes.

"I take it it's the stabbing at RYCE that's been keeping you?" He nodded. "Has there been any progress?"

"Not really."

"Well, get this down you while the food's cooking."

"Bless you." He sat up and drank deeply from the glass of beer she handed him. "It looks as if it might end up being a very long investigation," he said as she settled down at his side. "It's not as if we can be sure the killer is one of the people who were known to be there at the time of the murder."

"But it must have been – I mean, who else would have access to that knife?"

"The knife was used only occasionally, as part of a kind of grand finale to one of the more advanced courses. The last time was nearly three weeks ago. It could have been taken almost any time since then, which means we have to check on everyone who was there from then on."

"But surely someone would have noticed if it was missing. Josie spotted it immediately."

"Theoretically, yes, but we can't take anything for granted."

"And what about Jarvis? I thought—"

Jim gave a weary shrug. "We had to bail him for the time being. He faces charges over growing and probably supplying pot, of course, but we're satisfied he had nothing to do with the killing. We were right in one respect, though; when he waylaid you and Serena on your way back to the house, he did already know Burrell was dead. He said he was missing a pair of secateurs, remembered he'd been working the previous day in the private garden and thought he might have left them there. Knowing Burrell would be 'saying his prayers' as he put it and wouldn't notice if the SAS came charging in, he slipped back to look for them. When he saw the body he panicked and fled. The SOCOs found the secateurs during their search, which seems to bear out his story."

"It doesn't explain why he didn't raise the alarm immediately."

"That was put to him. His first thought was self-preservation, so he began trying to hide the cannabis plants in a disused shed. I don't think it occurred to him that he might be suspected of the murder, but he decided it would look odd if he didn't put in an appearance after all the shemozzle. His intention was to go back and finish the job before the police got there; he hadn't bargained for 'that effing bossy-boots' – that's you, my love – keeping him banged up until the police arrived."

Sukey chortled with delight. "Well, three cheers for clever old me!" She detached herself from the encircling arm he had slipped round her shoulders and stood up. "I'd better go and check on your supper – it should be nearly ready."

"That's good. I'm starving." He followed her into the kitchen and tucked in with gusto to the plate of food she put in front of him. "By the way," he said when he had taken the edge off his hunger, "what's this I hear from Radcliffe about you wanting a freebie therapy treatment at RYCE?"

Sukey blinked in astonishment. "Is that what he told you?"

"That's the impression he got."

"Not quite accurate, although it might be quite a pleasant experience. I just wondered whether I was the only one who didn't receive the special offer – which I assume was by way of compensation for the disruption to the course – and if so, why? And if Jennifer was the only one to get it, what could be the explanation for that?"

Jim shook his head. "No idea at the moment. Have you got a theory?"

"Well, one possibility is that somehow they knew Jennifer is Oliver Drew's widow and it was a kind of goodwill gesture – but if that's the case, you'd expect Serena to have said so, made some expression of sympathy, said she hoped their teaching had been a comfort to her, that kind of thing."

"That doesn't sound very convincing to me."

"Nor to me."

"So what else do you have in mind?"

"Did Serena just forget to make the offer to me, as Jennifer suggested, or was it a deliberate omission because for some reason they didn't want me anywhere near the so-called Rejuvenation Suite."

"Any idea why that should be?"

Sukey helped herself to a chip from the dish at Jim's elbow and munched it thoughtfully for a moment. "Not at the moment, but when I went back to Burwell Farm the second time, on the pretext of letting them know their stolen mower had been recovered—"

"Just a minute." Jim paused with a sausage halfway to his mouth. "What second time?"

"Oh, didn't I tell you?"

"You did not."

"It was probably because you'd made such a fuss about what Jennifer and Adrian had asked me to do."

"All right, let's not go over all that again. What were you about to say?"

She gave him a brief account of her conversations – first with Jarvis, who identified Vera as a woman he had seen emerging from the Rejuvenation Suite looking "put out", and then with Serena, who she felt was uncomfortable over the reference to Oliver Drew. "And there was something in the way she looked at me when she was doing her 'Welcome to RYCE' act on Monday morning that made me think she wasn't altogether happy at seeing me there."

"You think, knowing your connection with the police, she might have suspected your motive?" Jim frowned as he helped himself to the last of the chips. "It sounds a bit thin on the face of it. Just the same, I wish you'd listened to me, and stayed away from the place."

"And missed out on a commendation from DCI Lord?" Sukey teased, but there was no answering smile.

"All right, you did a great job at the time, but please, leave it to us from now on."

"A propos of that, there's one other point you might want to think about." She described the lame explanation that followed Jennifer's inadvertent reference to a third party.

For the first time, Jim showed an interest. "That does need looking into," he agreed. "Any idea who 'he' might be?"

"How about Loveridge? As I told you yesterday, Jennifer looked pretty shocked while he was making a scene at not being allowed out of the room – which was natural, I suppose, but it's occurred to me since that it might be more than shock. I thought she looked scared as well – almost as if she was afraid of what he might let drop. I've been wondering whether she might know him – or know something about him. Remember, her initial motive in going to RYCE was to try and pin responsibility for her husband's death on someone there. Next thing, the owner of the place gets topped. And Loveridge didn't strike me as the kind of man likely to suffer from 'internal shackles' as the jargon goes."

Jim laid down his knife and fork and pushed his empty plate aside. "You never know what goes on inside people's heads, but as you say, it's worth following up. I'll have a word with Andy Radcliffe and tell him to see what he can dig up on Loveridge."

Twenty-One

T owards the end of the following Monday afternoon, Sergeant Radcliffe entered DI Castle's office with a file of papers in his hand.

"Ah, Andy. Just the chap I wanted to see." Castle indicated a chair. Radcliffe sat down and put the file on the desk. "What have you been able to dig up on the Percy Burrell murder?"

"A few interesting tit-bits, but at first sight nothing significant. We're still waiting for forensics to complete their examination of the witnesses' clothing – initial reports indicate no trace of blood found so far, although all the shoes had picked up grass cuttings. Nothing particularly suspicious there – the lawns had been cut the previous day and they all admitted going into the garden before the start of the session."

"What else?"

"Serena Elford, who is supposed to be one of Percy Burrell's converts, turns out to be Edith Burrell's daughter. She claims to have studied various forms of alternative medicine and joined the team shortly before they moved to Burwell Farm from London. I looked up the reports of their earlier brush with authority – you may remember Percy and Edith had their knuckles rapped for making misleading claims about their treatments – and came across the fact that Elford was Edith's maiden name. Rumour had it that she was a bit of a wild child and Serena was the result of a teenage fling with a Spanish hippie. Maybe she became involved in some sort of cult religion, which would explain the attraction to Percy Burrell."

"Presumably they decided to conceal the relationship because they thought presenting Serena as a disciple would be a good selling point," Castle observed. "That might be a slightly dodgy marketing ploy, but it's hardly criminal."

"I'm not suggesting it is, guv. I just thought it was another indication that they're not above the odd deception."

"Point taken. Sukey seems to think Serena controls the business side of the enterprise, as well as giving some of the so-called rejuvenation treatments. Does that tie in with your information?"

"Pretty well. There's a young woman called Josie Garrard who handles the day-to-day admin and she's directly responsible to Serena. Edith and Serena give the treatments between them. Edith comes swanning into the office now and then to check her appointments, but Percy seems to have taken little interest in the hands-on side of things – Josie hardly ever saw him except now and again in the garden. I must say," Radcliffe added with a sigh, "Josie hasn't been a particularly useful witness. The job suits her because it's close to home, but outside office hours she hardly gives it a thought. She's not in the least interested in her employers' private lives, or those of the punters. She says Percy was 'a bit of an oddball, but a lovely man' and privately thinks the RYCE philosophy is 'a bit of a laugh'."

"She knew about the knife and she was quick to spot that it was missing," Castle pointed out.

"Only because it was kept in a place where her duties took her now and again. She happened to comment on it one day and Serena explained the part it played in the proceedings."

"I see. What about the others?"

"Edith Burrell once did a drama course, but never made the big time. Gave up her hopes of an acting career when she met Percy and threw in her lot with him. Lisa Crombie interviewed her, says she's devastated by his death but passionate in her determination to carry on his 'mission', as she calls it. Claims to be motivated by his spirit guiding her from 'the Great Unlimited'."

Castle frowned. "Either she's a genuine fruitcake or she's putting on an act. Is there any reason to suspect her?"

"None at all at the moment, but naturally we're keeping an open mind. Lisa said she sounded totally dedicated and sincere – and, of course, losing the key player out of a three-person act is going to present enormous difficulties."

"Do we know who benefits financially?"

"We checked with their accountant – they were quite happy for us to speak to him – and everything is already in the wife's name. Percy doesn't seem to have been interested in anything so sordid as money or worldly goods."

"Any other family?"

"They say not. Edith's an orphan and Serena's father probably did a runner years ago, but I suppose we'd better check on that." Radcliffe made a note before continuing. "Percy inherited a considerable sum of money from his widowed father – again, the only relative – which enabled them to buy Burwell Farm and convert it. Serena says left to himself, he'd probably have given it all away, but Edith managed to talk him into setting up the RYCE Foundation on the grounds that it would enable him to reach more people with his divine message."

"Apart from Jarvis the gardener, are there any other staff – cook, cleaner, that sort of thing?"

"They're all vegetarian and what cooking is done Serena and Edith do between them. A Mrs Robbins comes in for a couple of hours three times a week to do the laundry and cleaning and a window-cleaner calls every three or four weeks. They were both elsewhere on the day of the murder."

"Hmm." Castle got up and began prowling round the office, repeatedly tossing a bunch of keys into the air and catching it. It was a long-standing habit of his and Radcliffe knew better than to interrupt his train of thought. It was several minutes before he sat down again, replaced the keys in his pocket and said, "So that brings us to the people who made up the group that day. Jennifer Drew's background we know about and I think we can eliminate Sukey from our enquiries. What about the others?"

Radcliffe opened the file and handed the top sheet of paper to Castle. "Daniel Foster, human resources manager for an electronics company. Reason for attending the course: stress levels among the company personnel have been causing anxiety and the chairman's given him the job of sussing out a few places where they can be sent to chill out."

"That's interesting." Castle scanned the report briefly before returning it. "Sukey said she thought he had what she called 'leadership qualities'."

"Perceptive girl, Sukey," Radcliffe commented.

"Very," Castle replied dryly. "She's got me sized up. D'you know, Andy –" for the moment, he dropped his official manner and addressed Radcliffe as the man with whom he had enjoyed a close comradeship going back to their early days in the force. Radcliffe, with less ambition, had been content to remain a sergeant while Castle had always had an eye to further promotion, but outside their work the difference in rank had not affected their friendship – "she told me the other day that I was pompous."

"That's a bit steep," said Radcliffe with a grin. "What had you done to deserve that?"

"I suppose I was laying down the law a bit too strongly," Castle admitted. "Anyway, back to the job in hand. What have you on the other three?"

"The woman, a Miss Mary Hargreaves, is a teacher in a comprehensive school in Bath. Gives her reason for enrolling at RYCE as job-related stress, which sounds reasonable enough. Hubert Phillips was a little reluctant to divulge his profession – said it would look bad for him if it became known to his employers."

"Who are?"

"The church. He's a reverend gentleman."

Castle gave a soft whistle. "I can't imagine that would go down well with his bishop – he might suspect a whiff of paganism. If he was under stress, you'd have thought he'd have applied to go to some Christian retreat."

"That occurred to me," Radcliffe agreed. "So I had a few discreet enquiries made, and it turns out that Miss Hargreaves is a member of his congregation and – according to one garrulous old gossip of a churchwarden – 'rather sweet on our vicar'. And," the sergeant continued with a certain amount of grim relish, "it emerged that they were staying in the same pub on the outskirts of Tewkesbury, under assumed names. They were taken back for a change of clothing so that forensics could check the things they were wearing – separately as it happened and about half an hour apart because of the way the interviews were timed, so the coincidence wasn't spotted until the reports were compared later."

"And I imagine the reverend gentleman has a lawfully wedded wife?"

"You've got it. According to Josie, they registered at RYCE in their own names – he as plain Mister – but any correspondence went to Hargreaves's address."

"Is there any way that Percy Burrell could have known about their relationship?"

"It seems unlikely and there's no apparent reason why he should be concerned about it, but obviously we'll have to go into that in a bit more depth. It's going to come as a shock to Mrs Phillips, I'm afraid. She thinks her husband's been visiting a sick aunt in Carlisle."

"That leaves Loveridge. What have you got on him?"

"Not a lot. We haven't managed to speak to him since we took his initial statement; all our phone calls have been taken by a dragon of a secretary who claims his diary's completely full for the next few days. He enrolled at RYCE at the last minute, by the way. She says he came back from a very stressful business trip and told her to fix him up somewhere where he could unwind. They happened to have had a last-minute cancellation so they were able to take him."

"Any idea why she chose RYCE?"

Radcliffe shook his head. "Never thought to ask. Could be because it's conveniently situated – the firm's headquarters are in Birmingham. I'll check on that." He made a note. "I think I'll put DC Hill on this one – if Loveridge continues to be elusive he can see what he can get out of the secretary. Young Tony's got a way with women."

As he approached the glass front door of the headquarters of Loveridge International, DC Hill noticed that the young woman behind the desk in the reception area was filing her nails and looking bored. When the automatic panels slid apart to admit him she hurriedly put down the file and greeted him with a welcoming expression that appeared natural and spontaneous rather than the professional baring of the teeth that in similar situations so often passed for a smile. He guessed – rightly as it turned out – that the arrival of a personable man in his twenties held the promise of a pleasant if brief diversion during an otherwise uneventful period. She was blonde and blue-eyed with pretty, mobile features, and there was a slightly breathless quality to her voice as she said, "Good morning, can I help you?"

Hill treated her to one of the ingratiating smiles that had been known to disarm the least impressionable of female witnesses, held up his identity card and said, "Good morning. I'm Detective Constable Hill of Gloucester CID. Would it be possible to have a word with your Mr Mervyn Loveridge?"

"A detective!" Her tone was a mixture of awe and apprehension. Then the blue eyes widened in alarm and the smile faded. "Oh dear," she breathed. "I do hope it's nothing too serious. Poor Mr Loveridge has had so much worry lately."

Hill adjusted his expression to one of concern. "I'm sorry to hear that. Business problems, I suppose – what with the recession and so on."

"Recession?" The girl's brow wrinkled in perplexity and Hill had the impression that she was unsure of the meaning of the word. "I don't know about that, but he's always having to go off on trips – abroad mostly."

"Yes, I'm told that business people have to do a lot of travelling. It must be very stressful, with jet-lag and all that."

"That's just it. And then losing his Uncle Oliver, poor man . . ."

189

Hill's pulse gave a blip, but he kept his tone casual as he asked, "What happened to Uncle Oliver?"

"He died very suddenly. Mr Loveridge had only just come back from a trip abroad when he got the news. He was in reception, just rushing off out when his aunt phoned to tell him and he took the call right here." She pointed to the instrument on the desk with a shudder, as if blaming it for having been the harbinger of bad news. The recollection seemed to unleash a flood of emotion; the girl's mouth trembled and her eyes filled.

"Here, let me . . ." Hill took a tissue from a box beside the phone and gently wiped the tears away.

"Thank you, you're very kind." She sniffed, took a second tissue and blew her nose. Then she pulled herself together, assumed what she doubtless considered to be a correct, business-like manner and said, "I'm afraid Mr Loveridge isn't in the office this morning. You could have a word with his PA, Ms Nightingale, if you like."

"That would be very helpful." Hill treated her to another dazzling smile.

She gave him a shy smile in return and asked, "What's your first name?"

"Tony. What's yours?"

"Linda. My sister's boyfriend's called Tony – he's ever so nice. You must think it's silly of me to get so upset," she went on apologetically, "but if you'd seen Mr Loveridge's face when he got the call from his aunt . . . it must have been a terrible shock to him, being still jet-lagged after his overseas trip. It was very stressful, so Anne – Ms Nightingale said."

"I'm sure it was," Hill agreed sympathetically.

"I'll tell her you're here." Linda reached for the telephone, but Hill, sensing that he might glean a little more information from her, put a hand on the receiver.

"Do you happen to remember what Mr Loveridge said when he took the call from his aunt?" he enquired.

She thought for a moment before replying. "I think it was something like, 'Just keep calm and wait at home, I'll be with you

190

as soon as possible'," she said slowly. "I can't remember exactly. He never came back that day and he was away from the office every morning last week. Anne wouldn't say why, but I know she had to reschedule lots of his appointments."

"So you don't know what actually happened to his uncle?"

She shook her head and pouted. "Anne wouldn't tell me that either," she said with a touch of resentment. "She said it was none of my business and I wasn't to say anything to anyone, so I hope you won't let on I mentioned it."

"Don't worry, we detectives know when to keep quiet." Hill lowered his voice to a conspiratorial whisper and she gave a nervous little giggle. "As Mr Loveridge himself isn't available," he went on, "it would be helpful if I could have a word with Anne if she's free."

"I'll find out for you." Linda screwed up the tissues, threw them into an invisible bin under her desk and reached for the phone. This time, Hill made no attempt to stop her.

It turned out that Anne Nightingale was able to spare him a few minutes. Linda replaced the instrument and directed Hill to an office on the first floor. "You can take the lift if you like, or the stairs are over there," she said. He told her she had been very helpful and she simpered in delight. She seemed sorry to see him go.

Loveridge's personal assistant was a very different character from the impressionable Linda. When Hill knocked on her office door, her "Come in" sounded more like a command than an invitation and she continued – very pointedly, he felt – to study some papers on her desk before condescending to raise her head and greet him with a curt, "Detective Constable Hill?"

"That's right."

"What is it you want?"

"It's really Mr Loveridge that I wanted to see, but I understand he's unlikely to be available for a day or two. We're hoping he may be able to help us in our enquiries into the murder of Percy Burrell of the RYCE Foundation. As I'm sure you're aware, Mr Loveridge was there when it took place and—"

"—and was subjected to a considerable amount of questioning at the time," she interrupted, fixing Hill with frosty blue eyes. "He's aware that you wish to speak to him again, of course, and he has no intention of being obstructive or elusive, but he has many calls on his time and I think it's been made clear that he has nothing to add to his original statement."

"Oh, quite." Hill eyed a chair which was obviously intended to accommodate visitors, but received no invitation to sit down.

Ms Nightingale smoothed the collar of her severely tailored white blouse and fingered one of the stud earrings which matched the pearl choker at her throat. Her nails and lipstick were the colour of blackcurrant juice. "So how do you imagine I can help?" she asked.

"Am I correct in assuming that you made the arrangements for him to attend a course at RYCE?"

"You are."

"When did you make the booking?"

For the first time, her poise appeared momentarily affected, but she quickly recovered and said, "It was the day he got back from his Far Eastern trip. He was quite exhausted and his doctor recommended a complete break. He didn't feel able to take the whole week off, but it so happened that I knew about RYCE and their programme of morning or afternoon sessions, so I booked him in there."

Hill made a note. "So it was on your recommendation that he chose RYCE?"

"Haven't I just said so?"

Hill gave a conciliatory smile, which evoked no visible response. "I just want to make sure I've got it clear in my mind. Do I take it that you've attended a course there yourself?"

"I?" The carefully shaped eyebrows lifted in scorn. "Certainly not."

"Then presumably you know someone who has, and benefited from it?"

"Oh, I see what you mean." Again, she appeared vaguely disconcerted. "Yes, that's right."

"Could you possibly give me the person's name? It's just that we're trying to fill in as much of the background to the murder as possible. Obviously someone had a grudge against the victim, but we've drawn a complete blank as far as the people who were present at the time is concerned." Hill waited for a moment, but she made no comment. "The name of this person who recommended RYCE?" he prompted.

"I'm sorry, I can't remember. It was probably someone I met casually, at a business meeting, or maybe a party . . ."

She was definitely rattled. Hill was quick to press home the advantage. "Did you have any difficulty in making the booking for Mr Loveridge? It was pretty short notice, and I understand there's a considerable demand for the courses."

"That's right, but it so happened there had been a cancellation, which was very fortunate." She began shuffling the papers on her desk. "Now, if that's all—"

"Just one thing more. Apart from the strain of his Far Eastern trip, did Mr Loveridge have any other problems that you know of? His health? Worries concerning the business? Or –" Hill paused to give the impression that he was mentally seeking other possibilities – "some family difficulty, perhaps? A sudden bereavement, for example. Do you know of anything like that?"

Beneath the carefully applied make-up, Hill saw her colour rise and for the first time she avoided his eye. "Mr Loveridge never discussed his personal affairs with me and I wouldn't have dreamed of questioning him," she said. Her tone was dismissive, with an uneasy edge to it.

"Oh, I'm sure you're the soul of discretion," said Hill smoothly. He put his notebook in his pocket, turned and reached for the door handle. "Thank you for sparing the time to talk to me, Ms Nightingale, you've been very helpful. Good morning."

She responded with a brief nod. He left with the distinct impression that she was relieved the interview was at an end.

*   *   *

Shortly after eight o'clock that evening, while Sukey was writing out her reports on the day's cases, DI Castle put his head round the office door. Seeing her alone, he came in and sat down. "Had a good day?" he asked.

"Pretty routine. How about you?"

"Some interesting developments in the Burrell murder. Guess who's been having it off with the vicar?"

Sukey's eyes saucered as he regaled her with the saga of Mary Hargreaves and the Reverend Hubert Phillips. "Well, that's a turn-up for the book," she commented with a chuckle. "Not much help with the enquiry, but an interesting diversion. You know," she said thoughtfully, "I'd have sworn that their re-ponses to Freya's exhortations were genuine, but it seems odd for church people. Although, come to think of it, there's nothing in the RYCE teaching that's incompatible with religion – it simply boils down to a kind of 'heal thyself' philosophy."

"Maybe they've been kidding themselves that it was the Almighty's way of giving the OK to their amorous adventure," Castle observed.

"You old cynic!" Sukey said reproachfully. "It might be a genuine *grande passion* that they've been resisting for years."

"Maybe. Anyway, you're right; assuming there'll be a negative result from forensics we've written them out of the frame. Likewise Dan Foster." He sketched in the details that Radcliffe had turned up. "Your hunch about him was spot on, and the same applies to your doubts about Loveridge. You'll never guess who he's turned out to be." She shook her head. "Oliver Drew's nephew."

Her jaw dropped. "You're kidding!" She listened in growing amazement to his account of DC Hill's investigations. "Tony says it was pretty obvious the secretary knew more than she was prepared to admit, but the receptionist was much more suscep-tible to his charm."

"That accounts for Jennifer's change in attitude," Sukey commented. "The idea of persuading me to go to RYCE with her was to look for evidence of skullduggery and I fully expected her to be on the phone every evening wanting to rake over everything that had gone on during the day in the hunt for clues. When it didn't happen I put it down at first to a genuine change of heart, but as I told you I had some doubts about the way she reacted to Loveridge's ranting, and when she kept insisting that she was convinced she'd been barking up the wrong tree it didn't quite ring true."

"It's possible that when nephew Mervyn returned from his wanderings and learned about his uncle's suicide," Castle continued as she paused to consider the implications, "he agreed with Jennifer about the possible cause and decided to join in the hunt for the presumed blackmailer. That would explain why Jennifer gave you the brush-off." He glanced over his shoulder; the office door was closed and there were no sounds to indicate the presence of anyone in the corridor. He leaned towards Sukey, took one of her hands in both his and put it to his lips. "Got to hand it to you, Sook, you're a real little bloodhound at times," he murmured.

She leaned forward and kissed him lightly on the cheek. "Just put it down to feminine intuition," she said smugly. "I suppose you'll be pulling both Loveridge and Jennifer in for questioning?"

"Of course, although I'm a bit puzzled at the moment as to motive. On the face of it, it's difficult to see what they had to gain from killing Burrell, other than revenge for his supposed responsibility for Oliver Drew's suicide. Maybe somehow or other they'd turned up what appeared to them to be proof of that."

"You've probably hit on it. 'Revenge' is the name Jennifer gave her 'demon', remember?"

Twenty-Two

S ukey and Fergus were eating a late supper when Jim phoned.

"I thought you'd like to know we think we're on to something," he told her. "We pulled in Loveridge and Jennifer Drew for questioning and they both kicked up a great fuss. She became hysterical, he hurled abuse at the officers who brought him in and they both asked for a duty solicitor. That struck us as odd – you'd expect people like them, especially Loveridge, to have their own legal advisers."

"So?"

"So we started probing around. We got the name of Loveridge's solicitor from his secretary; he was extremely concerned when he heard what prompted the enquiry, but couldn't offer any explanation as to why he'd been passed over. And then Lisa Crombie said Jennifer Drew was in such a state that she sent for the FME, who was sufficiently concerned about her mental condition to arrange for her to spend the night in hospital. She gave her mother's name as her next of kin, so we contacted her. The result was very interesting."

Sukey swallowed the mouthful of grilled lamb she had been chewing and said, "But I understood they weren't on good terms because Mum disapproved of Oliver."

"That's what Jennifer kept saying, but we went ahead anyway. Lisa had a most revealing chat with Mrs Newlyn, during which it emerged that she objected solely because of the disparity in ages, but she was much more forthcoming about Mervyn Loveridge – says he's a nasty piece of work. It seems that as the result of some

196

dodgy business deal a few years ago, her son-in-law altered the terms of his will so that his nephew would no longer inherit a controlling interest in Drew's business. In recent months, Loveridge has been making great efforts to worm his way back into Uncle Oliver's good books – persuade him that he's seen the error of his ways and all that and try to get him to reverse the decision. He was also hoping to touch him for some more immediate help. Mrs N says Loveridge International has been going through a rough period lately."

"So when Uncle goes and tops himself before he can take the necessary action and Loveridge learns of Jennifer's suspicions, he decides Burrell is responsible for blowing his little scheme out of the water and kills him out of revenge. Is that what you're saying?'" Sukey speared a piece of potato with her fork and popped it into her mouth.

"It seems a strong possibility. Take a Brownie point for suggesting we go into Loveridge's background – you could well have saved us hours of spade-work."

"Thank you."

"By the way, your question about the free therapy session – all the others were offered one, so it looks as if Serena just forgot to mention it to you."

"I suppose she must have done," said Sukey absently. She reached for the last piece of grilled lamb and chewed it thoughtfully. While they were speaking, her mind had switched back to the events of that fateful Thursday morning in a series of impressions running before her mind's eye like a video on fast forward: the general lightening of the atmosphere: Serena's unaccustomed word of welcome as she circulated with her tray of drinks: Freya's normally sombre attire given a lift and sparkle with that scattering of sequins and the flowers in her hair: the positive response from some of the "initiates" and the almost palpable sense of excitement as they awaited Xavier's appearance. Then came the horror of the discovery: the arrival of the police and her own overwhelming sense of relief as responsibility was lifted from her shoulders. After that, the memory became less clear and she had a feeling that somewhere along the line there was something she had missed. She puzzled over it as she swallowed the last of the meat and reached for her glass of water.

"You don't seem all that interested." Castle sounded slightly put out. "I thought you'd be thrilled to know that your hunch looks like turning out to be correct."

"Sorry, of course I'm interested. Tell me more."

"That's pretty much it for the time being. You would have thought," Jim added, evidently well pleased by the early break-through in what had threatened to be a long and difficult inves-tigation, "that a man who's built up a hitherto thriving company would have weighed things up a bit more carefully before doing something as drastic as murder, but his run-in with you proved he doesn't take kindly to being crossed, and Sergeant Radcliffe and DC Hill confirm that he showed every indication of having an explosive temper. His brief warned him several times to cool it."

"Have you found any evidence to link either of them to the killing?"

"Not so far, but we're confident one or other of them will crack under questioning. We reckon it was Loveridge who actually committed the murder, but it's more than likely Jenni-fer's implicated in some way. Look, I've still got a mountain of paperwork to deal with so I'd better go now. I'll keep you posted." As further evidence that his thoughts were completely focused on the job in hand, he hung up without the usual exchange of endearments.

"What was that about?" Fergus asked eagerly as his mother put the phone down. "Has there been an arrest?"

"Jennifer Drew and Mervyn Loveridge, but only on suspicion. There's no evidence so far." Sukey repeated the gist of the conversation while Fergus cleared the table, brought plates for their dessert and took a tub of ice cream from the freezer while she began cutting slices of Bakewell tart.

"You don't sound very excited about it," Fergus commented, unconsciously echoing Jim's sentiment. "I'd have thought you'd be thrilled to have your hunch confirmed."

"I suppose I am, but the more I think about it the more it seems just a little too obvious. And not the way I'd expect a hard-headed businessman to go about getting his own back on some-one he suspects of doing him down."

"But if he was out for revenge . . ."

"Put yourself in his position. Uncle Oliver tops himself before he can be persuaded to reinstate him as his heir to the business. Furious at being thwarted in his ambition and persuaded by Jennifer that Oliver was being blackmailed by someone at RYCE, Loveridge sets out to find evidence. Assuming – as Jim seems to be doing – that he and Jennifer between them turned up that evidence, he would be in a strong position to expose them and ruin their business. If revenge is what they were after, surely that would be much more satisfactory – and far less risky than committing murder."

"Hmm, I see what you mean." Fergus polished off his portion of Bakewell tart and helped himself to another slice. "Unless the reason for the blackmail was something disgraceful in Oliver's past?"

"By all accounts he was a pretty upright sort of man. And in any case, how would the people at RYCE know anything about his private affairs?"

"Search me."

"I guess it'll all come out during the inquiry," said Sukey with a shrug.

Fergus gave her a questioning look. "You've got another idea, haven't you, Mum?"

"There's something bugging me, but I can't put my finger on it at the moment. And I'm still wondering why Serena offered a free therapy session to everyone but me. Maybe it was an oversight, but I think I'll chase it up just the same."

"You reckon it might have something to do with the murder?"

"Not necessarily the murder."

"Then what?"

A little wearily, Sukey passed a hand over her eyes. "I might be just imagining things, so please don't mention it to anyone for the moment," she said. "I don't want to make a complete fool of myself."

Timmy Tritton had two absorbing interests – a passion for gadgets and a desire to become rich. The two converged one day when he spotted a headline in the local paper reading "Farmer Unearths Buried Treasure". Fascinated, Timmy read the story of how a man using a metal detector had located a quantity of Roman coins estimated to be worth over £20,000. Timmy's fourteenth birthday was approaching; when his doting grandfather asked him what he would like he knew exactly what to ask for.

His initial search, in an uncultivated corner of the family's back garden, yielded nothing more valuable than a couple of old paint tins where a ramshackle shed had recently been demolished. He then approached the father of one of his school friends, who farmed a few acres in a neighbouring village, and was given permission to try his luck in a field recently turned over to pasture. Armed with his new toy and a spade, he set off to seek his fortune. He was an intelligent lad; knowing that the field had been regularly ploughed until a couple of seasons ago, and reasoning that anything of value in the cultivated area would have long since been brought to the surface, he decided to try his luck close to the boundary hedge. His hopes rose when within a very few minutes the machine signalled his first "find", but quickly died when further investigation in the undergrowth revealed nothing more valuable than a fifty pence piece, probably dropped by someone gathering blackberries. Still, fifty pence was better than nothing. He pocketed the coin and continued to work his way patiently and methodically along the hedgerow. Half an hour later, the machine responded again.

The first thing Timmy noticed was that, whereas his first find was merely concealed in the long grass, the second apparently lay beneath a patch of bare earth where the soil appeared loose and crumbly – possibly the remains of a molehill. That would make digging easier. In a state of great excitement he put down the machine, picked up his spade and began to dig. A few minutes' work exposed the source of the signal; that too was far from being treasure trove. Disappointed a second time, he was about to throw it back in disgust when it occurred to him that his mother would find it useful and decided he might as well keep it. He was about to refill the hole – having promised the owner of the field that he would leave everything as he found it – when he spotted something else, potentially more interesting. He picked it up, brushed off the loose, dry soil that clung to it and put it in his pocket with the coin before completing his task and moving on. He made no further discoveries that afternoon and returned home at tea-time, somewhat downcast at his lack of success but determined to resume his search another day. He put the fifty pence in his money-box, presented his second find to his mother – who expressed surprise that anyone should have taken the trouble to bury it but thanked him all the same – and decided to wait until after tea before investigating the third. His eyes nearly fell out when, on further examination, he realised what it was. It was only with difficulty that he managed to convince his mother, who happened to enter his room unannounced at a crucial moment, that he had come upon it entirely by accident.

The courtyard at Burwell Farm was deserted when Sukey drove in and parked her ten-year-old Astra alongside the office building. She pushed open the door and found Josie at her desk entering a pile of cheques in a paying-in book. Evidently, in spite of the tragedy, enrolments were still coming in. She looked up and greeted Sukey with a friendly smile that held a hint of surprise.

"Hullo, I wasn't expecting to see you again," she said. "I thought the police had finished their search."

"They have, as far as I know. This isn't an official visit."

"Oh, right. Just bear with me a second while I finish this, will you?" Josie totted up the amounts on a calculator and entered the total in the book, which she put in an envelope with the cheques. "What can I do for you?"

"I was wondering if I could have a word with Serena."

"She's in the Rejuvenation Suite at the moment, getting ready for a treatment later on."

"Would it be all right if I popped across?"

"I'm sure it would."

"I was hoping to have one of her treatments, but what with all the upset over the tragedy . . ."

"Yes, dreadful, wasn't it?" Josie shook her head sadly. "Have the police arrested anyone yet?"

"I believe they're making some progress," said Sukey cautiously.

"I assume you've come to claim your complimentary session – would you like me to make you an appointment? I'm not sure if we can fit you in this week, though."

"Never mind, it can wait. It will be something to look forward to." In a sudden flash of inspiration, Sukey assumed a serious expression and said, "I know how much poor Vera Masters was looking forward to hers."

Josie sighed. "Yes, it was so sad about Vera. She was to have come for an OSS treatment the day after she died. That's Oriental Spiritual Stimulation – something like aromatherapy, but a bit different I suppose. I haven't tried it myself."

Sukey was barely listening to Josie's explanation. Something had clicked in her brain. "Are you sure . . . about the date, I mean?"

"Oh yes, quite sure."

"Look, I'm sorry to bother you, but this could be quite important. Would you mind very much checking?" While she was speaking, Sukey was frantically trying to concoct a plausible reason for her request, but it did not seem to occur to Josie to query it. Jim had been right in his assumption; she was not of a curious disposition.

Josie opened her appointments book and flipped through the pages. "Here we are." She pointed to an entry. The name Vera Masters was clearly entered against the day after the discovery of her body. But Vera had been seen by Jarvis emerging from the

Rejuvenation Suite on the day of her death, apparently upset. Of course, she might simply have been annoyed at her own mistake, but on the other hand . . .

"That's right, isn't it?" said Josie.

"Yes, quite right. Thank you." As the girl took back the book she happened to glance over Sukey's shoulder through the open door. "I just saw Freya go into Rejuvenation," she said. "You'll catch them both there now if you want to discuss your treatment. I must get off to the bank now – our local branch closes at one." Her face clouded again as she added, "I do feel so sorry for them, but they're coping splendidly."

"It's what I would have expected. I'll go over right away, if you're sure they won't mind me barging in."

"Oh, I'm sure they'll be very happy to see you."

But that cheerful assumption was shortly to be proved dangerously wide of the mark.

Twenty-Three

S ukey crossed the yard and tapped lightly on the door of the Rejuvenation Suite. Receiving no reply, after a moment's hesitation she opened it and went inside. It led directly into the small reception area where she and the other five members of her group had assembled the previous Friday to hear Serena give a brief résumé of the nature and benefits of the therapies on offer before showing them the treatment rooms. The walls were papered in a soft shade of peach; to the left of the door was a couch upholstered in a deeper shade of peach damask, and a cloth of similar material covered a small round table on which stood an arrangement in a copper jug of silk flowers ranging in colour from deep bronze to pale alabaster. The lighting was soft with a flattering pinkish tinge; one or two prints of naturistic designs of clouds, rocks, leaves, birds and flowers hung on the walls and the air was perfumed with the same musky fragrance as the meeting room in the main building.

Sukey's recollections of her one previous visit were a trifle blurred; seven people crowded into such a small space had given it a slightly claustrophobic feel which, together with the shadow of the previous day's tragedy, had induced a desire – which she sensed had been shared by the others – to be back in the open air as quickly as possible. Serena had led them along the narrow, windowless passage which ran the length of the single-storey building and shown them briefly the three small treatment rooms which led off it. The furniture appeared conventional enough; each had a couch, an adjustable stool for the therapist and a table on which were arranged a selection of bottles, jars and other containers. One corner was curtained off to provide hanging space and storage for items of equipment appropriate for the various treatments. There were also the ubiquitous, discreetly positioned speakers pumping out the usual soothing, formless cascade of musical harmonies.

For the moment, presumably because the morning session was over and the afternoon's not yet begun, the music was stilled. It had become so much a part of the RYCE environment that its absence gave the atmosphere an uncanny quality of emptiness that sent a ripple of gooseflesh along Sukey's spine. As she moved hesitantly along the passage, the sound of her footsteps absorbed by the thick, milk-chocolate coloured carpet covering the floor of the entire suite, she found herself holding her breath like a child entering the haunted house in a fairground, half excited, half apprehensive. She had a momentary vision of Xavier, not as a murdered, bloodstained corpse with the fatal dagger protruding from its back, but of the charismatic, white-robed, monkish figure with the brooding eyes who had exerted such a powerful influence on his followers. For an instant she seemed to feel his spiritual presence, then told herself not to be so fanciful. Serena had said he played no part in the "hands-on" side of the RYCE programme and so would seldom, if ever, have had reason to be here.

The door of the first room stood ajar; within, the light was on and she was about to give a gentle tap before pushing it open when her arm froze at the sound of a woman's voice that seemed to be coming from the room at the far end of the passage. It was not so much the fact that someone had unexpectedly spoken – Sukey already knew that both Serena and Freya were in the building and to hear them conversing would have been natural enough – but the words themselves, spoken in a low but pene-trating voice that vibrated with emotion, made her throat tighten and set her heart madly racing.

"It's his blood, isn't it? Percy's blood!" In the short pause that followed, the words seemed to echo round the confined space like the sound of a fallen stone rising from the bottom of a well. Then the woman spoke again, and this time Sukey recognised the anguished shriek that Freya had uttered on finding the body of her murdered husband. "It was you, wasn't it? You killed him! In God's name, why?"

"Shut up!" Serena's voice was a sharp, staccato hiss. "D'you want the whole world to hear? Anyway, what were you doing rummaging around in my room?"

"I was only collecting the laundry for Mrs Robbins. Your wardrobe door was open and I noticed it on the floor at the back. You're always so untidy, I thought you'd forgotten to put it in the basket."

"Well, that should teach you not to be so nosey. I couldn't wash it myself or put it on the bonfire without risking you asking a lot of questions so I thought I'd bag it up and put it out with the refuse tomorrow."

"But why kill him?" Freya's voice dropped to a low moan. "Just tell me why!"

"He found out about our lucrative sideline, that's why." There was something chilling about Serena's matter-of-fact tone, as if committing murder to protect one's personal interests was a perfectly logical thing to do. "He walked in early Thursday morning while I was running through Henry's performance." She gave a low, sensuous chuckle. "It's pretty good – I can't wait to see his face when I show it to him. He'll cough up a mint—"

"Never mind Henry's performance." Freya was clearly on the verge of another outburst of hysteria. "Are you telling me you murdered your step-father – my husband, our leader – just because he was going to put a stop to your miserable little scam?"

"You mean *our* scam, don't you? I don't recall you refusing your share of the proceeds."

"We could have done without the extra money—"

"It wasn't just a question of the extra money." Serena's voice was harsh, urgent. "You should have seen him – he was incandescent with rage, said I'd sullied and defiled his life's work. For a moment I thought he was going to hit me, but instead he stood there with his arms stretched up to heaven, cursing away

206

like an Old Testament prophet. He said I was to be cast out of the Unlimited, I was nothing but a great whore, he'd never been happy about running RYCE for profit and as far as he was concerned that was the end of the road. Then he went rushing out; I thought at first he was going straight back to the house to tackle you and I followed him to try and reason with him, but instead he went off down the garden muttering about needing to meditate."

"And you knew he'd be squatting there with his back to you, a sitting target, so you fetched the knife and killed him!"

"He was going to pull the plug on our whole enterprise. Don't you understand, we'd have been left with nothing – I had to stop him somehow."

"And now, you evil cow, I'm going to stop *you*." This time, there was no emotion in Freya's voice, only an icy calm that was even more ominous. "In the name of the Great Unlimited, I'm going to make you pay for your wickedness."

"What are you talking about?" Sukey, straining her ears to listen, detected a hint of apprehension in Serena's voice. "And what's that you're hiding?"

"All they that take the sword shall perish with the sword," Freya intoned.

"Mum, you don't believe all that . . . Mum, you wouldn't!" Apprehension swiftly changed to alarm. "No, Mum, don't . . . you don't understand . . . we'd have had nothing left."

"Without him, I have nothing left."

"That's a load of crap. You've been doing brilliantly so far . . . we can keep it up, you know we can. It'll be difficult, we'll need a period of adjustment before we can . . . please, Mum, just put that away and . . . all right, if you want to play rough—" The next minute there was a sharp, whistling crack followed by a high, thin scream.

Fearing that unless she acted quickly there would be a second killing or at least a serious injury, Sukey sprinted along the passage to the end room and flung open the door, but was disconcerted to find it empty. Before she had time to figure out her mistake and check the middle room, a curtain in the far corner was pushed aside and Serena emerged backwards through another door concealed behind it. In one hand she held a three-legged metal stool by its seat; in the other was a whip with a black leather thong. Behind her was Freya, her face contorted with pain from the thin red weal on one bare arm. She too held something in either hand; one grasped a long cotton garment patterned in brilliant shades of red and orange, the other a kitchen knife, its long, narrow blade pointing directly at Serena.

For a fraction of a second the scene appeared unreal, almost ludicrous, as if the protagonists were acting out some bizarre, erotic ritual, but one glance at Freya's expression, eyes burning with hatred in a face the colour of marble, was enough to convince Sukey that this was no game. Unless she acted quickly there would at the very least be some serious blood-letting. Unable to think of any other effective action she shouted, "Stop it at once, both of you!"

Serena started and half turned to face the intruder, momentarily taking her eyes off her mother. At the sight of Sukey, her mouth fell open and she uttered a strangled gasp of astonishment, but Freya, whose gaze was still fixed with murderous intensity on her daughter, did not appear to have noticed the interruption. With Serena's attention thus distracted she seized her chance and lunged at her. In the nick of time, Sukey leapt forward, grasped her by the arm and deflected the blow. Freya stumbled and almost fell; the point of the knife hit the wall with such force that the blade snapped in two. Sukey, keeping a wary eye on both women, backed away and dragged her mobile phone from her pocket. "You're nicked – both of you!" she said.

"You reckon?" Serena's voice was scornful. In a sudden, totally unexpected movement she lashed out with the whip. The thong caught Sukey on the wrist, dashing the phone from her grasp and sending it spinning across the room. The shock of the searing pain in her arm put Sukey off her guard for a moment; then, realising that she was in deadly danger, she made a move towards the door, but Serena was there before her, cutting off her retreat. The next moment she was pinned by the arms and thrown face downwards on the couch. She thrashed out frantically with her legs but a second pair of hands held them in a grip of iron. Their quarrel momentarily set aside in the face of a common threat, the two women began working quickly and in silence to immobilise their enemy.

Sukey tried to scream, but her cry was stifled as a hand pressed her face into the pillow. For a few seconds she could barely draw breath; then the pressure was released and a cloth thrust into her mouth. Her wrists and legs were bound and a blindfold placed over her eyes. "Right!" Serena hissed in her ear. "We'll teach you to poke your nose into our affairs, you bloody snooper!"

"What do we do with her now?" It was Freya seeking instructions. Clearly, the daughter had taken command.

"In there for the moment. We'll decide later how we dispose of her."

Sukey felt herself being lifted bodily, carried a short distance and dumped on what felt like another couch. Hands seized her ankles; something hard encircled them and she heard a metallic click. Serena's mocking voice taunted her. "These are *external* shackles. I don't suppose you'll enjoy them as much as some of my clients do, but you've got plenty of time so you might as well make the best of them."

"What about her car?" Again it was Freya speaking. "Josie'll be back soon and—"

"Good thinking. I'll find the key." Hands rifled the pockets in Sukey's denim jacket. "Got it. We'll put it in the barn – let's get a move on." There came the sounds of a door closing and a key being turned in the lock, followed by total silence.

For several minutes Sukey lay motionless in her prison, almost overcome by shock and despair. Whatever plans the two women might be hatching for her, she had little hope that they included allowing her to survive. Calculating that they could hardly dispose of her in broad daylight, with Josie expected back shortly from her errand and the afternoon's initiates due to arrive within an hour or so, she might stand some chance if she could at least free her arms. The shackles round her ankles were another matter but . . . "First things first," she muttered grimly and began straining against the material that bound her wrists. It felt soft and, after a few minutes of determined struggle, she felt it give a fraction. Thanks to regular work-outs at her fitness club her arms were strong and muscular and little by little the bonds loosened until, with a muttered exclamation of triumph, she manged to extricate one hand. She tore the gag from her mouth and the bandage from her eyes, sat up and looked around.

She was lying on a narrow bed with metal bars at the head and foot. The room was small and windowless. Hanging on the walls was a bizarre range of garments in an variety of materials and styles from leather tights and thongs to filmy see-through creations of lace and chiffon, together with abbreviated versions of nurse's, housemaid's and school uniforms. On a shelf was a collection of canes and whips; glancing down at the floor, Sukey observed that it was tiled rather than carpeted. No doubt some of the more sophisticated activities resulted in a certain amount of body fluids being spilled. Seized by an uncontrollable wave of nausea, she rolled over to the edge of the couch and vomited. Then she lay still for several moments before sitting up again and unwinding the torn length of bandage still hanging from her arms – no doubt taken from the props for some erotic "nurse and patient" game, she reflected grimly as she threw it to one side and set about freeing her legs.

She slid forward to the end of the bed and inspected the shackles. They appeared similar in style to police handcuffs and were securely locked. She tussled with them for several minutes in the hope of finding some hidden quick-lease catch, but without success. She thought of shouting for help; then reflected that if it was Serena who heard her cries, she would end up in a more helpless position than before. Her eye fell on the whip that Serena had wielded to such devastating effect and left lying on a chair beside the bed. She rolled over as far as the shackles on her ankles would allow, reached out and just managed to grasp the thong. At least, when they came for her, she might be able to give them a taste of their own medicine. She glanced at her wristwatch; it was a quarter past two. She should have signed on at the office fifteen minutes ago. When she did not appear, George Barnes would call her, first on her mobile – which so far as she knew was still lying on the floor in the next room – and then, receiving no reply, he would try her home number. But Fergus – the only person who knew where she was – would quite possibly be out. There was little hope from that direction, so she lay back, stared at the ceiling and prepared to do the only thing left to her – wait for Serena and Freya to return. At least, she now had a fighting chance – albeit a slim one – where before there had been none.

How much time passed before she heard the sound of the key turning in the lock she had no idea, but she was immediately on the alert. Her heart thumping and her eyes on the door, she seized the handle of the whip and sat bolt upright, grimly determined to do whatever damage she could before being once more overpowered, then gave a cry of mingled astonishment and relief as DS Andy Radcliffe burst into the room. He stood for a moment transfixed with amazement, then clapped a hand to his mouth and uttered a strangled snort. "Well, get Miss Whiplash of the Millennium!" he exclaimed in a voice that wobbled with suppressed laughter.

"Not funny!" Sukey retorted through her teeth. "Just get me out of this lot, will you!"

Twenty-Four

"What I don't understand," said Sukey, "is why I never heard a sound until Andy unlocked the door and came bursting in. I suppose I must have dozed off or something . . ."

"I doubt it." DC Lisa Crombie handed Sukey a fresh mug of tea and sat down opposite her at the table in the interview room where she had been taking her statement. "For obvious reasons, that room was sound-proofed."

"Of course – why didn't I think of that?"

"Don't tell me you wore your lungs out screaming for help."

"As it happens, I deliberately kept quiet because I didn't want to advertise the fact that I'd partially freed myself."

"So you very wisely waited for DS Radcliffe to come to the rescue." In spite of herself, Lisa could not suppress a smile at the mental picture conjured up by Sukey's account of the way her ordeal had ended.

Sukey responded with a shaky laugh. "You should have seen his face when he saw me chained to that bed! Not that I saw the funny side of it at the time – to be honest, I've never been so scared in my life."

"I can imagine."

Sukey picked up the mug and drank half the contents before putting it down again. "I must be dehydrated – this is the first time I've enjoyed seconds of vending-machine tea. Tell me, how did Andy know where to look for me? That room's pretty well concealed."

"Aha, thereby hangs a very interesting tale. The so-called Rejuvenation Suite was given a quick once-over immediately after the murder, just to make sure no one was hiding there, but it didn't occur to anyone that there might be a fourth room – it's quite small, there aren't any windows and there was no reason at the time to make a more detailed check."

"Then what . . . ?"

"We have a bright young schoolboy called Timmy Tritton to thank for your deliverance – and for solving the puzzle of why Oliver Drew killed himself."

Sukey's jaw dropped. "Now you've completely lost me. Who's Timmy Tritton and what did he do that was so clever?"

"It wasn't so much cleverness on his part as curiosity. It was his mum who had the wit to contact us, with very surprising results."

"I do wish you'd stop talking in riddles."

"Sorry, I just wanted to fill in the background." Lisa gestured at Sukey's by-now empty mug. "Want another?"

"No thanks, just get on with the story."

"Right. Well, Timmy was playing with his new toy – a metal detector – and by a stroke of amazing luck for us he happened to be working on the edge of the field where Oliver Drew was found dead in his car. He struck oil – or rather, metal – and thought he'd found treasure trove, but all he unearthed was a small garden trowel buried under the hedge. Because it looked nearly new he thought he might as well take it home and give it to his Mum, so he picked it up . . ." Lisa paused for dramatic effect before continuing, "and guess what he found buried underneath it."

"Oliver Drew's signed confession?" Sukey suggested sarcastically.

"Not so far wide of the mark as you might think."

Lisa was obviously enjoying spinning out her tale, but Sukey was becoming increasingly impatient. "If you don't stop beating about the bush—" she began.

"OK, OK!" Lisa raised her hands in mock surrender. "What Timmy found was a cassette from a camcorder. He realised what it was because he's got a camcorder of his own. He's also got one

213

of those adaptor things you can plug into your video to watch what you've filmed on your TV screen, so he decided to take the cassette home to see what was on it. And it wasn't Postman Pat or the Teletubbies."

Recalling the use for which her temporary prison had obviously been designed, Sukey's brain had clicked into action while Lisa was speaking. "A highly explicit sex show starring Oliver Drew?"

"Got it in one. With Serena as co-star," Lisa added. "I haven't seen it myself but I gather the boys in CID found it pretty strong stuff."

"So Jennifer was right after all." Sukey's mind went racing ahead. "I imagine the trick was to film the proceedings with a concealed camcorder, show the results to the victim and threaten to send copies of the cassettes to wives or partners if they didn't cough up some pretty substantial sums."

"Something like that. They must have chosen their victims pretty carefully. Serena's being held in connection with Percy's murder and Edith Burrell on a charge of assault and false imprisonment. We'll get round to their other activities in due course."

"Did the boys find the camcorder?"

"They did – disguised as a smoke detector immediately above the bed," said Lisa. "It was all set up," she added mischievously.

Sukey covered her eyes in horror. "You don't mean . . . ?"

"Just kidding," Lisa said cheerfully. "The cassette was blank – the thing hadn't been activated."

"Thank goodness for that. Can you imagine what the lads in CID would have said if I'd been filmed doing my Houdini act and then brandishing one of Serena's whips – I'd never have lived it down. By the way, you said Timmy's mother was somehow involved."

Lisa giggled. "She walked into Timmy's room while he was getting the sort of sex education they don't give in school. The poor lad had quite a job to convince her that he hadn't bought it with his pocket money. She didn't know anything about the Oliver Drew case, but she decided it was a matter for the police and came straight down to the station to hand it in – the trowel as well. Drew's prints are on both . . . and Serena's are on the cassette."

"Well, good for Mrs T." Sukey's stomach contracted at the thought of what might have happened to her without Timmy and his metal detector.

"I don't think it's an exaggeration to say that you owe your life to the Trittons," said Lisa soberly, as if she had read Sukey's thoughts.

"I wonder why Oliver didn't destroy the cassette instead of burying it," Sukey mused.

Lisa pursed her lips and shook her head. "Search me. A man who's about to take his own life isn't going to be thinking too rationally. Maybe he thought that if he tried to burn it or break it up, it could still leave some sort of trace that Jennifer could find and start asking questions. I don't imagine it occurred to him for a moment that anyone would dig it up. Timmy would never have found it if the the metal trowel hadn't been thrown in on top of it." She glanced at her watch. "Sukey, it's nearly five o'clock and I think it'd be a good idea if you went home and got some rest. I'll drive you."

"Thanks. What about my car? I heard Serena say something about hiding it in a barn."

"I'll make a note of that and get someone to recover it for you. Shall we go?"

"Sure."

"By the way," Lisa added as they made their way to the station car park, her voice unconvincingly casual, "so far as I know, DI Castle hasn't been given any details of the arrests yet as he's been out of town all day on another case. No doubt he'll want a full report in due course."

"I'm sure he will," Sukey said drily. *And I'm going to get the telling-off of a lifetime*, she added mentally.

"What in the world am I going to do with you, Sook?" Jim Castle released Sukey from the bear-hug in which he had enfolded her the moment she opened the door to him and gave her a gentle shake. "You do realise you broke nearly every rule in the book, don't you?"

"How do you work that out? All I did was to enquire about a complimentary treatment I thought I'd missed out on—"

"You know very well what I'm talking about. The minute you twigged what was going on you should have bolted from the scene and called for back-up, instead of which you—"

"Prevented another killing," Sukey interposed as he dried up, evidently too exasperated to continue.

"You damned nearly precipitated one – your own," he reminded her grimly. "George Barnes says he'll be afraid to send you to a break-in at a playgroup after this."

"Tell George that some of the kids who go to playgroups can be pretty scary – and so can their mums."

"Will you be serious for once?"

"Sorry." Sukey did her best to look suitably humble. She wound her arms round his neck and looked up at him with a smile of contrition. "Don't be cross with me," she whispered. "I've had one hell of a day."

He held her close for a long time. Neither of them heard the key turn in the lock of the front door. "Sorry, am I interrupting something?" said Fergus blandly as he stepped into the hall.

"Jim's just forgiving me for stealing his thunder by clearing up one of his most difficult cases for him," Sukey explained as she disengaged from the embrace.

"You don't mean—?"

"The RYCE mystery is solved – and guess who cracked it?"

"My brilliant mother?"

"The same."

"Clever old you!" It was Fergus's turn to give Sukey a hug. "So who dunnit?"

"Jim will tell you the dénouement while I go and have a bath and change my clothes."

"Yes, you do look a bit scruffy." Fergus took in his mother's

216

dishevelled appearance with a disapproving eye. "Did you have to go through a hedge backwards to collect the evidence?"

"Something like that."

Later, when the three of them were relaxing after a takeaway meal – Sukey having refused point blank either to cook or eat out – Fergus said, "Do you suppose Anita's Auntie Vera got wind of what the RYCE people were up to? Could that have been the shock that brought on her heart attack?"

Sukey shook her head. "All we know for certain is that she turned up on the wrong evening and went away looking put out. It's possible that someone had been careless enough to leave the place unattended for a few minutes so that she was able to wander in and see all the sex aids on display – or the door might not have been properly closed during a performance so that she got some inkling of what was going on. She wasn't expected there that evening, remember. We'll never know the answer to that one."

"Perhaps one of them saw her and went after her, maybe with the idea of shutting her up . . ." It was evident that Fergus was seeking a dramatic explanation for the old lady's death, but Jim was quick to discourage the notion.

"Unlikely. Jarvis saw Vera drive off in a hurry, but according to your mother's statement he never mentioned anyone attempting to follow or stop her. I'd forget about that if I were you." Jim's tone made it clear that he was giving an instruction, not a piece of advice.

"Anyway, Adrian will be happy to know that RYCE is no more." Fergus got up and went to the phone. "Is it all right if I call Anita and tell her the news?"

"OK, but no details," said Jim sternly. "You can just say RYCE has been closed down and the police will be issuing a statement to the press tomorrow."

"And no mention of the part your mother played," said Sukey.

Fergus grinned. "Trust me, I'll be the soul of discretion."

As the door closed behind him, Sukey said reflectively, "I can't help feeling sad about the way it's ended. Xavier was totally sincere; he trusted those two scheming bitches to support him in his work and literally gave his life for it. Some of his teaching might have been a little bizarre – well, unconventional, shall we say – but there's no doubt he brought comfort to a lot of people." She sat fingering the stem of her empty wineglass. "Me among them," she added after a long pause.